Praise for these authors

Pamela Morsi

"Pam Morsi is wise, witty and wonderful!
I'm a huge fan."
—Susan Elizabeth Phillips

"Morsi is an extraordinarily gifted writer."
—*Romantic Times BOOKclub*

Karen Kendall

"Hilarious and downright sexy! Karen Kendall
will delight you!"
—*New York Times* bestselling author Carly Phillips on
Karen's books *First Date* and *First Dance*

"Sexy-hot delicious and laugh-out-loud delightful!
Karen Kendall is my new favorite author!"
—*New York Times* bestselling author Nicole Jordan

Colleen Collins

Colleen Collins' *Building a Bad Boy* is funny and tender,
and decidedly non-traditional hero Nigel
is hotter than sin."
—*Romantic Times BOOKclub*

"Colleen's books never disappoint—
they're sizzling, snappy and very sexy!"
—Nancy Warren, *USA TODAY* bestselling author

THE NIGHT WE MET

Pamela Morsi
Karen Kendall
Colleen Collins

ROM

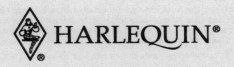

HARLEQUIN®

TORONTO • NEW YORK • LONDON
AMSTERDAM • PARIS • SYDNEY • HAMBURG
STOCKHOLM • ATHENS • TOKYO • MILAN • MADRID
PRAGUE • WARSAW • BUDAPEST • AUCKLAND

ISBN-13: 978-0-373-83728-1
ISBN-10:   0-373-83728-3

THE NIGHT WE MET

Copyright © 2006 by Harlequin Enterprises S.A.

The publisher acknowledges the copyright holders of the individual works as follows:

THE PANTY RAID
Copyright © 2006 by Pamela Morsi

FRAME BY FRAME
Copyright © 2006 by Karen Moser

THREE WISHES
Copyright © 2006 by Colleen Collins

This edition published by arrangement with Harlequin Books S.A.

® and TM are trademarks of the publisher. Trademarks indicated with ® are registered in the United States Patent and Trademark Office, the Canadian Trade Marks Office and in other countries.

www.eHarlequin.com

Printed in U.S.A.

CONTENTS

THE PANTY RAID

Pamela Morsi

Thanksgiving
Present Day

EVERY TUESDAY and Thursday, fifty-two weeks per year, the *Manohra Song,* a fifty-year-old rice barge now restored as a luxury travel vessel, makes the three-day round trip along the Menam Chao Phraya, the River of Kings, from modern Bangkok to Ayuthaya, the ruins of the capital city of ancient Siam. The ship, built entirely of teak and rare woods, is sumptuously outfitted with Thai tapestries, carvings and antiques. There are four staterooms onboard, and for this particular trip, on the fourth Thursday in the month of November, three were booked.

The first couple to arrive came by taxi from the Hotel Oriental. Perhaps they were anxious to get on board, or thought they might need extra time. But the spry seniors, easily pegged as in their mid-seventies, were as eager and excited about the trip as any young honeymooners. He was tall and lean and moved with the grace and confidence of a man at peace with the past and eager for the future. His wife beside him was a woman who'd grown handsome with time, the lines on her face reflecting a life spent smiling.

As they made their way up the gangplank, the

stewards and staff were immediately there to welcome them, putting hands together in a prayerful pose and offering a slight bow. The couple, obviously familiar with the local customs, expertly returned the traditional *wai* greeting. They were handed cold, lemongrass towels to freshen up and shown to their stateroom.

The second couple to arrive were in their fifties, a handsome pair reminiscent of Susan St. James and Sean Connery in his James Bond days.

The wife had shoulder-length hair, gorgeously streaked with silver here and there, but her face was youthful and seemed to glow from within. She was stunning in a green silk sarong that probably came from one of the local Bangkok markets.

Her husband appeared slightly older and more conservative, his bearing clearly military. Sharply observant, he maintained a trim, athletic build undisguised by his classic khakis and beige polo shirt.

The third couple to arrive was younger and emerged laughing from a tiny tuk-tuk, the motorized three-wheeled vehicles dotting Bangkok traffic. The man was likely in his mid-thirties and the woman seemed twenty-something.

He was strikingly handsome, with a strong, lean face and a thick thatch of salt-and-pepper hair. He toted what appeared to be expensive camera equipment. Before coming on board the *Manohra Song,* he pulled out a thirty-five millimeter camera and took several shots of the barge, after asking the staff's permission in stilted, American-accented Thai.

His wife waited patiently, a tender smile on her face. As he snapped away, she pulled a rubber band out of the pocket of her cropped khaki pants and pulled back her shoulder-length, light brown hair, exposing slightly asymmetrical eyebrows. "Pete, you're obsessed."

He finally stowed the camera in a carrier and took her hand to pull her up the gangplank. "Yes, but it's my job to be obsessed. *World Sophisticate* will want these photos, Natalie, see if they don't." And he kissed her, in full view of everyone. She kissed him back with enthusiasm.

"Please excuse us," she said to the steward after they exchanged greetings. "We're here to celebrate our first anniversary since we met here in Bangkok."

The couples got acquainted over fruity refreshments as the crew readied the boat. The six strangers would be in close company for the next two nights and three days as they made the fifty-mile trip through the waterway that was the pulsing lifeline of Thailand.

"We're the Brantlys," the elderly man introduced himself to the other couples. "I'm Henry and this is my wife, Dorothy."

"Mac Griffin," said the man with military bearing, extending his hand. "And my wife, Christie. Nice to meet you."

"I'm Natalie Sedgewick," said the twenty-something woman with a warm smile. She sent a teasing wink toward her husband. "And this is my old man, Pete."

He poked her in the ribs and then turned to the others with a shrug and a grin. "I'd never robbed a cradle before, but she was irresistible. And I figure she'll take care of me when I'm a doddering old fool."

Everyone laughed.

"So, we're all Americans," Dorothy said, stating the obvious. "I suppose we should wish each other a happy Thanksgiving."

With smiles and chuckles, they did just that.

"It's easy when you're on vacation to lose track of the days," Pete pointed out.

"Oh, my wife would never let me forget Thanksgiving," Henry Brantly said. "We got officially engaged over Thanksgiving dinner at her parent's house."

"That seems very sweet and old-fashioned," Christie said.

"Oh, yes," Dorothy said, not completely disguising a saucy grin. "We were always a very conventional couple. I met Henry while he was trying to steal my underwear."

All eyes turned to Henry, who actually blushed.

"There's a story here," said Mac. "And we'd love to hear it."

Dot's eyes twinkled and she took her husband's hand. "Well, if you insist…"

CHAPTER ONE

A BRIGHT FULL MOON illuminated the night sky, bathing the campus below her open second-floor window in a sleek silver glow. Dorothy Wilbur, known as Dot to all her girlfriends in the dorm, sat cross-legged on the end of her bed. Her dark brown hair was freed of its typical ponytail and the length of it hung loosely down her back. She was wide-awake, her chin in her hands, gazing outside sightless and worrying. That was not something she'd been prone to do in the past. But she was older now, twenty-one candles on her last birthday cake, and the future was headed in her direction at a rapid pace. The decisions she made about it now were going to be critical.

It was 1956 and Dot was in fall semester of her last year at State. She had excellent grades and a full scholarship. Tomorrow morning she'd write her first exam in Organic Chemistry class and she was pessimistic. Not about Chemistry. The sciences were more than just her major, they had always been her forte, her passion. It was what she been born to do. That's what she'd always thought.

Until now.

Until Dr. Falk.

Until the evil Dr. Falk.

She liked thinking of him that way. Like a mad

genius in a science-fiction movie—evil, diabolical, vil-
lainous—he was the devil in a rumpled white lab coat.
She suspected that in the anonymity of his office, he
rubbed his hands together in eager anticipation of some
dark deed and laughed in the maniacal manner pre-
ferred by the dastardly deranged doctorate.

Falk was dean of the university's Department of
Science and he was trying to ruin her life.

"Miss Wilbur," he'd said that very afternoon in class,
looking down at her over the thick lenses of his eye-
glasses. "Young ladies who enjoy assaying weights and
measures, should be coming up with recipes in a
kitchen, not taking up valuable laboratory space at the
university."

She'd felt her cheeks heat up, both with anger and
embarrassment. Every guy in the room was looking at
her. And it was all guys in the room.

"Is there a problem with my experiment, sir?"
she'd asked him.

He shook his head. "No, Miss Wilbur," he said. "It's
very good work, but good work that will come to
naught. Five years from now all the men in this room
will be out in academia and industry expanding the
frontiers of science. You'll be sitting in some suburban
house surrounding by a troop of noisy, babbling
children. The only thing you'll be expanding is the
width of your backside."

There was muffled laughter all around the room.
She'd wanted to burst into tears and run from the room.
That's what she wanted to do, but that's what they would
expect. She'd managed to maintain her seat and held her
chin high with difficulty.

It wasn't as if she hadn't had practice.

"Honey, boys like girls who are pretty and sweet," her father had told her. "You'll never catch a husband by being smarter than he is."

Her teachers in high school felt much the same way.

"So you're going to college," Mr. Peterson, the principal, had said when she'd asked him to write a letter of recommendation for her. "Lots of girls doing that these days. They say they're looking for a B.A. or a B.Sc., but most are just looking for an MRS."

He'd chuckled at his own little joke. It was all Dot could do not to roll her eyes.

Only her mother was on her side.

"Go after what you're wanting, Dotty," she told her. "When I look back on my life, I spend more time regretting the things that I didn't do than the things that I did."

Four years at college was a big ambition for a working-class girl like Dot. Her father was a laborer, spending his days shoveling scrap at a smelter. Her mother took in ironing. She was the oldest of four children and if her parents were going to pay for anyone's education, an unlikely scenario at best, she knew it would be her baby brother, Tom. Though at age ten, he'd yet to show any inclination toward schoolwork.

But Dot had never given up hope.

When she'd won the *Women in Science Foundation Scholarship,* she'd thought her troubles were over. But the attitudes she'd found in college were little different from those in her hometown.

"Science!" her roommate, Trixie, had shrieked. "Oh, you'll meet all the neatest guys in those classes, all the premed majors, predentistry, prepharmacy. That's my goal, marrying a doctor."

Marrying was not one of Dot's goals. It never had been.

Unexpected sounds from beyond her window interrupted her rumination and captured her attention. Curious, she walked over and looked down. There was movement in the bushes and trees on Theta Pond. Lots of movement, and even from this distance she could hear the whispered orders and directions.

A frown creased her brow as she stared in that direction. She couldn't really see what was happening, but it was as clear as springtime that something was going on. The sororities and fraternities were extremely popular on campus and there were only two main dorms for independents, those who eschewed the Greek life, Silas Baldridge for men and Elizabeth Compton for women. Baldridge and Compton were separated by the parklike paths and secluded benches of Theta Pond. But the Pond was off-limits after midnight and Dot was certain it had to be closer to two in the morning.

The buzz of voices was getting louder and the scurry of activity broader and wider.

"Trixie, Trixie," she called in a hushed whisper.

There was an unintelligible response from a tangle of bedcovers.

"Something's going on," Dot said. "Something's going on at Theta Pond."

"Huh?" Trixie poked her sleepy head out just an instant before they heard the battle cry.

"Charge!"

The call came from the shrubbery around the pond. A minute later the lawn area surrounding the dorm was swarming with people, male people, running, hollering, and they were carrying ladders.

From somewhere within the building she heard a young woman shriek.

"Panty raid!"

Bedlam broke out among the three hundred residents of Elizabeth Compton. Lights went on everywhere. There was yelling and clamor and chaos. The slumbering dorm was instantly a hive of activity. Every young woman in the building was awake and at her window.

"Oh, my gosh! It's really happening!" Trixie exclaimed beside her.

Her roommate, dressed in pink baby-dolls, her blond hair knotted up in bobby-pin curls all over her head, seemed almost as pleased as she was horrified.

"Hide your underwear," she advised.

"What?"

"Hide your underwear," Trixie repeated as she hurried to her chest of drawers. "They're coming to steal our panties."

The new innovation in campus hijinks was the rage at colleges and universities everywhere. Young men were forcing their way into female residence halls and sorority houses and stealing undies. These bits of young ladies' lingerie would then be hoisted on flagpoles to fly like triumphant trophies on the breeze, or worse yet to be used as a decoration for some frat house wall.

When the top of a ladder found its perch upon their sill, Trixie let out an ear-piercing squawk.

"They're here!"

Someone hit the fire alarm. The ensuing noise and flashing lights resulted in more screaming, more running, more frantic actions. Adrenaline flooded Compton like a deluge.

Trixie cleaned out her lingerie drawer and tried to stuff the contents behind the texts on the bookshelf.

Dot, instead, hurried to the sink. She dumped the

trash in the wastebasket on the floor and quickly began filling it with water. The halls were filled with screaming, running, squealing young women garbed in cotton pajamas and chenille robes.

"Men on the floor! Men on the floor!" was the warning they called out.

Beyond the open window, Dot could hear the night air filled with shouts of encouragement and raucous laughter.

"We want panties! Give us your panties!" they chanted.

When the wastebasket was filled with water, Dot hurried to the window.

From the third-floor windows above her, the girls unable to be reached by ladders were raining their underwear down upon the grateful crowd below.

"We're giving them our underwear?" Trixie asked, confused. "Are we hiding our underwear or giving it to them?" she called out in general.

Everyone was too busy to answer.

At a ladder two rooms down from theirs, Dot saw a young man hoisting himself into the room of her friends, Maylene and Eva. The two girls didn't seem to be making it easy for him or handing over the unmentionables. Dot took her cue from them.

Not more than an arm's length below her window, an intruder was on the ladder. He looked up at Dot. She looked down at him. There was one instant of vague recognition by both. Then he spoke.

"Give me your panties," he demanded.

She turned the wastebasket upside down and doused him on the head with cold water.

CHAPTER TWO

THE LAST THING Hank Brantly needed to be doing the night before his first Organic Chemistry exam was participating in a panty raid. For one thing, he was too old for that kind of nonsense. He was, after all, a senior. And before college he'd done a two-year stint with the army in Korea. He was not only three years older than most of his buddies at Baldridge but in life experience he felt like an old man among children.

Maybe that's why he had done it.

He'd listened to their plans around the dorm for days. They had vague ideas of marching over to Compton and being let in. They would mill around on the lawn, throw pebbles at the windows to get the attention of girls and just see what happened. They had no organization, no tactics—they were even short on goals or what might constitute a success. Hank had been a draftee, not a great fan of military life and happy to have his compulsory service behind him, but at least he'd picked up a few notions about strategy, logistics, intelligence. If he left it to the other guys in the dorm, the operation was doomed to failure. He felt he had no alternative but to take charge.

He put every guy who could handle a hammer and saw to making ladders. The first-floor windows sported burglar bars, but the second floor was less than twenty feet from the ground. They scavenged lumber all over town and came up with six usable ladders.

Hank recruited Mary Jane Coulter, a girl he'd dated a few times for inside treachery. She wasn't that difficult to convince. Hank was not at all certain that she understood either the danger of the job or the possible ramifications.

"So, when I hear the signal," she said, "I'm supposed to run down the hallway and hit the fire alarm."

"Yes," he told her. "That's all we need you to do."

Mary Jane nodded slowly. "What about refreshments?" she asked. "If we're going to have a party, shouldn't there be refreshments? Punch and little sandwiches at the very least."

"I don't think we're going to have much time to eat," he assured her.

Mary Jane was not the sharpest knife in the drawer, but she was the only female inside Compton Hall that he could ask to do the job.

Pulling the fire alarm accomplished two things: it raised the noise level in the building, which would lessen their ability to organize a defense and it would unlock all the outer doors. The intended purpose of the fire locks was getting girls out of the building. But in this case, it would let guys in.

He set up a staging position under the relative cover at Theta Pond. The guys were not particularly adept at stealth. Some had been consuming beer, though Hank had specifically warned against it. Those he suspected of imbibing were relegated to rear guard action. One of those fellows was supposed to have been the lead on ladder number three. Reluctantly, Hank took his place.

Which was exactly why he found himself at the edge of a windowsill, unexpectedly staring up into the eyes of the one girl who'd haunted his fantasies for months. Miss Wilbur.

Miss Wilbur was not the only woman studying science. Out of perhaps three hundred majors, there were probably a dozen girls. But Miss Wilbur was, in Hank's vernacular, a bonafide dish.

He'd thought about asking her out. He'd thought about it more than once. But in class she was all business. She was the most diligent, attentive, exacting student he'd come across at State. She was serious, very serious. Probably way too serious for dating. Way too serious to date him.

So, having her suddenly appear at the top of the ladder in the middle of a panty raid was incongruous at least. Completely unexpected was more like it.

Hank was momentarily stunned into silence. Then he blurted out exactly what everyone else was saying.

"Give me your panties!"

He saw the wastebasket, but didn't interpret its purpose until it was too late to dodge. The cold water hit him full force right in the face. He lost his footing and was suddenly hanging by one hand on the side of the ladder. Afraid that he'd bring it down, along with the guys behind him, Hank let go and dropped about ten feet, landing unpleasantly in a shrub of holly. The prickly bush cushioned his fall, but it also virtually imprisoned him. It felt like every branch had attached itself to his body and barbed edges of the leaves dug into his flesh. He was still attempting to extricate himself when he heard the sirens.

Campus police were on the job. With spotlights and

a bullhorn, they quickly took charge of the situation. The men were ordered to line up on the lawn. Many were able to manage a hasty retreat. Hank was not one of them—he hardly managed to roll himself out of the clutches of the holly bush. He was wet and scratched up and generally very annoyed.

"You!" one of the cops called out to him. "Get in line."

Hank was in no position to argue.

Meekly he stood shoulder to shoulder with the other captured rowdies.

Now the girls had the upper hand. Catcalling from their open windows, they were clearly enjoying the humiliation of the invaders.

Hank glanced up toward the second-floor window where Miss Wilbur had been. He didn't see her there. Instead, a blonde with her hair up in curls was waving a brassiere like a flag of victory.

A small consolation came moments later when the housemother began restoring order. The woman's shrill, commanding voice could be heard all the way to the lawn. In short order, all noisemaking ceased. The windows went down and the lights went off.

The cops, outnumbered about ten to one, made no attempt to detain their prisoners, they just shone a flashlight in each face and requested the student's registration card.

Hank handed his over like all the rest. He knew what it meant. No admittance to football games, university facilities, the library, not even the dorm cafeteria, was possible without the card.

"You can pick it up at the dean's office tomorrow," the policeman told him.

Which was why, that very next afternoon, he was

sitting on the row of seats in the hallway of the second
floor of Chariker Hall.

Character Hall was the student's nickname for the
place. The office building housed most of the adminis-
tration, including the registrar's office, which took up the
entire first floor. Upstairs was the Dean of Men and Dean
of Women, each office having a long row of chairs for
students waiting. There was no one waiting for the Dean
of Women that afternoon, while the Dean of Men's side
was standing room only. All of the guys from Baldridge
were taking their turns to be dressed down by the dean
and find out what they'd have to do to get their cards back.

Hank had been contemplating his shoelaces and
counting floor tiles for twenty minutes when he heard
the tap of ladies' pumps coming down the hallway. He
glanced up and did a double take. Miss Wilbur.

He'd seen her that morning in class, but as usual, she
never glanced up from her work and never gazed around
at the guys in the room—even when she finished the
test, earlier than everyone else. She quietly turned her
paper over and sat staring at the back of the page until
time was called.

Hank knew all this, because anytime Miss Wilbur
was in the room, a large part of his attention was
focused upon her.

She was dressed as she had been that morning. The
standard low-heeled pumps were what separated college
women from teenage bobby-soxers. Her only conces-
sion to youth was the white anklet socks she wore with
them. Her skirt was slim and straight, devoid of the
usual yards of cancan petticoats favored by other girls.
Her sweater would not have been described as tight, but
fit closely enough that he had a general impression of

the soft mounds of her bosom. She had, what Hank liked to think of, as a neat figure. Not busty and over-blown or sexily big bottomed, she was long and lean with all the requisite curves. She was definitely female without the necessity of calling attention to the fact. And she was pretty, in a wholesome kind of way. She'd tied a small colorful neckerchief above her collar. Her dark brown hair was pulled back in a ponytail. And there was a smear of pale pink lipstick on her mouth. But what grabbed his attention now, as always, was her eyes. They were not doelike and loving, or sparkly and full of humor. She had intelligent eyes. They seemed to look out into the future with hope and optimism.

Hank noticed all these things in an instant. The instant before he realized that she was walking right past him to the office of the Dean of Women. Hurriedly, he rose to his feet.

"Miss Wilbur," he called out.

She stopped, surprised and turned to look at him.

"Ah…hi," he said, foundering.

Her brow furrowed as she eyed him curiously before pointing a finger. "You're the guy outside my window," she said.

"Yes, I—"

The door to the dean's office opened.

"Brantly," the secretary called out.

He gave a nod of his head in that direction.

"I'm just going in to talk to the dean about that now," he said. "I'm charged with Attempted Lingerie Larceny."

She nodded. He could almost see a hint of humor hesitating on the edge of her businesslike demeanor.

"And you?" he asked. "What are you up for? Discharging a Wet Substance Down a Second-Floor Ladder?"

She did smile then and it was better than he imagined. Her grin was wide and bright and her nose wrinkled slightly, making her seem suddenly less goddess, more woman. Something rich and warm and wonderful opened up inside Hank's heart.

"They don't discipline you for that," she assured him. "They award you a medal. Heroism in Defense of Underwear."

Hank nodded.

"I guess that's the university's version of The Order of the Garter."

"Mr. Brantly," the secretary called more sternly.

"Got to go," he said.

"Hope they don't throw the book at you."

He shrugged, unconcerned. "Aren't books what college is all about?"

Miss Wilbur laughed. It was a wonderful sound.

At that moment, as Hank stepped into the dean's Office the echo of it still in his ear, he first managed to put his jumble of feelings into one single thought.

I'm going to marry that woman.

CHAPTER THREE

DOT HAD FOUND the hallway distraction to be surprisingly welcome. Her worries of the previous night had not dissipated with morning. In fact, they'd gotten worse. After finishing the exam, she'd waited to speak to Dr. Falk alone.

Once all the other students had left the classroom, she'd approached him. He'd glanced up, but instead of giving her his attention, he began thumbing through the book on his desk.

Dot had spoken up, nonetheless.

"Dr. Falk, I understand that representatives from Dupont will be visiting campus next week," she said.

"Yes," he answered. "Two gentlemen will be coming in on Thursday."

"I understand that they'll be scouting for employment prospects."

He shrugged. "The big companies are always on the lookout for promising young men."

"What about a promising young woman," Dot suggested. "I would really like to meet these people."

He looked up at her then, his expression hard as nails.

"Oh, I'm so sorry, Miss Wilbur," he said. "The list of students they'll be meeting has already been put together and I'm afraid you're not on it. Maybe if you'd mentioned your interest sooner."

Dot's own expression hardened.

"I did tell you sooner, sir," she said. "I spoke to you about it the second day of class, as soon as the rumor went around. I mentioned it again to you two weeks ago and last week as well."

"Oh, did you? Well, I'm sorry. I must have failed to make a note of it."

He picked up his book again. "You're dismissed, Miss Wilbur," he said, without even looking at her.

Dot knew she couldn't just let that go. She needed Dr. Falk. Without his support, his recommendation, there wouldn't be a chance for her, as a woman, to find a job in research. She was a senior. Most of the men in her class, certainly the men with grades nearly as good as hers, had already been scouted for positions by major companies in the chemical or pharmaceutical industry. Her name had never been suggested to anyone.

And if Dr. Falk had his way, she was fairly certain it never would.

So she'd called the office of the Dean of Women and made an appointment. All the way across campus to Chariker, she'd practiced what she was going to say. She chose her words carefully. She phrased, rephrased, stopped to make notes about it and then practiced expressing it all again.

By the time she got to the dean's office it was such a total jumble of thoughts and ideas that her mind could hardly keep it in a linear direction of conversation. Dot had no problems remembering every element on the periodic chart. But the fears and emotions that swirled inside her defied any attempt to be compartmentalized in a neat, ordered fashion.

The panty raider who interrupted her thoughts just

outside the dean's office was an unexpected respite. Laughing had forced her to relax, approaching the problem more academically and less emotionally. She found she was still smiling as she walked in to give her name to the secretary. She was shown right in.

Dr. Barbara Glidden, the Dean of Women, was a tiny little woman with such unflagging energy she reminded Dot of a hummingbird. She was in her sixties, bright eyed, with silver-gray hair piled in a bun on the top of her head. She seemed to always be smiling, but there was a strength in her that drew young women. They felt confident that she would be on their side.

Dot hoped that would be true today.

Calmly, accurately, she explained in detail the unpleasant reality of life in Dr. Falk's class. Dr. Glidden listened quietly until Dot was finished. She was nodding.

"Dr. Falk is very old-school," she told Dot. "And his department is so overwhelmingly male, he has very little experience with women's education."

"But surely he can't be opposed to it," Dot said. "It's unfair not to treat me with the same respect and offer me the same opportunities that a man would get."

Dr. Glidden smiled. She had a beautiful smile. It was rumored in the dorm that she'd been a beauty queen in her youth. Now, however, she was a tenured professor, university administrator and a spinster.

"If someone told you that life was fair, Dorothy," she said with a certain amount of humor, "then, my dear, I'm afraid you've been lied to."

"Is there some way I can make it less unfair?" Dot asked.

"You have to think of it from Dr. Falk's perspective," Dr. Glidden told her.

"What's his perspective? He hates women?"

"He doesn't *hate* women," Dr. Glidden assured her. "He simply believes that with limited time and facilities, it's a mistake to waste effort on those whose education will come to nothing."

"My education won't come to nothing," Dot insisted.

Dr. Glidden shrugged. "Most women only work until they are wed," she said. "That's a reality of our time. We, in higher education, expend much effort and resources preparing young women to take their place in the work-force. Then a man comes along and they marry and stay at home. It's an unpleasant fact of life that everyone in the field struggles with. Dr. Falk finds it less disappointing to confront it directly."

"But I want to work," Dot said. "I'm good in science. It's what I want to do."

The dean nodded. "That's how you feel now," she said. "But when you fall in love and your husband asks you to stay home, you'll feel differently."

"My mother works," Dot insisted. "I mean, she takes in laundry. But she gets paid for that. It's the same as a job."

"Your mother is *working* class," Dr. Glidden said. "As a college woman you naturally should aspire to more. And a middle- or upper-class husband will be diminished in the eyes of the community if it appears that he's not a good provider and his wife is forced to work."

"But I wouldn't be forced to work," Dot said. "I'd be working by choice."

"No one would know that," Dr. Glidden said. "No one would understand it or believe it. And even if they did, marriage means children. What would you do about your children? Would you be able to work while they stay home and rear themselves?"

Dot had no idea how to respond to that.

"I'm the first person in my family to ever go to college," she explained to the dean. "This is a big opportunity. I can't just take it and throw it away. I have to make something of myself."

"Companies aren't looking for temporary female employees in their research labs and corporate hierarchy," Dr. Glidden said. "If you want to work until you marry, you'd be better off taking typing."

"No, I don't want to be in the typing pool," Dot told her firmly. "I love science."

"Well," she said, "then there is the College of Education. There are many small towns and rural areas that might hire a woman to teach high school science. And of course, there is nursing, which is truly the practical application of science."

"I don't want to teach or be a nurse," she said. "I want to do research in a big laboratory, expanding the boundaries of biology and chemistry."

The dean nodded. "Dorothy, you need to think that through very carefully. Research is a lifelong vocation," Dr. Glidden told her. "If you truly want to pursue that and be treated equal to men in the endeavor, then you have to be willing to say that you will never want a husband and children."

"What?"

"The only way that you can pursue a vocation like a man," she said, "is to give up all the aspirations of womanhood. It's not an easy thing to do. As a woman who's done it, I can tell you that."

Dot was momentarily stunned into silence.

"So that's why you never married," she said at last.

"I never wanted to give a man the right to tell me

what to do," she answered. "And I don't regret it. I have friends and colleagues. I have a half-dozen nieces and nephews. My life has been far from the empty wasteland people imagine with the term *spinster.*"

That word conjured in Dot's own mind images that were equally negative.

"A woman who truly wants a career cannot marry," Dr. Glidden said. "Marriage means taking care of a husband and family and having a baby every few years. By the time that's over, the woman is far too old and worn to do anything else. Wife and work don't mix. You'll have to choose one or the other."

"Men don't have to choose," Dot pointed out. "They have both families and careers."

Dr. Glidden sighed and shook her head. "As I said before, Dorothy, the world is not a fair place. I know that. Dr. Falk knows that. You're a senior in college—it's time you understood it as well."

Dot left the office a few moments later with an admonition from the dean.

"Think about what you really want and decide the direction of your life."

It was a monumental choice. And one that was not easily faced. Dot truly did not want to give up hope of actually pursuing her gifts, her talents. But she was not so immersed in the world of academia that she couldn't imagine herself with a husband and family. Dot had dated, both in high school and college. There had been a couple of boys she'd liked a lot. But she'd never really been in love.

Not that she didn't believe in it.

Her parents, for all their cares and struggle, obviously loved each other very much. Sometimes, late at night, she'd hear them laughing together, sharing the day. There was no question in Dot's mind that the joy they had in their marriage, their children, was the most valuable and fulfilling aspect of their lives. But then, smelter work and ironing were not vocations that people went into for the love of the job.

Dot hoped to do more important work. To discover medicines that would cure diseases or design products that would make life safer, easier. She had the God-given talent and aptitude for such work. Surely it would be wrong not to pursue it.

Still, the thought of her younger brother gave her pause. When she'd held little Tom as a baby in her arms, she had yearned for motherhood. Did she yearn for science more?

Dot had much to consider. As she left the building, headed down the bricked lane in front of Chariker Hall, she became vaguely aware that someone was walking next to her. It was nearly half a minute before she realized it wasn't a coincidence.

"Don't want to interrupt your thoughts," he said as she glanced over at her panty raider, Mr. Brantly.

"Are you following me?"

"Escorting you, I hoped," he said.

He was cute. There was no getting around that. He was tall and muscular. In the sunlight his wavy brown hair looked almost red. He had bright eyes that crinkled at the corners, as if he were smiling all the time.

"To where are you escorting me?" she asked.

He considered the question. "Dorm?" he asked. "Library? No wait, Swimms," he said. "After a conference with the dean, you've got to go to Swimms." He dug down in his pocket. "I even think I've got a quarter."

He pulled out the shiny coin and held it up for her inspection. "Why don't we take Lady Liberty here over to Swimms and see if we can bust her up?"

Dot's first reaction was to say no. She had things to think about, things to consider. But her head ached from thinking, considering. There was nothing she needed more than vacation from her own worries. This guy had made her laugh in the hallway. Maybe he could do it again.

"All right, Mr. Brantly," she said. "Lead on."

To Dot's surprise, he took her hand. "I'm not that kind of guy," he assured her, smiling. "I never lead on. A girl always knows where she stands with me."

"Oh, really," she said, as she pointedly withdrew from his grasp and folded both arms across her chest, her books held tightly against her heart. "And where is it that I stand?"

He was smiling, but there was some seriousness in the softness of his tone.

"On the brink of an amazing romance," he said.

Dot laughed in his face.

"Does that sort of talk work with other girls?" she asked.

He shrugged. "I don't know," he said. "I never tried it with other girls."

"Oh, so I'm the guinea pig," she said. "Hmm. Well, I'll try to think of myself as a scientific subject."

They walked toward the edge of campus.

Swimms Malt Shop was just across Bow Street, an off-campus hangout, close enough to hear the bells from Founder's Tower, but far enough away that the rules of university life need not apply. The tiled corner doorway led into a huge building lined with booths along two sides, an array of tables in the middle; everything was matched to the university's colors, and the team's wily mascot adorned the walls. The place was busy, noisy, hectic. But there was an exuberance that was pure optimism. Perhaps because all of the customers were college kids, relaxing among friends.

Since all the tables were filled, he led her to the long marble counter and helped her up on one of the dark green vinyl stools. The soda jerk came over with a rag and wiped the area in front of them.

"What'll ya have?" the guy asked Brantly.

Her escort turned to look at Dot, his eyes narrowing.

"Hmm, should I try to guess?" he asked.

Dot laughed lightly. "You can try," she told him.

"Well, an ordinary girl would probably go for vanilla malted," he said. "But you, Miss Wilbur, have never impressed me as an ordinary girl."

He hesitated. She gave no hints.

"Cherry-pineapple shake?" he suggested.

"Not even close," she answered. "Chocolate-coconut malt," she told the soda jerk.

He nodded and turned to Brantly. "You?"

"Just bring me an extra straw," he said, laying his shiny quarter on the counter. "I think I've got a lot to learn about Miss Wilbur. Do I have to keep calling you that? Miss Wilbur."

"That's my name," she said. "You don't like it?"

"It doesn't suit you," he said. "It sounds like some dried-up old maid."

"Ah…well, we among the dried-up prefer the term *spinster*," she said.

"I prefer the term *sweetheart*," he told her. "But I'm not sure you'd be willing to let me call you that."

"No, not hardly," she stated flatly. "You can call me Dot."

"Okay, Dot," he said, "you can call me Hank, as long as you call me."

His mischievous grin made the words seem charming rather than bluster. She chose to ignore them.

"So, how did your session go with the dean?" she asked him. "I suppose that bringing me here means you weren't restricted to your dorm."

"No, that would have been cruel and unusual punishment," he said. "I requested a firing squad at dawn. They give you a last cigarette, you know. It's the only time we get to smoke on campus."

The solemnity feigned in his explanation brought a burst of laughter from her throat.

"No seriously, what happened?"

"Well, the truth is, it's worse than execution. We're being punished by party making."

"What?"

"The dean wants the men of Baldridge to learn how to interact with ladies in a more socially acceptable manner," Hank explained. "So we're required to hold a formal dance and invite the ladies of Compton to attend."

"Oh, my gosh!" Dot said.

"And it gets worse."

"How?"

"Because some snitch, under torture no doubt, revealed that I was the ringleader of the panty raid," he said. "I've now been drafted as dance committee chairman."

"Oh, no!"

"Oh, yes," Hank said.

Dot was really laughing now. The image in her mind of the loud, clumsy, boisterous residents of Baldridge

Hall sedately sipping punch and passing plates of petits fours was too funny to keep a straight face.

"I'm glad you're enjoying this," he said. "To me it's similar to the feeling of having cold water doused on my head."

Dot put her hand over her mouth in an attempt to stifle the hooting that threatened to break out.

"I'm sorry," she managed. "Not for defending my dorm, but for imagining your punishment to be a great joke. I'm sure you guys will give a lovely party."

He nodded with a sham of solemnity. "Yes, it will be charming, no doubt. What do you think, gardenias or chrysanthemums for the table decoration?"

"It depends on what time of year you plan it for."

"It's got to be before Thanksgiving break," he said.

"Then autumn leaves would be your best bet."

"See, that's just one of those basic things that a guy doesn't think about," Hank said. "I told the dean I thought it would be impossible."

"What did he say?"

"He said that he thought it would be impossible for a bunch of Baldridge boys to get inside Compton Hall in the middle of the night."

Dot shrugged. "Maybe you are just the man to do it."

The soda jerk brought the chocolate-coconut malt in its tall glass and set it between them. He picked up the shiny quarter and replaced it with a nickel in change. The drink was topped off with two bright green straws and a cherry.

Hank reached over and carefully picked up the cherry by its stem.

"I believe the crowning glory always goes to the lady," he said.

She liked his hands. They were large, sun browned and seemed no stranger to hard work. The ripe, red fruit was delicate, but there was no clumsiness in the way he held it.

"Yum," she said, reaching to take it from him.

He tutted and shook his head, preferring to carry the prize to her lips. She bit.

"Sweet," she told him.

"Yes," he agreed.

"I was talking about the cherry."

"I was talking about you."

Dot ignored that comment and focused her attention on her soda straw. She took a sip of the ice-cream concoction and made appreciative noises.

"This is really delicious," she said.

Hank leaned forward slightly, putting his mouth on his own straw to taste it as well.

"It's good," he agreed. "And I'd never have known that if I hadn't run into you."

"So the cold water was worth it."

"Some guys tell girls they'd march through hot coals to get to them," he teased. "You already know that I'd shiver up a wet ladder."

They shared their shake, sometimes talking, sometimes laughing, sometimes complaining about the shreds of coconut that got caught in the straws.

"You know what I like about sharing a soda?" he said to her as they neared the end of the glass.

"Saving half the price?" she suggested.

He shook his head. "Being so close to a girl I like. And the way I see it, there's not a much better way to spend time together out in public. Seated close enough to smell the scent of your hair, our faces almost touching, our mouths open, our lips pursed. When you think about it, sharing a soda is almost like kissing."

Hank's eyes were all soft and dreamy. Dot was sure he needed another cold douse of reality. She jumped to her feet and grabbed the nickel off the counter.

"Let's dance," she said.

They made their way toward the back of the joint, where a half-dozen couples were crowded together on a square of hardwood dance floor.

Dot walked directly to the brightly lit jukebox that was spinning out rock and roll. She leaned against it, reading the tunes available for play. She felt Hank's presence right behind her. He didn't so much as graze her, but he was standing so close it somehow felt more intimate than touching. When he spoke, his words were very near her ear and the whisper of his breath sent a shiver down her body.

"Three songs for a nickel," he said. "You pick two and I'll pick one."

"Okay," Dot said. Carefully she chose both for content and dance style. She wanted to keep moving and send a message.

"Why Do Fools Fall in Love?" by Frankie Lymon and the Teenagers was her first choice, A7. Followed by C14, Patience and Prudence singing "Gonna Get Along Without You Now." Both tunes were good for bop or jitterbug jive.

"My turn," Hank said, quickly punching the buttons for Elvis Presley's "Love Me Tender," unmistakably a romantic waltz.

Her choices played first. Dot had never been a great dancer, and Hank was not exactly the suave, debonair type who could really lead a girl across the floor. But they were well matched. Dot lost all sense of being self-conscious and together they managed plenty of one-handed swings, twirls and sugar pushes.

They were both laughing and exuberant by the time the slow dance began to play. Hank pulled her into his arms, snuggling his chin against her hair.

"You're holding me too close," she protested.

He moved away slightly, just enough to look at her.

"I'm just practicing for our Panty Raiders' Cotillion," he explained. "I'm sure the dean won't want any rock and roll at a formal dance."

"If you want to stay out of trouble," Dot told him, "then you guys should definitely stick to the fox-trot."

"Whatever it takes to keep you in my arms," he answered.

In his arms was exactly what the dance felt like to Dot. He'd clasped her palm traditionally, but held it close to his shoulder. His other hand was at her waist, but instead of being at the side, he laid it along the small of her back. There was barely an inch of daylight between their bodies and the space crackled with electricity.

Dot closed her eyes and tried to breathe in the essence of the sensation. She tried to understand it. There was sweetness and a languid quality that was almost lazy. But there were also huge waves of excitement and a thrill that nearly overpowered her.

She opened her eyes to meet his, looking directly at her. Mirrored there was the same ravel of longing and uncertainty that twisted inside her. It was frightening.

Dot pulled away. Fortunately, her retreat coincided with the last notes of the love song, so she had hope that her withdrawal might have been interpreted as natural.

"I...I need to get back to the dorm," she said.

There was a question in his eyes for just a moment and then he nodded.

"I'll walk you," he said.

It wasn't the ideal escape, but Dot didn't argue.

He picked up their books at the counter and they headed out the door together. She felt very nervous walking next to him. She wasn't sure what had happened between them on the dance floor, but she was certain she didn't want to talk about it.

Hank must have understood what she was feeling, because he made it easy for her.

"So, I told you what the dean said to me," he pointed out. "What about your visit to Chariker Hall?"

CHAPTER FOUR

HANK BRANTLY WAS a guy who knew what he wanted. He'd known it since he was ten years old. He wanted to be a man.

As clearly as if it were yesterday, he could remember his father squatting down beside him to wipe Hank's tears.

"You can't cry," Henry Brantly, Sr., had told him. "I have to leave and you can't cry. You're the man of the house until I get back. I'm counting on you to take care of your mother for me."

Hank had bit down on his lip to stop the tears and nodded bravely.

"You mind your mother, do what she tells you, and take care of her for me. That's your job. You have to be a man. Can I count on you for that?"

"Yes, Daddy," he had assured him.

His father leaned forward and kissed him on the lips, just like he was a baby. Then he stood up to take Hank's mother in his arms.

Five minutes later, the bus took Henry Brantly away. Hank and his mother stood in the snow watching until it was completely out of sight. They never saw him again. And Hank never forgot his promise. But it was a hard one to keep.

For one thing, his mother didn't seem to want or

need his help. Quite the opposite, in fact. Hank was never involved in any decisions. His mother was a grown-up adult woman—she didn't need a child to give her advice.

They moved to the city so that she could work in a defense plant. After the war was over, she lost her job. They moved a dozen times after that. The world had no plan for a woman on her own. His mother was constantly searching for steady employment and a chance at security. She worked long hours, sometimes at two jobs. Hank had taken care of himself until he was old enough to work, as well. His mother finally found some security, but not with the money he'd sent home from his meager paycheck. While he was in the service, she'd married an elderly widower. The old man had health problems and required a lot of care, but Hank's mother felt she was set up for life. Hank felt somehow he had failed.

But that was not what he revealed to Dot on their walk back to the dorm that night. When he talked about himself, his family, there was more fact expressed than feeling.

"My father was killed in World War II. He's buried in Foggia, Italy," he said. "I remember trying to find the place on the globe at school. Apparently, it's not large enough to have it's own dot. I'd like to go there sometime, just to see, you know, where it happened."

Dot nodded.

"When I was drafted, I hoped that maybe I'd be sent to Europe," Hank said. "But it doesn't work that way. If the army gets the tiniest hint that you want to go to Europe, they send you to Korea. And if they think you want to go to Korea, you're Germany bound or the Canal Zone or the Arctic Circle. So, you've got to really push for a transfer to a place where you don't want to go, so they'll be sure not to send you there."

She was smiling at him. Hank already loved that smile. A man could spend a lifetime looking at a smile like that, he thought.

"Did you like military life?"

"I hated it," he answered. "I was proud to serve, glad to be done. It just wasn't my cup of tea. Some guys really like the camaraderie and soldiering. And there's an edgy thrill to the combat zone that really gets under a guy's skin. In between hating it, you almost love it. But I've had enough of that to last me forever."

They talked all the way to back to the dorm. Hank, who had never thought of himself as a big talker, suddenly discovered he had a lot to say. And he felt comfortable saying it to Dot Wilbur.

When they got to Compton, they sat on the porch and continued their conversation. All through dinner and until dark. They talked about school, home, travel, families, the world at large and the quality of cafeteria food.

At ten-thirty the porch lights blinked the signal for lockup. Girls had to be in their dorm rooms early. The guys were allowed to come and go as they pleased. The rules were based on the theory that young men should be treated like adult human beings, and young women should be held within the restraint and protection required for their gender.

"I've got to go in," Dot told him. "Our door monitor is a real stickler. If you're a half minute past time you get demerits."

"Wouldn't want you to get in trouble," he said. "You've already been to see the dean this week."

She smiled at him, but there was a vagueness to it, as if she'd just remembered something worrisome.

"Can I call you?" Hank asked.

"Sure," Dot said, hurrying to the doorway along with other girls, and told him the phone extension number.

Hank stood there on the steps of the porch for a moment. A young woman with a huge load of books whizzed past him, but she was too late—the door was closed right in her face and she had to ring the bell.

He turned and walked back to his dorm, thinking about the day, thinking about Dot. As he entered Baldridge, he was immediately surrounded by questions, problems, suggestions. The whole place was abuzz with discussion about the dance they were to give.

Hank could hardly listen. His thoughts were completely focused on something else.

"We'll have an organizational meeting tomorrow," he suggested. "We'll talk about all of this stuff then. Right now, there's something else I've got to do."

They let him pass and he hurried to the small closet at the end of the hallway with a narrow wooden bench. He went inside, shut the door, sat down and picked up the phone.

He gave the extension number to the operator. It rang several times. "Compton Hall, second floor," a female voice answered.

"Dot Wilbur, please," he said.

Hank waited several moments as her name was called out.

"Dot Wilbur! Telephone for Dot Wilbur!"

Finally she was there. "Hello, this is Dot."

"You did tell me I could call you," Hank said by way of greeting.

There was a moment of startled silence and then he heard her laugh. "I don't think you've had time to miss me," she said.

"Oh, yes, I have," he told her. "The minute you were out of sight, I thought of a million things I wanted to say to you."

The two of them stayed on the phone for over an hour. The operator in Dot's dorm finally came on the line to warn them that it was almost "Lights Out" and that their call would be terminated.

"Can I see you tomorrow?" Hank asked her.

She said yes, but clearly, the next morning when she walked out of Compton's front door, she was surprised to find him waiting.

"You did say I could see you," he pointed out.

She laughed and shook her head. "I guess I was thinking afternoon, not after breakfast."

"I thought we could walk to class together."

The morning was bright and crisp, and the stately oaks and maples around campus were ablaze with the colors of autumn. The smell in the air was all harvest moon and pep rallies. Dot fit perfectly in the picture in her shirtwaist gabardine with the circular skirt.

Hank asked to carry her books, but she declined.

"You've got a tall enough stack of your own to manage."

"Carrying my books is an effort," he told her. "Carrying yours would be an honor."

Dot laughed and shook her head. "I don't need so much honor," she said. "I just want to be a classmate, a friend."

Hank raised an eyebrow at that statement. *Class-mate* and *friend* were not descriptions of the relation-ship he wanted. And last night, it didn't seem like the direction they were headed. This morning, however, she was all business.

"I'm headed to the science complex," she told him. "You don't need to go that far if it's out of your way."

Hank chuckled. "I know exactly where you're going. And I am headed in that direction. We're in the same Organic Chem class—I guess I failed to mention that."

Dot appeared completely surprised. "I can't believe that I never noticed you," she said.

"You never notice anybody in class," he told her. "You keep your eyes straight ahead and all your focus on Dr. Falk, which is a good idea. I don't think you could put it past the guy to sneak up behind you and put a knife in your back."

He'd meant the words as a joke, but he could tell by the color in her cheeks that she found it too true to be funny.

"Falk's a jerk," Hank declared. "The way he treats you is lousy and everybody in class knows it."

Dot glanced quickly in his direction. "If that's true, then why do I always hear laughter all around me?"

Hank looked her directly in the eyes. "I've never laughed," he said honestly. "And I've never understood it. Dr. Falk would be the first to say that women are the weaker sex, yet he singles you out for abuse. It's bullying. And it's like having things both ways. He won't treat you like an equal, nor will he give the gender deference that he's supposed to believe in."

"It's because female students have disappointed him so much in the past," Dot said.

"Really?"

"That's what Dean Glidden says," she told him. "Dr.

Falk has invested time and effort into promising women students, only to have them throw it all away for marriage and children."

"Nothing we ever learn is thrown away," Hank said.

"Of course not," Dot agreed. "But great scientific breakthroughs are not made in suburban kitchens."

She had a point, Hank thought. Not one that he really wanted to pursue.

"I think you and Dean Glidden give Dr. Falk too much credit," he said instead. "The man doesn't act like a dispirited educator, just a coward and a bully. He doesn't talk to male students that way, because one of them would catch up to him after hours and pop him a good one right in the kisser."

"Well, that's an idea," Dot said. "If I want to be taken seriously as a college woman, I can always resort to fisticuffs."

"It would probably be a fair fight," Hank said. "The prof is, more than likely, the kind who hits like a girl."

Dot was smiling as they made their way to the second-floor lab. Hank felt strangely proud of that. He didn't remember seeing her come into class in such a happy mood.

They took their seats across the room from each other. She gave one final glance in his direction, still obviously in a pleasant frame of mind.

Unfortunately, Hank wasn't the only one who noticed.

"Miss Wilbur!" Dr. Falk boomed out. The room quieted immediately. "Have you discovered something about Organic Chemistry to giggle about?"

"No, sir," she answered. "I was thinking of something else."

Dr. Falk snorted a huffy, disapproving sound. "Undoubtedly you were daydreaming about feminine nonsense and trifling folderol."

There was no reasonable response Dot could make to such an accusation.

"No, it was me, sir," Hank said, speaking up.

The entire class, including Dr. Falk and Dot Wilbur, turned to stare in his direction.

"You're saying Miss Wilbur was thinking about you?"

That suggestion was offered even more snidely and with unveiled derision.

"No, sir," Hank answered, feigning complete innocence. "I just thought that if you were reading student's minds, you must have got your wires crossed. I'm the committee chairman planning Baldridge Hall's cotillion, so if you're picking up brainwaves from the classroom, I'm the one thinking about 'feminine nonsense and trifling folderol'. What do you guys think?" He directed his question to the rest of the room. "Crepepaper mums or dogwood blossoms made of ribbon?"

CHAPTER FIVE

COMPTON WAS ABUZZ with the excitement. The panty raiders were holding a formal cotillion on the night before Thanksgiving recess. Handwritten invitations arrived, personally addressed to every resident of the dormitory.

> The Gentlemen of
> Silas Baldridge Residence Hall
> request the honor of your presence
> at a supper dance
> on Tuesday, the twentieth of November
> in the Baldridge Main Living Room
> We will arrive to escort you
> at 7 o'clock in the evening

Dot found herself getting annoyed at all the excitement and giddiness. The girls at the dorm were so easily impressed. It was a simple, ordinary party with food, flowers, music and dancing. It wasn't as if they were splitting the atom!

She managed to keep these thoughts to herself, partly because she didn't want to be a damper on the enthusiasm of her friends, but mostly because she had other things to think about.

The other *thing* she thought mostly about was named Hank.

Since the day she'd seen him at the dean's office, he had been a persistent part of her life. Dot liked that. It also bothered her. If she truly planned to devote her future to a research career, then the right thing to do was to give a guy like Hank the brush-off, before he got stuck on her and she had to break his heart.

Every night after he walked her home from the library or the quadrangle or the student union, she'd tell herself this was the last time. Tomorrow she'd send him on his way. But the next day, he was right there again and she couldn't resist him. The days passed into weeks and more and more the entire campus began to see them as a couple.

Even Dr. Falk had ceased baiting her. Hank had never said one word. When it became clear that they were a couple, the professor backed off. Dot had gone from lightning rod to completely invisible. She wasn't sure that was really a step in the right direction.

So it was understandable on Saturday, with a room full of girlfriends all seriously discussing what to wear, that Dot's mind wandered.

Trixie, who had a wardrobe large enough to clothe a small country, was sorting out her formal gowns on the bed. Maylene and Eva were trying to help her decide what to wear.

Dot was sitting there, watching, listening, just not seeing or hearing.

When she noticed everyone was looking in her direction she sat up abruptly.

"What?" she asked.

"I asked if you'd given any thought to what you're going to wear," Maylene said. "You are the only one of us who's actually dating someone from Baldridge."

"Oh, no, I haven't thought about it," Dot admitted.

"Are you interested in Trixie's dress?"

Her roommate was holding up a lavender taffeta cocktail gown with a sweetheart neckline and a bouffant skirt.

"Oh, Trixie, you'll look very pretty in that," Dot said.

"I'm not wearing this," she said. "I'm asking you to. Dot, you're not paying any attention at all, are you?" she accused.

She blushed, admitting the truth. "Sorry."

"Don't scold her. She can't help it," Eva said. "She's in love."

Dot shook her head firmly. "Don't be silly," she told them.

"We're not being silly," Maylene said. "Only observant. You spend every waking moment with the guy. When you're with him, you're all dreamy eyed. When you're not with him, you're walk around like a zombie."

"I'm not dreamy eyed and I'm not a zombie," Dot defended.

"Nobody's criticizing you," Eva assured her. "Merely observing."

"That's right," Trixie said. "Of all of us, who'd believe that you'd be the one to find the right guy first."

"He's not 'the right guy,' he's just a guy and I'm really not that interested in guys. I'm going to stop seeing him. I'm going to stop seeing him really soon."

Her friends gave one another knowing glances, which was almost as frustrating to Dot as her own lack of follow-through on her intentions. Until she'd decided for certain whether she wanted a family or a career, she needed to stop leading Hank on.

Sally, a girl from down the hall, stuck her head in the door.

"Dot, telephone," she said. "It's him."

She hurried out of the room with a chorus of speculative ooh's behind her.

"Hello," she said, when he picked up the phone.

"Hi, sweetheart," Hank responded. "I'm up to my eyebrows in party favors over here and if I don't get out of this building, I'll go stark, raving mad."

Dot laughed.

"Meet me on the corner next to Ketchum Street in five minutes."

"Five minutes?" Dot glanced down at her clothing. "I'm wearing dungarees."

The denim slacks made popular for women by Rosy the Riveter and other WWII working girls were what all the female students wore in the dorm, but they were absolutely forbidden as appropriate attire for ladies on campus.

"That's perfect," he said. "We're going on a picnic."

In all of Dot's college days, she had never once even considered sneaking out of the dorm in such casual clothes. She hurried back to her room for reinforcements.

"Hank wants me to meet him on Ketchum in five minutes, dressed like this," she announced.

If she'd been hoping somebody would try to talk her out of it, she was disappointed.

Maylene grabbed a head scarf and tied it around Dot's hair. Eva helped her into her car coat. And Trixie stuck a straw hat on her head for good measure. The four young women hurried her down the stairwell.

"I'll distract anyone at the office," Trixie promised. "You two get her out of here without anybody seeing."

As luck would have it, the housemother was nowhere

in sight. The desk was manned by a student assistant who was easily distracted by Trixie.

"You've got to help me, I'm desperate," she said, dramatically. "I'm writing a bread-and-butter letter and I can't remember if I'm supposed to address it to my girlfriend who invited me or her mother, who's the lady of the house. Could we check the *Emily Post?*"

"Sure," the assistant said.

As the girl turned to get the huge reference books from the shelf behind her, Dot hurried past with Maylene and Eva on either side.

Once outside the door, they shooed her like a bird.

"Hurry, have fun."

Dot set off at a loping run but stopped herself at the sidewalk. Nothing would draw attention like running. Slowed to a normal pace, she thought about what she was doing. She was excited, a little nervous, but she failed to summon up any feelings of guilt, an amazing feat for a good girl like herself. She was breaking a rule, not something she could ever remember doing. But it was a ridiculous rule, made up by someone who obviously hadn't thought it through. It deserved to be broken and she decided that only by refusing to abide by it was she giving it the deference it deserved.

Just before she reached Ketchum, a green '49 Chevy pulled up to the curb. Hank was driving. Dot opened the door and slid onto the seat.

"Right on time," he said.

"And nobody saw me."

"It's their loss," he assured her.

Hank drove out to the edge of town, crossed the wide river bridge and turned off onto a narrow road that curved around a high bluff. The narrow lane dead-ended into a patch of worn grass, obviously frequented by numerous cars.

Hank parked the Chevy and they got out. Dot was entranced by the view across the water of the little college town. The sky was clear blue with only a hint of clouds on the horizon. The trees were adorned in their brightest autumn colors—red, orange, yellow and gold. She could see a half-dozen church steeples rising from the distant landscape. The twelve-story Crenshaw Hotel, Main Street's tallest structure, and the cluster of limestone and red brick buildings that made up the university campus. It all seemed as idyllic as a painting.

"This is beautiful," she said.

"You should see it at night," he responded.

"Oh, yes, it must really be something."

There was a moment of hesitation and Dot glanced his way. Hank was grinning ear to ear.

"What?"

"Sorry, I'm having a joke at your expense."

"A joke?"

"This place is known on campus as Petting Peak," he said. "If you come up here after dark, it's a crowded parking lot. And all the cars have the windows steamed up."

Dot felt herself blushing. She'd, of course, heard of Petting Peak. It was said that just driving past the place was enough to ruin a girl's reputation.

"Don't worry," Hank told her. "We'll be out of here long before the sun goes down. For us, it's just a picnic spot."

From the trunk of the Chevy he got out a tablecloth-covered basket and a plaid blanket.

"There's a nice place up this way," he said, indicating a narrow footpath that went up among the trees. "It's not too rough going and you impress me as a girl who's not afraid of a challenging climb."

Dot put her hands on her hips. "Lead on," she told him.

The trail they went up wasn't tricky or dangerous, but it was plenty steep and Dot was pretty sure that it would have been inaccessible to young ladies in heels. But with Keds on her feet and the freedom of dungarees, she had no problem at all.

They reached the top to find that the view was even better and, without the shade of the trees, it was pleasantly warm. A lazy south wind blew an occasional breeze that barely stirred the air.

Together they laid out the blanket and settled down on it.

Dot removed her hat and her head scarf.

"No further need for disguise?" he asked.

She laughed. "I want to feel this breeze on my hair," she admitted.

He nodded. "Take the ponytail down, then you'll really feel it."

Dot pulled the rubber band out of her hair and combed the loose locks with her fingers. It did feel great. She glanced over at Hank. His smile had disappeared, and his expression was very serious.

"What?" she asked.

The solemnity remained in his eyes, but he managed to pair it with a mischievous grin.

"I was just thinking," he said, "that the last time I got a good look at that beautiful hair, I was immediately doused with cold water."

Dot laughed and shook her head. "Unless you've got

a bucket with a long enough rope for me to dip it down in the river, I think that you're very safe up here."

He reached over and caught a strand of the long brunette length and twirled it gently around his finger.

"I'm not sure either of us is safe up here," he said.

Dot might have asked him what he meant by that, but his faint touch and the huskiness of his words somehow had her trembling.

She became peculiarly aware of how alone they were and how closely they were seated on the small square of woven fabric. He continued to twist her hair, slowly inching her nearer.

He began leaning forward, urging her toward him. Dot knew he was going to kiss her. She wanted him to kiss her. She ached for him to kiss her. She'd been waiting since the day they'd met for him to kiss her. But was it fair? She didn't know what she wanted yet; she wasn't sure if romance could be included in her life.

In the last instant before their lips met, the final second before she would taste him, the ultimate last chance before it couldn't be stopped, she could feel his breath on her skin, their faces only inches apart, she hesitated.

"There's something I have to tell you," she said.

"Tell me later," he answered, and pulled her into his arms. Hank's mouth came down on hers and all thoughts of qualifiers and explanations vanished.

His lips were warm and welcoming, there was tenderness but also passion, power. She had kissed before, but never like this. He moved his mouth on hers, tugging ever so gently, as if he would pull her soul into his own. It was more than just a gesture of affection or even desire. There was an instant of wholeness of finding home and recognizing it as exactly that. Dot gave herself up to it.

She wrapped her arms around his neck, urging him closer. He moaned against her lips and she felt the vibration of it in his chest. Momentarily she felt exuberant, in control. That was followed, almost immediately, by a sense of being swept into a tide of longing.

Dot wasn't sure who called a halt, but as they separated, the loss was too much for her. She nestled her face in the crook of his neck. He tightened his grip around her as if he never wanted to let her go.

"I knew it would be like this," he whispered. "Somehow I just knew that you had to be the one."

He began to feather little kisses along her temple and down to her jaw. Dot's heart was pounding, her senses finely alert and her brain inexplicably foggy. She raised her head, offering access to the length of her throat. Hank explored the territory eagerly.

The feel of his mouth so distracted her, she didn't realize that she was leaning until her back touched the blanket. He was above her, his expression lazy but with the hint of a satisfied smile.

"Dot," he told her, "I think I've fallen in love with you."

A like declaration sprang to her own lips, but inexplicably the image of Dr. Falk, in his superior, judgmental voice, flashed through her brain, silencing her words and sobering her inclinations.

"Wait!"

"It's okay," Hank assured her. "I'm not going to push you. I know when to stop."

"No, it's not that," she said. "Well, yes, it is that, but it's more."

Hank ceased placing kisses on her eyebrows and regarded her more seriously.

"What?" he asked.

"Let me get up."

He released her and moved away. Dot sat up, primly straightened her blouse and smoothed her hair. She pulled it back tightly and reattached the rubber band.

She glanced over at Hank. He was eyeing her curiously.

"Did I do something wrong?" he asked. "Did I speak too soon?"

Dot nodded.

"I can't have a boyfriend," she said.

Hank's brow furrowed momentarily and then he laughed. "Of course you can," he said. "I'm sure that's within the rules and regulations, even at Compton Hall."

"No, I don't mean I can't *can't*. I mean I can't *shouldn't*."

"Why not? You're not worried about your grades— you're tops in all your classes."

"It's not grades."

"Then what is it?"

"It's my future."

"What about it?"

"I…I have to think about it," Dot said. "I haven't decided about it."

He shrugged, unconcerned. "We've still got seven months before graduation. A lot of us haven't got our plans worked out yet."

"It's more than plans," she said. "For me…well, it's different."

"How so?"

She didn't know quite where to begin. She turned the question back to him.

"Tell me what you want for your future, Hank?"

He was thoughtful for a moment.

"I'd like to get a good job," he said. "By good, I mean something that I'd enjoy doing and that would have some purpose to it. I don't have to make tons of money, but I want enough to get by and build up some savings for a rainy day. Someday I'd like to own a house with a yard and have a couple of kids to grow up there. I want to be healthy, live to old age and have good friends. But more than any of that, or all of it, I want the right woman to share a life. I want a wife who's smart and funny and serious and impetuous and…well, it sounds like I want you, doesn't it?"

She didn't pick up on his suggestion or comment on his declaration.

"I guess I want what everyone wants," he continued.

Dot nodded. "I don't know about everybody," she said. "But that's what I want, too. Unfortunately, I can't have it."

"Why not?"

"Because that's not how the world works," she said. "You know that a woman can't have a career and a family."

Hank thought about that and nodded. "Sure she can—she must," he said. "If she doesn't marry, how will she afford to live? It's hard enough for a woman to even get offered a job, let alone one that pays more than pin money. She'll need a husband to pay the bills whether she chooses to work or not."

"But any chance of being taken seriously at work disappears if she has Mrs. in front of her name," Dot countered. "Any company will treat a married woman as a temporary employee, because they know that any day she might get…in the family way. If she does, they'll have to replace her, because you can't have a woman who's going to have a baby working in public. And after her baby is born, she'll have to stay home to take care of it."

"Children eventually go to school," he said.

Dot nodded.

"One child goes to school in just six years, but there's no way to predict how many you'll have," she pointed out. "It could be two, it could be twelve. Either way, you're not in the clear until well into your forties. And nobody hires middle-aged matrons. That's like a comedy skit."

Hank could only shrug in agreement.

"That's what I went in to talk to Dr. Glidden about," she explained. "I mean, initially I went there to complain about Dr. Falk and not getting appointments with job recruiters. But she made me see that Dr. Falk is not some strange, offbeat aberration that I need to get past in my classwork. He's the norm out in the world I want to work in. His attitudes are their attitudes."

"He's a creep," Hank said adamantly.

Dot appreciated his sentiment.

"Dr. Glidden explained to me that a woman can't be like a man. She can't do whatever she wants. She can have a career or a family, but there is just no plan, no mechanism in society for her to have both."

There was not any way that Hank could disagree with that and he didn't try. Instead, he asked the question that Dot had been asking herself.

"Which do you want more? A family or a career?"

Dot shook her head. "That's the problem," she admitted. "I want them both. I can't seem to choose. I love kids. I always thought I'd want to be a mom. But I love science, too. And I'm the first person in my family to go to college. Can I just throw that away and say it's not important to me? That it changes nothing?"

"No, of course not."

"So, I haven't decided what I'm going to do yet. And until I do, it's unfair for me to get involved with someone," she said. "I don't know yet if I'm willing to fall in love. I don't know if I can let someone fall in love with me."

"Oh, sweetheart," Hank said, "I think you're too late."

CHAPTER SIX

THE MAIN LIVING ROOM of Baldridge Hall was off-limits to anyone who wasn't tying bows, hanging lights or cutting the thousands of autumn-colored paper leaves that were the main staple of the theme's decor. Hank, and the residents under his command, were approaching the festivities of the formal dance with all of the organization and dedication they had put into the panty raid. And Hank was pretty sure that had been exactly what the dean had wanted.

Hank had tried to use everybody's strengths and interests. The Ag and Forestry majors gathered a full half mile of wild grapevine from every fallow field and woods within miles around campus. Premed, Botany and Biology cleaned it and twisted it into garlands that Math students strung up precisely two feet apart across the width of the room. Each yard had an eighteen-inch drop where a brightly colored leaf, sparkling with glitter, dangled down to create an atmosphere of intimacy. The guys studying Drama and Music were in charge of the bandstand, which had to have a raised dais, lights and a gossamer background of orange, brown, red and gold. The future engineers put together an amazing water feature that was expected to be the "wow factor" of the entire decor.

The whole operation as it progressed, was both eye-opening and surprisingly fulfilling. Chemistry majors discovered cooking and athletes had the opportunity to utilize the muscles they'd honed. The fellows in the College of Business were uniquely challenged on how to produce such a lovely occasion within the tiny budget that had been previously collected for pep rally snacks.

Everyone seemed to be gaining from the opportunity. Especially Hank. Hank needed something to fill his hours since Dot had sent him on his way.

He was being dumb, foolish, a knot-head, he told himself. Dot was just a girl—the university was full of girls. If she didn't know what she wanted, if she wasn't sure what her future should hold, then Hank should forget her, stop looking for her and move on. There were plenty of fish in the sea, and most of them wanted a bright young man to wed and have a home.

That's what he told himself, again and again. But that's not what he'd felt. He had listened to her explanations, her motivations, and he tried to understand. He wasn't sure he did. Wasn't marriage and children a biological imperative for females? That's what everyone thought. Wasn't the woman uniquely made to fulfill domestic duties? His mother hadn't reared him to believe such fallacies, and watching the men of Baldridge Hall step up to the plate so admirably to *women's work* quashed any lingering doubts he had.

So he knew that she was right, he supposed. But he still didn't like it. He hadn't been able to keep his eyes off her, even before they'd met. Now she was at the edge of every thought that went through his mind. She was the one with whom he wanted to share every dream that came into his head.

But it wasn't to be.

Late at night in the darkness of his dorm room, he'd imagine that she'd have a sudden change of heart. That she'd come running to him, declaring that she didn't want to live without him. Completely convinced that what she truly longed for was a little house with a white picket fence and a brood of rowdy children. But he couldn't honestly say, even to himself, that he wanted her to give up her dreams. Her dreams were as much of what he loved about her as every other aspect of her person. He didn't want some women who just looked like her or talked like her. He wanted her—Dot Wilbur, chock-full of personal hopes and ideals and ambitions.

Sometimes he told himself that in a few years, out working in some impressive science laboratory, she'd realize everything that she imagined for herself—a renowned research, a dozen breakthrough patents, a Nobel Prize. That when it was enough, she'd seek him out, telling him that she'd made her choice and she chose him.

In the stark light of day, however, he knew that once they left campus, headed their separate ways, they would most likely never see each other again. Just the idea of that felt like a nightmare. But Hank wondered if it was more frightening than seeing her every day.

Class was the worst. He'd sit at his desk, his notebook open, his pencil at the ready, intent on writing down every significant word that dropped from Dr. Falk's lips. Instead, he'd find his attention drifting toward the far right desk in the front of the room, where lips that he'd tasted now pursed in concentration as she stared at the blackboard. He watched her small, delicate hands now clutching her pencil. Those hands had caressed his shoulder blades, rested upon his chest. He had wanted those hands against his skin. He wanted those hands...

The distraction was untenable. How was a guy supposed to concentrate on Organic Chemistry when such beautiful hands were in view?

Deliberately, Hank forced his attention to the floor. But then, along the floor his eyes drifted to the sight of her feet. Elegant, tantalizing feet, slim ankles in sensible pumps, the enticing curve of calf, the hem of her skirt. Hank imagined what was beneath that skirt and accidentally broke his pencil in half.

Don't think about it! Don't think about it! he admonished himself.

Being in the same room with her but so forcefully separate, he could hardly think of anything else.

When they'd been a twosome, he had been so relaxed, so full of hope and ambition. He had been no stranger to desire. But the edge to it had been less. He'd been waiting, wanting, confident that time would bring that around. He could kiss and hold her, knowing that, in the not so distant future, they could be together sexually as they were romantically. He'd believed it was their future. It was inevitable. And it would be well worth the wait when every feeling was shared and experienced.

Now it seemed that it was never going to happen. He was never going to touch her that way. They would never put their bodies together as one. The loss was devastating.

Dot had been good for his studies. Now, without her, he just felt empty. But it was an emptiness that was more than hollow—it was wrenching with unfulfilled longing.

Hank was jolted back into reality when they were dismissed. He glanced down at his papers and saw that an hour lecture had only produced two sentences for study and one of them didn't make sense.

He let go a huff of self-disgust. If he kept this up, by the end of semester, his entire class notes could be written on the head of a pin.

Mutely he filed out, letting Dot get far ahead of him and trying not to pay attention to which way he was headed. A guy from the dorm stopped him and asked to borrow a pen. Hank loaned him one and belatedly realized that his slide rule wasn't in his pocket. He'd need it for the next class. Annoyed, he backtracked to Dr. Falk's classroom to retrieve it.

"Ah...Mr. Brantly," the professor said as he saw him. "I'm glad I caught you."

Hank didn't care how amiable the guy tried to be with him. He'd always hold him in low esteem for the way he treated Dot. Still, respect came naturally to him.

"Yes, sir?" he responded politely.

"I wanted to let you know that the recruiter from Universal Research Labs will be here on Thursday and Friday," he said. "If you'd like to talk with him, I'd be happy to put you on the list."

"Yeah, great," he answered immediately.

He was being offered a chance at the brass ring that every guy in his class was reaching for. Lining up the dream job while still on campus was the senior class ambition. Everyone wanted to walk across the graduation stage and straight through the employee's entrance of a company.

He ignored Falk's pretense at bestowing such an honor. Hank knew it was no gift. He'd earned his place in the class. The opportunity to meet with company representatives visiting campus was nothing more than he deserved.

It was only later when he wondered if Dot was on the list, if she was going to get a chance to interview. He thought not. He couldn't imagine Dr. Falk going out of his way for her. When that thought occurred to him, Hank's eyes narrowed.

Self-important, closed-minded Neanderthal, he said to himself. He wished he could kick the creep's white-coat-covered backside all over campus. Of course, he could not.

But he could help Dot. If no one else at the university was going to lift a finger for her, Hank decided he must do it himself.

SPIFFED UP in his brown suit, white shirt and gray-and-brown striped necktie with the yellow dots down the center, he was fashionable but not flashy. He made his way to the third floor of the Student Union where the interviews were being held. There were three other guys waiting, each as overdressed for campus life as Hank was himself.

The talk as they waited was inconsequential and everyday. The weather. Football scores. The swell lines of the new Lincoln Continental. Nothing of any importance or any pertinence to their future was said. But Hank knew it was what was on everyone's mind.

One of the other fellows he didn't know, someone he'd seen around on campus, and one had been in a class with Hank the previous semester. The fellow with whom he was familiar was, to Hank's mind, no great prize. So, he wasn't in particularly good company. And the fact that apparently that guy was chosen over Dot really had him steaming. He'd never really thought about how unfair things were, that a half-wit jerk got more breaks than the smartest girl in school. But he was thinking about it now and it made him mad. Not just for Dot, but for all the girls. Even for his mother. He'd always known how hard his mom worked for so little. Now he saw more clearly what she'd been up against every day of her life.

By the time it was his turn to talk to the recruiter, he'd forgotten completely about getting hired and walked in with a chip on his shoulder as big as the university clock tower.

What the man, Clifford Wojciechowski, might have wanted to ask him, Hank never knew. Hank was the guy with the questions and he wanted answers.

"How do you choose your employees?" Hank shot off first. "Based on their clothes or their ability at the track?"

The recruiter was momentarily startled.

"We try to find the best academic prospects who—"

"The *best?*" Hank interrupted. "Are you aware that one of the top students in our class, perhaps the best mind in the whole university, has been shut out of these interviews?"

The man seemed genuinely startled.

"No, I wasn't aware of that," he said.

"Someone I think might be a very valuable asset to your company has been unfairly left off your interview list."

Mr. Wojciechowski's brow furrowed. "Our policy has been to rely on experienced academicians for recommendations," he said.

"Well, that policy," Hank insisted, "does not necessarily present you with the most qualified or suitable candidates. Certain professors can be guilty of favoritism and prejudice."

The man nodded. "That is true," he said. "Partiality

can undo all the most productive efforts. You run into that type in every line of work. Who do you think we've missed? I'll make a personal effort to speak with him myself."

The recruiter had his pen poised above the paper, ready, eager, to write down the name.

"Dorothy Wilbur."

The movement of the pen hesitated, and Wojcie-chowski quit writing. He smiled at Hank.

"Girlfriend?" he asked.

There was a part of Hank that wanted to answer affirmatively and with pride. But it wasn't wholly true and it wasn't what would help Dot.

"No," he said. "She's a really smart, hardworking student who wants a career. Professor Falk disapproves of that and won't give her a chance."

The recruiter eyed Hank thoughtfully.

"This woman has a gift for science," Hank continued. "She ought to be allowed to use it."

The man shrugged. "Women do use their talents," he said with a wry grin. "Cooking is chemistry. Washing is physics. And having children, that's multiplication."

Hank wasn't amused. He shook his head.

"I've heard all the arguments," he said. "They don't add up. As a citizen, she's got a right to the pursuit of happiness. Maybe a career won't make her happy, but she's capable and qualified. Denying her even a chance, well...well, that's not why I got shot at in Korea."

Mr. Wojciechowski straightened slightly and glanced down at the papers in front of him.

"I didn't realize you were a combat veteran."

Hank shrugged. "I was just a draftee," he said.

"Me, too," the guy answered. "In the big one. D-Day

plus two," he said, indicating he'd landed on Normandy beach during the third day of assault.

Hank whistled appreciably. "Glad to see you here," he said.

They both laughed, grimly, as if there were some strange dark humor to survival. Then they quieted, thoughtful.

"Okay," Wojciechowski said, handing Hank his card. "I'll see your Dorothy Wilbur. I can't promise anything. Even if I like her and recommend her, it probably won't go anywhere. But I'll talk to her."

"It's a step in the right direction," Hank said.

Outside a few moments later, Hank was nearly gliding on air as he hurried over to Compton. He left the man's card and directions to the interview room for Dot at the dorm's desk. He didn't want her to see him, to thank him. He just wanted her to have her chance.

It was only afterward, making his way back to Baldridge that his emotions began to well up in him. He loved Dot. He wanted her with him. But he was helping her get away.

What else could he do? he thought. When you love someone you have to want what they want. Even when it breaks your heart.

CHAPTER SEVEN

THE NIGHT OF THE Panty Raiders' Cotillion was perfect. A surprising Indian summer had appeared with night temperatures so moderate that a mere stole or shawl was sufficient cover over strapless gowns.

"I'm not going," Dot had declared to her girlfriends on a daily basis since the day at the river.

She wouldn't listen to any of their arguments. Eventually they gave up wasting their breath. She'd made a mistake even keeping company with Hank. If she couldn't decide between love and marriage, then the last thing she needed to do was tempt herself with gorgeous dresses, fancy parties and romantic dances in a gentleman's arms.

Amazingly, the interview with Mr. Wojciechowski had put a kink in her resolve.

She'd been walking around determined and keeping a stiff upper lip. It was the only way to fend off the sadness and gloom of being without Hank. When the buzzer went off in her room, to let her know she had a message at the desk, she didn't think much about it. She assumed it was from her parents. Her father was sending her a bus ticket so she could make the six-hour trip home for Thanksgiving. When she went down later, heading out to the library, she stopped to pick it up.

Her heart-in-the-throat excitement when she saw her message had nothing to do with the content, but rather with seeing Hank's handwriting on the accompanying note. She read it over several times. His words weren't cryptic, but she knew there was much to read between the lines.

She walked into the dorm's long parlor and sat down in a comfy armchair. This time of day, the place was deserted except for a game of canasta at the far end of the room. She stared at the card and the sparse sentences attached, trying to sort out the meaning. Not the actual meaning—she understood that she now had an opportunity to interview with a recruiter for Universal Research. Dot searched for the deeper meaning, the illusive implication that women have always looked for in the words and actions of men.

Was this just a simple notification? He'd heard about the recruiter and he was just spreading the word. Or was he being the great rescuer, rushing in to save the foolish, incompetent damsel, too weak to help herself? Was this a ploy to win her favor? Rather than candy or flowers, he was gifting her with what she really wanted to make her think the better of him. Or could this be his sacrifice to her love? He cared so much that he was willing to give her up, to let her pursue her dreams without him.

Somehow, the last alternative was the one that she liked least. She didn't want him to nobly let her go. Yet, letting her go was exactly what she'd asked for. Dot threw the papers down in self-disgust. This girl-boy stuff was more complicated than nuclear propulsion!

The meeting with Mr. Wojciechowski didn't help. He was polite, interested, but he didn't give her tremendous hope.

"You appear to be a very knowledgeable and qualified candidate," he told her. "If you were a young man, my company would undoubtedly come up with a very attractive salary offer. But you're a woman. Hiring and training employees is very expensive for corporations. No one wants to devote that time and money on a person who isn't committed to the company."

"I could be committed to the company," Dot assured him.

He shook his head. "Can you honestly tell me that you'll never want to marry?" he asked. "That you'll never want to have a family? Never put your personal life ahead of the goals of the company?"

Dot stared at him for a long moment.

"Do you ask men to do that?"

Wojciechowski was so embarrassed by the question, he never answered it.

"Men are men and women are women," he said. "They have different talents, different skills. They are made to do different things. If you're interested in being in the typing pool, I'm sure I could find something. Perhaps I could hire you and your boyfriend both."

"I assume that he wouldn't have to start in the typing pool."

"Look, Miss Wilbur," he said, "I'm sure you're a very bright girl. I could sugarcoat it for you, give you false hope. But the truth is, science careers will never be open to women. Go into teaching, it's a field where you could be useful and helpful. It's really your only option."

As Dot walked back to the dorm, she should have been fuming. But somehow, she wasn't angry anymore. Who was there to be angry at? Wojciechowski? Dr. Falk? Her high school principal? Her dad?

All the men in the world? Most of the women, too, for that matter? If she started being mad, where would it ever stop?

That was why, on the night of the Panty Raiders' Cotillion, she changed her mind.

"I'm going," she announced to her girlfriends, all of whom were already in mid-preen.

A startling chorus of screams erupted and all three of them jumped into action.

"We don't have much time," Maylene complained.

"Oh, we'll make it," Eva assured her. "Trixie, where's the dress?"

It was immediately produced from the closet. A confection of bright lavender taffeta, it had an abundance of matching tulle petticoats.

"Here, try it on, let's see if it's going to need any adjustments."

"I'm sure it's fine," Dot said.

"Fine is not good enough," Trixie told her. "Tonight you've got to be positively dreamy."

Dot thought the dress fit very well, but the girls agreed that the strapless sweetheart bodice needed a little tightening in the waist. Maylene hurried down the hall to get Barbara, who was an excellent seamstress. Barbara's roommate, Esther, came along as well.

"What's going on?" an anonymous voice asked from the hallway.

"Dot's going to the cotillion after all," Trixie answered.

The word spread from doorway to doorway and, within minutes, Dot and Trixie's room was shoulder to shoulder and a dozen more watching from the entrance. The noise, the exuberance, the excitement, was extremely contagious and within minutes, Dot and all those around her were giddy with jitters.

A half-dozen hands worked to twist Dot's hair into a dramatically upswept French roll. Dot hardly recognized herself in the mirror.

"Do you think it's too much?" she asked.

"Trust me," Trixie told her. "You look just like Grace Kelly."

"Grace Kelly is blond," someone pointed out. "Dot looks more like Jane Wyman."

"Not Jane Wyman, Natalie Wood."

"Natalie never wears her hair this way."

"Well, she should."

Two dozen would-be makeup experts argued about her face. Dot was among the group that wanted to go with her basic peaches-and-cream with some powder for the shine on her nose and a smudge of pale pink lipstick.

"This dress is just too dramatic for that," Eva insisted. Instead they plucked her eyebrows to a thin line and darkened them with pencil. Mascara and an eyelash curler gave her a sleepy, sexy look. And the vivid red that Eva chose for her mouth drew immediate attention to the fullness of her lips.

"I don't even look like me," Dot complained.

"You do, only better," Trixie said.

"This is what you could be," Maylene told her, "if that's what you wanted."

Tonight, Dot decided, it was exactly what she wanted.

The dress fit perfectly after Barbara's adjustments, the heavy boning in the bodice as rigid as a corset. Trixie loaned her a pair of white opera gloves that came up past her elbow. The flair of the ballerina-length bouffant skirt emphasized her small waist. The hair and heels made her seem majestically tall and willowy. The bare shoulders were daring and very grown-up. She was no bobby-soxer, but a fully adult female, confident and desirable.

The image practically took the wind out of her sails.

"Are you sure?" she asked Trixie.

"The poor guy will never know what hit him," she replied.

It was only a couple of minutes before seven when the girls of the second floor made their way downstairs. The noise from the hallway was deafening and the gathering of gowns in the living room was as colorful as an exotic flower garden. The scent in the air was a heady mix of Chanel No. 5, My Sin and Evening in Paris.

"They're here!" Mary Jane Coulter screeched from near the window.

She was uniformly shushed by the more mature upperclasswomen in the room. The housemother, Mrs. Livingston, looked at her disapprovingly and then gestured with her hands for silence.

"Young ladies," she began. "I wish that Miss Elizabeth Compton could be here herself tonight." The housemother gestured toward the nineteenth-century portrait above the fireplace. "As hostess for her father, Governor Compton, she set an example of modesty, gentility and prudence that each of you should strive to emulate."

As Dot gazed up at the woman in the painting, the face appeared to be one of squinty, hard-lined unhappiness. She'd been honored by having her name grace a women's dormitory. What were her achievements? Dot was aware of none, except being born in a prominent family. Was she exactly what she appeared, a dried-up, humorless old maid? Was that the life Dot was expected to esteem? But most probably, she had no opportunity to be anything else. Like Dot, Elizabeth Compton's place in the world was most likely not at any time in her own control.

"I expect each of you," Mrs. Livingston continued, "to behave yourselves in a fashion that honors your school, this group of women and most of all, your upbringing. Have a lovely time!"

She clapped her hands and the beautifully attired residents formed one long line. Outside, the men from Silas Baldridge had done the same.

For the sake of propriety, each of the gentlemen would be presented to Mrs. Livingston. She would then introduce the gentleman to the young lady next in line. He would then escort that girl to the dance.

As they slowly moved forward in the line, Dot heard Trixie's whispered prayer aloud.

"Please don't let it be somebody short," she pleaded. "No short guys. He can be stupid, he can be ugly, he can wear glasses, but nobody shorter than me, please!"

As they neared the door, Trixie began counting. She was sixth from the doorway. She counted out six white sport coats beyond the door.

"Oh, my God!" she muttered under her breath. "He's a shrimp. He'll come up to my shoulder. He's practically a dwarf."

Dot counted out for herself and saw that, indeed, the guy Trixie was numbered up for was a couple of inches shorter than Trixie herself.

"Trade places with me," Dot said.

"He's shorter than you, too," Trixie said.

Dot shrugged. "Not so much," she said. "And it really doesn't matter."

Trixie hurried to comply, showering words of gratitude on her roommate.

When Dot stepped onto the threshold, she pulled her shawl more tightly around her shoulders against the coolness of the night air. She smiled warmly at the short, red-haired, freckled-faced guy who stood in front of her.

"Buzz, do you mind if I cut in here?" a familiar voice said to the side.

All eyes turned to Hank, who'd been handling the introductions.

"Sure thing," the redheaded guy said. "Mrs. Livingston, this is Henry Brantly."

"Mr. Brantly," the housemother acknowledged him with a nod. "May I present Miss Dorothy Wilbur."

Hank bowed. "Miss Wilbur," he said. "You look beautiful tonight, as always. I'd be so honored to escort you to the dance."

Dot took the hand he offered.

CHAPTER EIGHT

ALL WEEK LONG Hank had devoted himself to the prospect of the dance. It was his salvation, his distraction. Every idle moment was somehow filled up with the image of Dot. She was the first thought that entered his mind when he awakened in the morning. And the last, heartbroken sadness that kept his nights sleepless and long. When big things happened, like his acceptance to a very good graduate engineering program, she was the one he wanted to tell. When little things happened, like the construction-paper turkey that had been hung up in the stairwell, Dot was the person with whom he wanted to share that story.

He also wanted to hear what she had to say. He was anxious to know if she had met with Mr. Wojciechowski. He wanted to know what the man had told her, if she thought he might give her a chance. He wondered if her bus ticket to visit her parents had shown up. If she'd talked to Dean Glidden again. But mostly he speculated about whether she'd attend the cotillion and if he'd get a moment alone with her.

As committee chairman, he took on the task of doing the introductions. There were more boys at Baldridge than girls at Compton, so more than two dozen guys would be going stag. He volunteered to be one of those.

And he'd had every intention of fulfilling his duty. That is, until he caught sight of Dot standing in the doorway.

He'd always thought her pretty. Hank had noticed that the first time he'd laid eyes on her. But tonight, tonight, wow! She was flat-out, knock-down, crazy-man gorgeous. Suddenly, the idea of some other guy walking her to the dance was completely unappealing.

"Do you mind if I cut in here?" he'd blurted out.

Hank was sure he looked like an idiot. He wasn't supposed to be cutting, he wasn't supposed to be escorting. His job was introducing and he was just walking away from it.

Buzz, ever steady and unflappable as he was, didn't even bat an eyelash. He did the introduction perfectly and as Hank took Dot's arm, Buzz turned to the guy behind him to get an introduction to Dot's roommate.

Each man standing up for the next was probably not in the etiquette book, but Hank was past caring. He had Dot on his arm and a lazy ten-minute stroll for just the two of them.

The color in her cheeks was bright. He thought her hand trembled against his bicep. But maybe it was his own arm. He had never felt so jittery around a woman before. He'd never cared as much as he cared for Dot.

"I'm so glad that you decided to come," he said.

"I hadn't planned to," she admitted. "But at the last minute...well, I just couldn't miss it." She lowered her tone perceptibly. "I missed you."

Hank felt his nervousness melt with a sigh of relief.

"I missed you, too," he said.

She smiled up at him.

"Thank you for getting me the interview with Universal Research Labs," she said. "It was very kind of you to do that."

"Kind?" he responded. "It was kind to *them*. They'd be lucky to have you. And you deserved a shot at their company. How did it go?"

Dot shrugged. "About as badly as you'd expect," she said.

Hank shook his head, disappointed. "It's their loss," he said.

Dot ignored the comment and changed the subject. She asked him about his Thanksgiving plans, of which he had none. She talked about her impending bus ride to see her family.

Hank told her about the graduate engineering program.

"You have to go," she said.

"Maybe," he told her. "It's a good opportunity. But my money from the GI Bill runs out about halfway through, so I'm not sure I can afford it. But I'm thinking about it."

"I'm sure there's a way," Dot said encouragingly.

Hank was buoyed by her confidence.

They joined the line of couples when they arrived at Baldridge. The conventions begun at the girl's dorm were carried out here. The gentlemen presented the young ladies to their dorm mother, Mrs. Pritchard. She welcomed them and invited the couples inside. The civilities only took a couple of minutes, but it was formal enough to keep both sexes on their best behavior.

With Dot's hand still in the crook of his arm, he led her through the foyer where the office was being used as a coat-check room. Dot removed her shawl and handed it to Hank. The sight of the exposed flesh of her shoulders hit Hank like a fist in the solar plexus. His Dot, the person that he loved, was the smartest girl in school, the most beautiful woman on earth and also the sexiest creature he'd ever imagined. It was all he could do not to take her in his arms that very moment.

He did manage to maintain his gentlemanly composure as he offered his arm once more and escorted her into the main living room.

There was gushy appreciation from most of the young ladies as they entered the room. Hank turned slightly for a glimpse of Dot's reaction.

The canopy of vines and leaves gave the feeling of a sheltered forest glade. The magical aspect was enhanced by the curved bench seating in little grotto niches with pagan statues. In the far side of the room, a waterfall cascaded down a rock face and flowed along a tiny river that separated the refreshment tables from the dance floor. A dainty little bridge, just wide enough for two, was the only connection of the two areas. The five-piece band was setting up in what appeared to be a cliff cave hidden behind gossamer curtains.

Dot's mouth dropped open and then, amazingly, she burst out laughing.

"Do you like it?" he asked.

"Yes, yes I do. But it's unbelievable," she admitted. "It's so...so much. It's fussy and girly, yet all this greenery and wood, you know that only guys would do that."

"I think the difference is, when you ladies put on a party, you know it's only one of many. We knew this might be the only one we'd ever do. So we had to get all our ideas in at one time."

"It may be just once, but I don't think any of us will ever forget it," she said.

Hank was pleased.

"Let me get your corsage," he said, and led her over to a nearby table.

The corsage was actually a collection of brightly colored, painstakingly collected autumn leaves, stacked from the largest, the maple, on the bottom to the poplar and hawthorn on top. They were sewn together with contrasting ribbon that was fashioned into a pom-pom on top.

"These are wonderful," Dot said.

Hank nodded, feigning solemn sincerity. "We hold them very dear. Before these bows were finally completed, we had several freshman contemplating a jump from the water tower to end it all."

Dot chuckled lightly and shook her head.

"May I do the honors?" he asked, holding up the leafy adornment and a long, stickpin.

"Oh…please," Dot agreed.

Now that he had the opportunity, Hank almost balked at the task. The material of her gown came up only slightly higher than her bosom, which, Hank couldn't help but notice, looked equally tempting in this fancy, bright lavender dress as it did in her everyday sweaters.

The fabric curved along the rounded edges of her breasts, drawing attention to the hint of cleavage between them. Hank's reaction to that nearness was physical. Deliberately, he cleared his throat and wished he could clear his thoughts as easily.

His hands were shaking so badly he feared he might jab her with the pin. He managed not to. And with only a bit less dexterity than an engineer should be expected to have, he got the silly piece of greenery attached to the highest part of the material that covered her right breast.

Hank no longer knew what to do with his hands. He wanted to use them to touch her, caress her, discover her.

None of those things were acceptable in the middle of the main living room of his dorm. Fortunately, at that moment, the band began to play.

"Let's dance?" he suggested.

"Okay."

They were the first couple on the floor. An encouragement, undoubtedly to the hesitating young people on the sidelines. The opening number was "When My Sugar Walks Down the Street." Hank's fox-trot was not as good as his jitterbug, but the thrill of holding Dot in his arms was sufficient incentive for him to give it his best.

He tried to keep her at a respectable distance. It was the polite thing to do, of course, but Hank wasn't motivated by that. He was afraid that if he held her in his arms, he'd never be able to let her go. But as the dance floor became more crowded, he had to hold her closer. Even in the up-tempo numbers, they hardly had space to separate them.

It was a slow, tender rendition of "Allegheny Moon" that finally had her snug and safe in his arms, her head resting against his shoulder. The seductive scent of her was too alluring. In the dim light and the privacy spawned by the crush of those around them, he leaned down to plant a simple kiss on her bare shoulder. She shuddered and surprisingly moved closer against him. Hank could feel the curves of her body. Dutifully, he kept his hand at her waist, but there were so many other places that he wanted to touch. One dastardly moment, as the music playing got the best of him, he allowed his hand to drift lower to the roundness of her backside. Through the slick fabric and a thousand yards of stiffened petticoats, he felt absolutely nothing. But apparently Dot did.

Her chin shot up and her mouth opened slightly in a startled O.

"Sorry," he said, quickly, and moved his hand back to where it belonged.

To his complete surprise, Dot grasped his hand in her own and moved it down on her rump. That, in itself, was shocking enough, but to Hank's surprise and delight, Dot went up on her tiptoes and wrapped both of her arms around his neck and plastered her body against his.

Hank now had two hands free. One he kept down on her bottom. The other he eased up along the bodice of her gown, slowly, hesitantly, giving her every opportunity to push it away. She didn't. In an epoch or an instant, he found himself actually caressing her breast.

Suddenly, everyone around him was applauding. The music had apparently ended and he'd not noticed. Guiltily he stepped away from her. The color in her cheeks was high and hot. He silently cursed the undignified reaction that was straining at his trousers. He was as bad as some pimply, teenage kid getting an erection on the dance floor.

He glanced around to see if anyone was looking at them. Nobody'd noticed. All the couples seemed to be intent only upon each other.

Hank glanced back at Dot. She was smiling shyly up at him. She was so beautiful, so generous, so vulnerable.

Let the next number be a swing number, a bunny hop, something fast moving and far from your partner, he pleaded silently with heaven.

The band started up the first bars of "True Love," a very seductive waltz. Just the idea of dancing it popped beads of sweat on his brow.

"Would you like to step out on the porch?" he suggested. "It's getting pretty warm in here."

"Sure," she agreed.

He took her hand and led her through the throng of dancers and across the little bridge. He escorted her among the chatting groups, around the heavily laden refreshment tables and across the room, this time less formally, his fingers at the small of her back.

The porch side of the main living room had a series of ten-foot french doors, several of which were already open to coolness of the evening. Together they stepped out. The huge porch ran the entire length of the dorm. Japanese lanterns offered only enough light to make the area romantic. There was an abundance of dark corners and shadowed benches, most already occupied. Hank and Dot walked the length of the tiled porch and seated themselves on the steps to the garden. Hank slid his arm around her shoulders and she laid her head against his neck.

"Are you cold?" he asked. "I can go find your wrap."

"No," she assured him. "Being close to you like this, I'll always be warm."

Hank liked the sound of that. It was much the way he felt as well. Tenderly, he placed a playful kiss on her forehead.

She moved away to turn and look at him. Nervously, she wet her lips. It was, undoubtedly, an unintended signal. He angled his head slightly sideways and met her mouth with his own. She tasted warm and sweet and luscious. Hank wanted to draw her completely into him. He urged her, implored her, until he heard the little moan deep in her throat that set his already reeling senses afire.

Fearing they'd both be burned, he pulled away, but couldn't resist taking tiny nips at the corners of her mouth, teasing, testing. She returned his affection with her own. Dot's kiss was just like her—genuine, guileless, enthusiastic. She held nothing back. The sheer sensuality of it nearly unmanned Hank. It had him gasping for breath and straining for self-control. Dot was apparently not interested in his retaining his aplomb. She wrapped her arms tightly around his neck and strained to get closer to him. Hank attempted to accommodate her, but found that even tightly pressed against him, he couldn't hold her near enough.

He encircled her waist, picked her up from the step and set her squarely upon his lap. That was such sweet torture, he groaned aloud. Her pretty bottom was right on top of the aching hardness in his pants. It felt *so* good, but not nearly good enough.

Straining against each other, Hank knew that they had to stop. He forced his lips away from her mouth, but got distracted from his gallant sacrifice by the naked flesh of her throat and collarbone. He feathered tiny sweet-tasting pecks down the length of her sternum. His hand could feel her hardened nipples even through the thick boned fabric. When his kisses reached the treasured hollow between her breasts, he wanted nothing more than to peel back that fabric, reveal the evidence of her desire and put his mouth there. When Hank hesitated, Dot's own hand snaked in between them and she tugged down at the bodice herself.

Hank might have let things go even further, if the sound of high heels on the tiles not far away hadn't brought him to his senses. He grabbed her hands, as much to stop where his own were going as to shackle her.

"Whoops, 'scuse us," a voice said behind them.

Neither Hank or Dot looked up until the footsteps had walked away.

"Wow!" Dot said, barely above a whisper. "I didn't...I'd heard, but, I didn't know it...it could be like that."

"It's never been like that for me with anybody else," Hank told her honestly.

The two just stared into each other's eyes in the dim light of the shadowed stairs. Hank was trying to remember who they were, where they were and why he couldn't just throw himself on top of the woman in his arms. She was still sitting pertly on his rock-hard erection and that was not doing his good sense any good at all.

"Let's walk," he suggested.

Hank set her on her own two feet. Dot seemed to be suffering from jelly legs, but he didn't offer his hand. Hank didn't feel all that steady himself, and having her lean against him could lead them straight into what he was hoping to stroll away from.

He clasped his hands together behind his back and walked beside her among the squarely manicured box hedges.

Hank tried to collect his thoughts. He tried to grasp some kind of intellectual understanding of his feelings for Dot. He had only hoped that tonight he might see her, dance with her, admire her from across the room. Instead, he'd held her in his arms. He'd kissed her, caressed her. He never wanted to let her go. Was that selfish? It probably was, but he couldn't conjure up a smidgeon of regret. Still, he apologized.

"I'm sorry that...I mean, I'm sorry if...if I pushed too much," he said. "I usually have better control of myself."

Dot shrugged and shook her head. "I usually have better control, too."

"And, Dot," he told her sincerely. "I promise that, if

you'll continue to see me, I'll not put such pressure on you in the future."

"You won't?"

"No. That is, I'll really try not to," he said. "I know that you're still trying to figure out what you want. I'm not going to push you into anything. I want you to be free to make your own choice."

"I have," she said. "I choose you."

Hank stopped in his tracks. He turned to look at her. She was smiling up at him.

"Say that again, so I know my brain is not playing tricks on me."

"I decided that I want to be with you," she said.

"You mean, steady until we get out of school or marriage until death do us part?" he asked.

"I don't remember hearing any marriage proposal," she pointed out. "So I can't answer that last one. But I can tell you that I love you. I want to be with you, laugh with you, make a life with you and have children with you."

Joy bubbled up inside of him.

"That sounds like a marriage proposal to me," he said. "I accept."

He wrapped his arms around her, lifted her feet from the pavement and spun around like a crazy man. They were laughing, hollering, kissing.

"I am so happy, so happy," he told her. "I can't even imagine our life together."

"I can," she said. "I've been thinking about it all evening."

"Really?"

"I think we should get married right after graduation," she said. "Then you should accept the chance at engineering school. We can move into a little apartment near campus and I can get a job. I can clean houses or wait tables. I can even type if the truth be told. Financially, it'll be tight, but I'm used to managing on no money. After you go to work, I can stay home and raise kids."

Hank was still smiling. This was exactly what he wanted. It was his dream come true. But something inside him just felt wrong.

"What about your dreams, Dot?" he asked her. "What about your future, your career? After all this hard work, you'll still want to pursue science."

"No," she said, shaking her head definitively. "That was just a silly, girlish whim and I've forgotten about it completely."

Hank felt cautious now, his exhilaration suddenly as fragile as spun sugar.

"A whim?" he asked. "You're the first person in your family to go to college. You're one of the top students in our class. You're the winner of the *Women in Science Foundation Scholarship*. When did you start thinking that is a whim?"

"Actually, I have you to thank for that, too," she said. "I realized it after my interview with Mr. Wojciechowski. He made it clear to me that I would never be accepted in the world of science. Society is not going to allow women to compete with men for important top level jobs in the workforce. Even if I got hired, I'd never be taken seriously. I'd never get the kind of research challenges that I'm capable of completing. It's just never going to happen. I'm always going to be second-class and therefore second-rate. And what was I going to have to give up for that? I was going to have to give up you, our future together, the children we might raise." She shrugged. "It was simply too high a price for no chance at the prize."

Hank stepped back from her. "So you're just giving up," he said. "You're not even going to try?"

"I'm going to try to be the best wife and mother that I can be," Dot said. "I'm going to channel all my goals and ambitions into your life. Your success will be my success. And I'll do everything I can to help you be successful."

"Dot, will that be enough?"

"Of course," she insisted, a little too brightly. "It's enough for all the rest of the women in the world. Why wouldn't it be enough for me?"

"Because you're not anybody else," he said. "You're unique, special, brilliant, talented."

She chuckled. "Believe me, Hank," she told him. "The suburbs are full of brilliant, talented women. I'm sure I'll fit in fine."

"I don't know if I want you to fit in," he said.

"What?"

"You're different from any girl I ever met," he said. "I love you for that, Dot. I love you for all that you want, for all that you are. If marrying me makes you give that up, then I'm not sure I want to marry you."

"What?"

"I mean if, at the very first obstacle, you can give up on something you been working toward all your life," Hank said, "what's to keep you from throwing in the towel at the first tough patch of our marriage."

"That's not the same thing," she insisted. "And Wojciechowski wasn't the *first* obstacle. If you run into a brick wall again and again and again, only a fool never decides to change direction."

"There is nothing foolish about going after what you want, what you deserve," he said.

"What I deserve?" Dot's color was high and her tone

was infuriated. "What I deserve is a man who loves me without question. A man who is willing to let me make my own decisions and who will stand behind me or beside me or wherever I need him to be."

"And what *I* deserve," Hank shot back, "is a woman who's not sacrificing her life to some ideal of marriage martyrdom."

CHAPTER NINE

DOT WAS OUT of breath by the time she got to the doorway of Compton Hall. That was to be expected. She'd walked out on Hank and left Baldridge intent on returning to her dorm alone. Unfortunately, Hank was not satisfied with just letting her go. He came after her, ostensibly escorting her home.

"Are you just going to leave?" he asked. "You're not going to try to talk it out, work it out. Are you just going to throw us away?"

Dot didn't answer. Instead, she walked faster and faster until she was practically trotting with him beside her, asking question after difficult, unarguable question.

She didn't even glance in his direction.

She had volunteered to accept the limitation of being his helpmate. She'd chosen to give up everything she'd ever wanted for him. And he'd thrown that offering back into her face, as if he didn't want it.

Dot vowed silently never to speak to him again as long as she lived.

When she reached her dorm, she walked inside without even a look back. Mrs. Livingston was in the office.

"You're home early. Did you have a nice time?" she asked.

"It was lovely," Dot answered. "But I'm tired."

She made it all the way to her room and had the door shut safely behind her before she burst into tears. She threw herself down on the bed and cried off every bit of mascara that she wore.

Why was it like this? Why was everything in her life so hard? Dot was tired of fighting. She wanted to be like other girls. To have a normal life where she did what was expected of her and other people approved. That's what she was trying to do. Why wasn't it working? It worked for other girls—why didn't it work for her?

She'd been honest with Hank, or mostly honest at the very least. She did love him. She did want to marry him. And she wasn't willing to give that up. All that was true.

But part of what he said was true as well. Giving up on her hopes and dreams was a tremendous sacrifice. It proved everyone right and everything she'd tried to do as wrong. She knew that there was good, valuable work she could do that would never get done. But she couldn't change the world. If Hank didn't understand that. Then…then why was she thinking of marrying him?

Her thoughts and hopes, her sadness and her tears dragged her down for hours. But she'd managed to change out of her fancy clothes, to wash her face and present a reasonable appearance by the time the rest of the girls made it home. She didn't want any questions from anyone about anything.

Fortunately, luck was with her. Or love at least. Trixie was floating on air. Buzz, the red-haired, freckled-face shrimp, had turned out to be Prince Charming.

"He's clever and funny and he's premed," her roommate told Dot, excitedly. "He's going into general practice with his father."

"Sounds perfect," Dot agreed.

The other big news of the evening was that Esther, Barbara's roommate, had gotten pinned. Her boyfriend, Ned, who was in the Civil Engineering fraternity, gave her his Chi Delta Chi pin. The status was more serious than going steady, but less than engaged.

The girls of Compton Hall held an impromptu candlelight ceremony. Dot was urged to join them. She tried. The pajama-clad women sat in a circle near the stairwell, passing a white candle as they sang, "When I Fall in Love." Each girl would hold the candle, stare into the flame, looking for her own true love. The sentiment of a forever kind of love that was complete oneness and totally reciprocal brought shy tears to the eyes of many of the girls, including Dot. As they came to the last line of the song, a commitment to forever and a belief in love as the greatest power on earth, the candle was handed to Esther. Accepting both the joy of the moment and the obligation of the future, Esther blew out the candle. Everyone applauded and hugged her.

That was the way love was supposed to be, Dot thought, as she slipped away from the group and returned to her room. You were supposed to find the right person and live happily ever after. There was no abandonment of what you wanted, no grief for the dreams you'd have to leave behind. There was nothing but a perfect, magical meeting of hearts and minds.

Dot went into her room and closed the door behind her. She worried that she might start crying all over again. She leaned over the small sink that was wedged between the two overflowing closets and gazed at her reflection in the mirror.

In truth, she had no doubts about what she wanted. She wanted everything. She wanted the career, the children, the little house with the picket fence *and* the Nobel Prize. Why couldn't a woman just have a chance at everything? That was what was fair, what was just. It simply wasn't what was easy.

Dot silently vowed that she would never allow herself the lazy luxury of being limited by what other people thought her capable of. That's what she'd been doing. She was as wrong in that as Dr. Falk was wrong. And Dr. Glidden was wrong, too.

Dot was not certain exactly who was right, but so far, Hank had come the closest.

At that moment she was startled out of her thoughts by a noisy bump at the dorm-room window. She hurried over to discover the top of a wooden ladder perched upon the sill. She raised open the window and leaned out to look down. Hank was already halfway up.

"What are you doing?" Dot called out to him.

He didn't answer, just kept coming.

Dot went back into the room, dumped the trash on the floor and hurried to the sink. She filled the container to the brim and returned to the window to view his upward progress once more.

"I've got a wastebasket full of water and I know how to use it," she threatened.

He hesitated, but only long enough to look up at her.

"I don't care if you douse me with benzene," he said. "I'm coming up there to talk to you."

Dot didn't pour the water on him. When he reached the window ledge, she set the wastebasket down, turned her back to him and walked across the room.

"I have nothing to say to you," she announced.

"Okay," Hank responded. "Then I'll do the talking. I

love you. I want to be married to you. I want to spend my life with you. But I don't want to give up my life for you. And I don't want you to give up yours for me, either."

She spun around to face him.

"What else can I do?" she asked him. "What choice do I have? Do you expect me to change the world?"

Hank shrugged. "Maybe," he answered. "It certainly could use some changing."

"Yeah, well that would be nice, but I'm not sure I'm up to the task," she said.

"But you can try," Hank said. "I can try, too. Together, the two of us. It's a start."

"I want everything," Dot admitted. "But I just don't know how I can get it."

"I don't know, either," Hank said. "I don't know what we can do, what we'll face, how successful we'll be. But I know that we love each other and if we're together and we're both willing to try, we can face whatever it is that comes our way."

Hank stepped forward, took her hands in his own and dropped down to one knee.

"Marry me, Dot," he said. "Marry me, but don't give up yourself. I want the real Dorothy Wilbur for my bride. Not somebody else's idea of who she ought to be. Be my wife and my lawfully wedded scientist as well."

Dot looked down into his eyes. She was reminded so vividly of the first time she'd gazed into them. She's doused him with cold water. But she loved him now and he loved her. She wouldn't throw cold water on this declaration.

"All right," she answered.

He rose to his feet and took her in his arms. He opened his mouth over hers. Their kiss was full of love, longing, and tenderness. Equally in love, their love was an alliance of equals.

Unexpectedly, the door opened. Trixie, and a half-dozen other girls, froze on the threshold.

"Man on the floor!" someone hollered out.

"Panty raid!" someone down the hall speculated.

Echoes of female screeches were heard all up and down the hallway.

Thanksgiving
Present Day

THE *MANOHRA SONG* moored for the night near the temple of Wat Bang Na. All three couples lounged together on the sundeck, enjoying a cool refreshment as they watched the late autumn sunset, a vivid display of light through feathery clouds that seemed painted with watercolors of blue and pink. The occasional splash of fish or fowl and the voices from passing families on tiny houseboats were the only sounds to encroach upon the solemnity of the evening on the river.

It had been a busy day. They'd cruised through the towers of modern-day Bangkok and out into the countryside. They'd visited the Temple of Dawn, one of the most remarkable structures in Thailand. Later they'd been wowed by the artistry of the boats in the Royal Barges National Museum. They'd felt as if they were sailing backward in time as they watched the life on the river, almost unchanged over aeons, move past on the water. They journeyed upriver toward the ancient capital of Siam.

The assistant steward brought out spring rolls and dried beef in tomatoes for a repast.

"This is good," Mac Griffin said. "Although I guess

we can't plan on Thanksgiving dinner like Grandma used to make."

Dorothy Brantly turned to the young waiter and questioned him for several moments in his native language.

"Well, no big American turkey," she reported to the group. "But I think a roasted duck in curry will probably be a very acceptable substitute for a traditional holiday meal."

"You speak Thai?" Natalie asked her.

"Yes, but I'm a little rusty," Dorothy admitted.

"Dot and I lived here for ten years," Henry Brantly explained. "It's a very special place to us."

"How interesting," Christie said. "Did your work bring you here?"

Her question was addressed to Henry, but Dorothy answered.

"We were in the Peace Corps."

"We were among the first team into the country," Henry told them. "We arrived here in January 1962."

"That must have been quite an adventure." Christie's eyes were bright with curiosity.

Dorothy nodded. "Yes, it was. And even more than that, it was a great experience."

Henry Brantly agreed with his wife. "It was a real surprise to us when it came up. The Peace Corps was desperate for qualified scientific and technical volunteers and they offered a lot of opportunities for women. Dorothy is an Organic Chemist, so they snapped her up to do research and testing on local water resources purification. When they found out she was married to an engineer, well, they gave me plenty to do as well."

Dorothy smiled at her husband. "Yes, Hank got the

water out of the ground and piped into the villages. I made sure that it was safe to drink."

"After we turned over the project here to the locals, we formed our own company and spent the next twenty years doing similar jobs all through the third world."

"So we've lived a lot of places," Dot said. "But Thailand is special for us. It's here where we found our life's work. And where both our children were born."

Henry added, "This little cruise is their gift for Mom and Pop's big fiftieth wedding anniversary."

"I love it!" Pete grinned. "A panty raider. Guy after my own heart." He turned to his wife. "Of course, if I'd ever tried to get my hands on Natalie's underwear, she'd have thrown another shoe at me."

"Another one?" Christie Griffin asked, her brows raised.

"Yeah. You wouldn't believe the way she treated me when we first met."

Natalie looked outraged. "For very good reason!"

The steward appeared before anyone could ask her what she meant. He removed the dishes from the hors d'oeuvres and invited the group to seat themselves for the main course of their Thanksgiving dinner. Under the canopy toward the stern of the boat, the three couples relaxed against the cushions adorning wicker benches around the dining table.

Mac Griffin asked, "So what did Pete do to make you throw a shoe at him, Natalie?"

She laughed. "You really want to hear this story?"

"Yes!" everyone said in chorus.

"Okay. Understand that I *now* truly give thanks that I met Pete. He's the love of my life. But let's just say that I didn't look forward to it…."

FRAME BY FRAME

Karen Kendall

CHAPTER ONE

"PETE, WE CAN'T have a *re*peat of what happened in *St. Pete*," Natalie Moore's boss said, in the general direction of her phone.

Nat raised an eyebrow, thinking of an old childhood prank kids used to play on one another: *Pete and Repeat were walking along a bridge. Pete jumped off. Who was left?*

Addison Fry, executive editor of *World Sophisticate Travel and Lifestyle* magazine, crooked a finger at her, pulling her up by an invisible leash into the vast corner office of her boss's domain.

Every piece of furniture in the room was modern and upholstered in leather. A lot of cows had given up their lives for Addison's posh posterior, and Natalie suspected that a couple of chairs were draped in the skins of her former assistants. But for some reason, Fry liked her, for which Nat was grateful.

Not for the first time, she squinted at examples of her boss's strange taste in art: a green-painted brick inside a Lucite box; a white canvas with a huge red dot in the center; a stainless steel-bucket hanging on the wall; a painting that consisted of nothing but sixteen squares of blue in various tints.

Nat didn't get it. Not that she was sure there was

anything *to* get. Outside the tempered-glass walls, a scaffold came into sight, and the two window cleaners on it seemed to share her opinion of the art.

A pair of thousand-dollar reading glasses slid down Addison's nose, and she sipped at an unappetizing moss-green liquid in a crystal tumbler.

Nat refrained, just barely, from wrinkling her nose, and followed the indication of Fry's finger that she should seat herself. On the speaker phone, a man groaned.

"I was *not* verbally abusive, Addison," he said in a deep, whiskey-rough voice.

"You made the girl cry, Pete. You were the catalyst for my stylist leaving Russia immediately and quitting her job. That doesn't smack of a kind, gentle approach."

"Add, she tried to put a *teddy bear* into my shot of the Hermitage. A blasted teddy bear! And besides, I apologized. I even sent flowers. Of course, I didn't know she'd gone straight to the airport, for Chrissakes."

"Regardless, you will not make young Natalie cry when you work with her in Bangkok."

Nat's eyes widened. *I'm going to Bangkok?*

"Is that understood?" Addison continued. "You may be a brilliant photographer, but I can't have you terrorizing my staff. Practice smiling into a mirror, my dear. Pretend to be affable."

"Affable," Pete repeated. "Bloody hell." He sighed. "Well, I haven't frightened a small child for months, now. That's an achievement, isn't it?"

"Absolutely, darling. Now, just remember, when you bare your teeth for a smile, the corners of your mouth should turn *up*."

"Ha-ha."

"And remember that 'please' and 'thank you' are useful little words."

"Brilliant. So I should have said, '*Please* get the friggin' teddy bear out of my architectural shot, you little twit.' Is that it?" The unknown Pete sounded so outraged that Natalie's mouth twitched.

This time it was Addison who sighed. "Something like that."

"Fine. So when does your sweet young thing arrive to make my job a living hell?"

"I'll e-mail you the information. She'll arrive a day after you do. That will give you time to…" Addison's voice trailed off. "Get acclimated and check things out."

Pete remained silent, and the atmosphere became oddly heavy. "Only for you would I return to Thailand, Addy. I hope you realize that."

Natalie was fascinated to see her boss's somewhat reptilian eyes go soft over the power glasses. "I do, sweet Pete. I do. Goodbye, darling."

The connection now dead, Nat sat quietly mystified while Addison made a couple of notes. She, Nat Moore, aka Sweet Young Thing, was flying to Bangkok to work with this grumpy photographer? To make his life a living hell? She swallowed. *Gosh, I can't wait!*

At last Addison pushed up her glasses and looked at Natalie. "Well, that was your introduction to Pete Sedgewick. Are you pleased to make his acquaintance?"

"Um," said Natalie. "Not…exactly."

"He's really not a bad sort. Heart of gold. Just don't let him push you around."

"Of course not." Nat did her best to look tough.

Addison laughed. "You look a bit confused, and rightly so. Natalie, you've done a good job here as a stylist for the last few months, so I'm sending you to work on your first foreign assignment. It's in Bangkok. We're covering the grand opening of the Continental Hotel on the banks of the Chao Phraya River. You'll stay in five-star luxury and have a generous expense account. Isn't that exciting?"

Nat nodded. *Yes, except it sounds too good to be true. And the catch is obviously Pete Sedgewick.*

"Now, I'll be honest with you. The only downside is a touch of jet lag and of course the fact that you'll be working with a difficult creative genius."

Bingo.

"I know you've heard of Pete—after all, he's world-renowned. He really is quite brilliant at what he does, but we need his photographs to have a shade more warmth and human appeal."

Great, so he's inhuman, too?

"We need to *personalize* the architecture of the Continental Hotel for our readers at *World Sophisticate,* so that they'll want to visit Bangkok and book a room. But our darling Pete is, ah, something of a purist."

"A purist…?"

Addison sipped at the nasty green liquid in her glass. "Pete doesn't like to put people or props in his photographs. Your job is to get them into the pictures anyway. That's all."

That's all, huh? You want me to wrest creative control over his own work *from a world-famous, difficult creative genius. That'll be a snap. No problem. Because I'm sure he's not territorial or anything.*

"Do you think you can handle that, Natalie?"

No. But she produced her best I'm-so-competent

smile. "Absolutely." *I really want to see Bangkok, and it's hard to make me cry on the job.*

Addison beamed at her and handed over a manila file and a first-class ticket in Nat's name to Thailand, which she just happened to have sitting on her desk. She was nothing if not efficient, but what if Natalie didn't have a passport? Apparently that had never crossed Fry's cosmopolitan mind.

"Excellent," she said. "I'm counting on you."

Euphoria tangled with dread in Nat's stomach. "Thank you so much for giving me this opportunity. I can't tell you how much I appreciate it."

"Well, I've had my eye on you since you started here, so enjoy the trip. Just try not to let Pete depreciate all that appreciation, darling." Addison hesitated for a moment, which was uncharacteristic of her. "Cut him some slack, all right? He's had a difficult year."

What does that mean? But Natalie nodded. "Okay." She got up and made her way to the door. Her boss's parting words followed her from the room.

"And for God's sake, no teddy bears!"

THREE DAYS LATER, a cold, early-November wind sliced through Nat's light jacket as she waited for a cab to take her from her tiny studio apartment on the Upper West Side to the airport. The smells of Manhattan eddied around her: pungent exhaust, autumn leaves, warm bread from a nearby bakery, hot grease from local restaurants and the occasional ripe whiff of a Dumpster.

She wondered what sort of face went with Pete Sedgewick's whiskey-drenched voice. He'd sounded older and, well, sexy, in spite of his gruff words.

His voice had rasped over her skin, teasing the tiny

hairs on her upper arms and raising prickles of aware-
ness. It had then shot straight to the center of her
spine and up to the back of her neck, where it blos-
somed into heat. Sound had become sensation with
the speed of light.

Nat's musings were interrupted by a dirty flash of
yellow: a cab occupied by a driver whose most remarkable feature was his utter lack of expression. He
emerged from the cab to throw her suitcase into the
trunk and slam it closed. She climbed into the back seat
and told him her destination.

Countless bumps, jolts and emergency brakings later,
they arrived at LaGuardia with a screech and a jerk of the
wheel, which indicated that she should get out while the
getting was still good. She handed the expressionless
cabbie his fare, waited for her receipt and got out of the
cab. The guy didn't move himself, just popped the trunk
again and waited while she pulled her own bags out.

She certainly wasn't in Atlanta anymore—but then,
she'd learned that over and over again in the three
months since she'd come to the city to work for *World
Sophisticate*. Men were different here. The first time one
had let a door shut right in her face, she'd thought he
was being deliberately rude. Soon she learned that most
New York men were oblivious and wrapped in their
own high-stress plastic business bubbles.

Natalie checked in with her airline, went through
security and arrived at her gate with plenty of time to
spare. She'd packed a book of Pete Sedgewick's photographs into her carry-on, to get some idea of what to
expect. The tome peeked spine out of her bag and it
occurred to her that there was probably a head shot and
short bio of him in the back. She settled into a hard

plastic chair, pulled the book out and flipped to the end, her pulse kicking up. And there he was.

Pete looked about thirty-five and had a lean, very handsome face that served as a nice canvas for the three days of growth on his chin and cheeks. Deep grooves ran from under his nose to the corners of a poet's mouth, sensual but sardonic. His dark eyes tilted slightly down at the corners, and were punctuated by faintly exclamatory crow's feet.

But the most remarkable aspect of Sedgewick's appearance was his shock of wavy salt-and-pepper hair. It would have curled over his collar if he'd worn one, and contrasted with the black T-shirt he favored instead.

Pete Sedgewick looked like a cross between George Clooney and Richard Avedon. He looked like a chain smoker, a hard drinker...and an unforgettable lover.

From the moment she met that challenging gaze and saw the angle of that dangerous chin, Natalie knew he was trouble—and that was before she took in his photographs.

She'd always thought of photography as more of a recording science than an art, but Pete changed that perception immediately.

The force of a complex personality penetrated every one of his shots, whether high-rise or historical, commercial or residential—as if he could compel the metal and stone and glass and concrete to reflect his own vision. He certainly didn't pay homage to the architecture; somehow he bent it to his will and exposed its pretensions as well as its beauty.

Nat paged through the pictures slowly, riveted by each one. Not only were they masterpieces of technique, but they were full of suppressed emotion.

Frame by frame, this was Pete Sedgewick's vision,

a force of nature that she'd been sent to tangle with. She closed her eyes and unwillingly began to laugh at the idea that her predecessor at *World Sophisticate* had brought a teddy bear anywhere near the man's camera. Maybe to call her a "twit" had been an act of great restraint on his part.

By the time Nat boarded her flight for Thailand, she'd begun mapping out a strategy for approaching and dealing with Pete. If she stuck with it and remained professional, she should be fine.

1. Start with a compliment. Tell him how much you admire his work.
2. Do not let him get the upper hand or treat you like an idiot.
3. Communicate clearly what the magazine needs and expects of him.
4. Make creative suggestions and stand by them.
5. Do not, under any circumstances, allow the man to know you are even faintly attracted to him.

Natalie felt satisfied with the plan, written out in a fresh travel journal she'd bought just for the trip. It told her plainly in blue ink, in her neat, loopy, slanted-to-the-right script, that she was in control of the coming situation and knew what to do.

CHAPTER TWO

PETE HAD GONE to great lengths to sit in an exit-row seat, far forward in the plane. Exit-row seats offered more leg room for his tall, rangy frame, and he figured that in the unlikely event of an emergency, he could push people down an inflatable chute just as well as anyone else.

Despite the fact that he should have been among the first coach passengers off the flight, Pete was the very last passenger to leave the plane. And when he did, his legs were rubbery.

He was guilty of weaving rather than walking, since he'd consumed several vodka tonics during the long hours in the air.

His intention had been to take the edge off, make returning to Thailand a blurry, fuzzy experience rather than a sharp, painfully focused one. Like most attempts to avoid emotion, it backfired. The vodka traveled straight from his gut to his memory and unleashed it like a starving, rabid dog.

He'd last flown this airline with Hannah, and he almost saw her sitting in one of the first-class seats, coiling her long, straight blond hair into a knot on her head and securing it with a pencil. He saw the bare back of her neck, and the funny little indentation high on her nape where her skin met her hairline.

He'd kissed her there often enough.

She'd have been wearing a sundress, probably one of the ones with the Balinese prints, and she'd have snuggled into her mangy jean jacket, the one she'd spilled green paint on but refused to part with.

She'd have worn a gift from him, her favorite necklace: three chunks of polished turquoise on a strip of leather, but no earrings. She'd avoided them ever since her little nephew had yanked one right through her left lobe.

At some point during the flight, he'd have stepped on her toes in their flat brown sandals, and she'd have yelped, "Off, Oaf!" She'd said the same thing to him when she wasn't in the mood for late-night attention.

Bitter regret and powerless longing all but knocked Pete down in the aisle, and he dropped his bag of expensive camera equipment, gripping the seats to either side.

"Are you all right, sir?" Behind him, a British Airways flight attendant touched him on the shoulder.

Pete started to nod. Then he sprinted unsteadily for the lavatory, barely getting the door closed behind him before he threw up. Damn Addison Fry. Returning to Thailand had been a very, very bad idea.

He shoved back his unruly hair and washed his face in the tiny, cramped little space. He dried himself and stared into the micromirror. *Hey, Good Lookin'. You are one-hundred-percent man, now aren't you? Can't hold your vodka or your memories.*

Pete rinsed his mouth several times. He opened the door to find the flight attendant patiently waiting with his camera equipment. "Thank you very much," Pete said as he took it from her.

"Are you all right?" she asked again.

"Good as new. Just a little morning sickness. I'm

still in my first trimester, you know." He flashed her a grin, but she only stared back at him, puzzled.

"That was a joke," he explained.

The light dawned and she emitted an obligatory tinkle of laughter. "Oh, yes. Ha ha!"

"Ha," Pete agreed. Then he reluctantly left the haven of the plane and set foot again on the soil of a country he'd cursed countless times in his nightmares.

Don Muang Airport was crowded but efficient as usual, and getting through customs went smoothly. But outside, the hot, humid air and the crawling, exhaust-ridden traffic oppressed him as much as his memories.

The sky overhead was a deep cerulean-blue, the sun smiling cheerfully from the middle of it. Pete glared upward, loathing beautiful days. They brought nothing but heartbreak. September 11, 2001, had been a lovely, sunny, blue-skied day. And so had December 26, 2004.

Give me a foggy morning and a gray afternoon, and I'm a happy man.

Doing his best to ignore the troubling weather, Pete avoided various rogue taxis and negotiated a reasonable fare for an airport-run to the Continental Hotel. It was a twenty-five kilometer trip that could take anywhere from twenty minutes to three hours, depending on traffic.

Finally settled into the car with his luggage and equipment, he tried to pass the time by gazing out the window. He still felt nauseous.

Hannah. The last time he'd been in Thailand, it was with Hannah. Swimsuit model, amateur Buddhist, devotee of Dr. Pepper. Her smile cut into his consciousness again and he missed her so much he could taste her mouth.

There'd been no warning, not the slightest indication

that he'd never see her again that gorgeous post-Christmas morning he'd headed inland from Phuket with his camera equipment. He'd only wanted to get a few less touristy shots of the local villages.

And before he'd gotten back, a vengeful ocean had taken Hannah, along with hundreds of thousands of others. He'd left her sleeping peacefully, so they'd had no goodbye. He now had no grave marker...no closure.

All Pete had were his goddamned cameras and her still images—both his curse and his salvation. Without Hannah, he didn't think he'd ever feel anything again.

And without his cameras, he honestly didn't know how he'd see. He thought in compositions, in still frames. He thought in terms of light/shadow and f-stops and film speeds.

Life didn't unroll for Pete passively like a film—he chased it frame by frame, capturing bits and pieces, freezing them in time and piecing them back together later. He compartmentalized.

Even as he hated Thailand now, and didn't want to carry any bits of it home, Pete couldn't help himself. As the taxi crept along in the heavy rush-hour traffic, he pulled a Nikon out of his bag and began taking shots: a building here, a *songthaew* (open air van) or a *tuk-tuk* (a small, noisy three-wheeled car) there.

By the time the driver brought him to the door of the grand Continental Hotel, Pete was back in his element; his ghosts, nausea and vodka were somewhat under control.

The Continental was unremarkably glitzy. It loomed pretentiously overhead, another pile of concrete and glass. Pete got his bags out of the taxi, paid the driver and walked into a pavilion of sorts, dominated by an entire constellation of cut-crystal chandeliers. He blinked, and not in appreciation: it was brighter inside than it was outside in the sunshine.

Under this blaze of light stood the hotel's registration counter and concierge desk. The clerks welcomed him effusively, especially after discovering that he was there to photograph their hotel for a prestigious American magazine. Pete signed in with a cynical flourish.

He found fresh flowers in his room, along with a chilled bottle of champagne in an ice bucket. He threw his bags on the bed and stared at it balefully. *Just what I want to do: celebrate my return.*

Hannah's voice came to him clearly at that moment. *It's not Thailand's fault. You're not being rational. The tsunami affected many countries.*

Pete didn't feel like being rational. He unpacked, tossing his few items of clothing into a drawer. He thought about calling Addison to bitch at her for putting champagne in his room. But chances were that the hotel staff had done it, not her.

He glared at the stuff again.

You know, most people adore sunny blue skies and deluxe accommodations and champagne, you ornery man. Hannah's voice came again.

He longed for the fuzzy oblivion of the vodka, but ordering up a bottle to drink alone in his room seemed truly pathetic. And he couldn't face the thought of sitting in the bar, having to make small talk with strangers.

Pete walked over to the champagne bottle and lifted it out of its icy bath. High-end Piper Heidsieck. There were worse things to drink.

He wandered into the bathroom with it and filled the tub, needing a good scrubbing after the long flight. He stripped naked and stood in front of the sink, working

the cork out of the champagne bottle. Finally, with a pop
it rocketed into the mirror, hitting his reflection square
in the right eye.

"Cheers," said Pete to the other Pete. "Mighty nice
of you to join me in my little Thai nudist colony."

The other Pete seemed to toast him back.

"Glad you've got your own stash—this is mine," he
told him. Then, still somewhat drunk from the plane, he
climbed into the tub and drank the wine straight from
the bottle, even though what he needed was water, not
more alcohol.

FORTY-EIGHT MINUTES later, Pete set down the empty
champagne bottle and congratulated himself on resem-
bling nothing more than a giant scrotum with feet.
Sitting in a tub of water for any length of time would
do that to a person.

Hannah's extremely unimpressed voice swam into
his head again. *Get out of that tub, you dumb-ass,
before you drown.*

Pete had to admit it was a good idea. He lurched out
of the bathtub and wrapped himself in a towel. See?
There was nothing that a drink and a hot bath couldn't
fix. He was feeling more cheerful and chatty already.

You've got to move on with your life, she'd said. *I've
been in my next one for almost a year now.*

Next life? Oh, right—the amateur Buddhist thing.
"Weren't you brought up a Christian, sweetheart?" he
asked. "Shouldn't you be bouncing around heaven,
skipping rope with all the other angels and making
divinity for St. Peter?"

No. I'm a giraffe now. I eat the leaves off of trees.

Clearly, he'd pickled his brain. "A *giraffe?*"

It's really convenient—you know how I always hated to cook, Pete.

True. And she'd been a vegetarian.

Plus there's no need for mascara! Giraffes have the longest eyelashes.

Pete didn't know quite what to say to that. "Are you happy, Hannah?"

I am. Now go on with you. You've got life, liberty— how about pursuing some happiness?

"I don't want to. I miss you like hell."

No response.

"Hannah? Are you there?"

There were obviously limitations to having a talk with a dead fashion model who was now a giraffe, at least in his alcohol-impaired, pseudo-Buddhist mind. Pete gave up, but her voice had come to him one last time.

Get out of that tub, you dumb-ass, before you drown. So he did.

PETE GOT HIMSELF DRESSED and decided that if he could have a conversation with his dead fiancée, then he could brave the bar and chitchat with strangers now. After all, the bar would be stocked with vodka, and God forbid he should sober up. He didn't have to start work until tomorrow, when Addison's girl would arrive.

What was her name? Natalie. She was probably about twelve, wore a ribbon in her hair and had majored in Nuisance. And if she was working for the pittance that *World Sophisticate* paid their entry-level employees, chances were that she was heavily subsidized by her daddy.

Pete's lip began to curl, until he fastened it firmly to the rim of his double old-fashioned glass. Baccarat? It was nice, heavy crystal, like his unused champagne glass had been. Perhaps the architect and interior designer of the Continental should be shot, but the smaller details of the hotel were very fine.

He ran his hands over the smooth mahogany of the bar and exchanged a few basic pleasantries in his stilted, limited Thai with a couple of businessmen to his left. On the curved wall behind the bar a reproduction of a nineteenth-century temple mural depicted a party of happy people seated on the floor around a low table laden with food.

Food is probably a good idea. Pete's blurry brain registered the thought. Tempting aromas rose from the restaurant downstairs. He was positive that he smelled Kaeng Som, a hot-and-sour curry with fish. And his mouth watered for Kung Mangkon Phao, a grilled lobster dish that he and Hannah had shared in Phuket. Or how about a crispy Khao Na Ped? He sure did love a nice roast duck. And for dessert…he'd loved the Kluay Buat Chi, or bananas in coconut milk.

But the thought of going into the restaurant alone and sitting down to dinner with nobody to talk to…even for a well-marinated and starving tourist, the thought was daunting. Pete ordered another double vodka instead, and almost heard Hannah sigh in disapproval.

He'd inhaled about half of it when the bartender eyed him warily and put a large dish of nuts in front of him. Pete tried to control his swaying on the bar stool and thanked him. "Hey," he said. "I got a good one for you. Did you know that my dead fian-shay is now a giraffe?"

Not so long after that, a couple of terribly nice

fellows from the Continental's staff helped Pete find his room again, where he slept like the dead—even if he couldn't join them.

CHAPTER THREE

NATALIE STARED at everything around her, behaving like
a typical gawking tourist. Every detail, color and smell
of crowded, chaotic Bangkok fascinated her, and she
tried to drink them all in at once while not breathing in
the pollution, which was horrific.

In the shadow of modern traffic and skyscrapers,
there were traditional wooden houses, sacred *wats* (re-
ligious complexes) and palaces adorned with *cho fas,*
architectural details meaning "tassels of air."

Street vendors sold all kinds of wares, from fresh
coconuts to knockoff watches and goods to wreaths of
jasmine that were hung in shrines.

As her taxi approached the hotel along the Chao
Phraya, Nat noticed the river was clogged with boats.
Some sat low in the water, loaded with fresh fruits, vegetables, cloth and other goods. Others were fishing
trawlers and odd little crafts. Ferries transported masses
of people, from businessmen to housewives, tourists
and student backpackers, to various stops.

Operators of food carts cooked all manner of things
over charcoal, from grilled meats to fried bananas to
fried insects like grasshoppers, worms and even cock-
roaches. At a traffic light, she watched a tourist buy a
soda, taken aback when the vendor poured it into a

plastic bag, stuck a straw in it and sealed it with a rubber band!

She arrived at the Continental Hotel with her mouth open, and didn't close it again until she was by herself in her room. The hotel itself was an interesting marriage of the modern with traditional Thai architecture, the contrast reminding her of the contemporary I.M. Pei structure outside the Louvre in Paris.

In awe of the huge chandeliers and ornately framed art everywhere, she didn't even think to ask if Pete Sedgewick had checked in on schedule. She should have been exhausted with jet lag, but excitement coursed through her and she couldn't wait to get out and explore the city.

She took a quick shower, changed and downed a protein bar and the remnants of a soda she'd brought in her carry-on. Then she adjusted her watch to local time and headed out the door for the main lobby. They'd have to get a shot of that with a tourist standing inside to show the scale.

Natalie ducked her head through the strap of her nylon messenger bag so that it crossed her chest securely. She walked toward a grove of large potted trees that lent an outdoor air to colorful benchlike seating adorned with lots of embroidered throw pillows.

She was admiring the handiwork on them when she heard Pete Sedgewick's whiskey-roughened voice again and saw a shock of salt-and-pepper hair. He sat with his back to her.

"Christ, Addison!" He growled. "I get it, okay? I'll make nice. I'll even buy Miss Scarlett some dinner. Not that I know why you're saddling me with her to begin with. You want people in the shots, I'll put people in the shots. Warm and fuzzy, that's what I'm all about. I don't need some teenager getting in my way."

Natalie stood without moving, torn between her sense of humor and annoyance. *Remember your list, Nat!* Number one on the list was: Start with a compliment. Tell him how much you admire his work.

She should back up, retrace her steps and go out a different entrance. That was obvious; it was the tactful choice.

"Professional!" Pete scoffed. "Tell me another one. You said she's just out of school."

Nat gritted her teeth and noticed that her annoyance was rising over her humor, and her body's reverse gear didn't seem to be working.

"Okay, okay. Don't scold, Addy. I have a wicked hangover. *World Sophisticate* bought me a few drinks last night, and I'm not apologizing because you know why."

So the man was a grump and a drunk, too? Natalie's indignation began to bubble close to the surface. She tried to tamp it down, reminding herself of that list again. *Compliment his work.*

Pete snorted into the phone, and at this point she was sure the snort expressed his opinion of her. Nat's chin went up and her hands unconsciously curled into loose fists. *Yeah, I've got a compliment for you right here, genius.*

"I," said Pete, "am the very soul of sweetness. I'll go practice purring into a mirror right now, big pussycat that I am. Just let me have some ibuprofen first, okay? And I'll let you know when your sweet young thing gets here. I'll be charm personified. I promise."

That's it. Nat's anger at the patronizing jerk boiled over. Instead of going into reverse, her body shot forward full throttle and rounded the bench. "Hi," she said. "I'm Natalie Moore."

Pete blinked.

"You know, the teenager? The sweet young thing? Reporting for duty, Sedgewick, to make your life hell."

The moment was all she'd hoped for. Pete's mouth dropped comically open. "Oh, *fu*—"

Nat raised her brows.

"Addison, I gotta go. Something's, er, come up."

It took Pete a minute to recover. He snapped shut his cell phone. Then he leaned on his knees, head down, and laughed weakly. At last he raised his face, produced a sickly grin and held out his hand. "Uh, hi. I suppose no further introductions are necessary?"

Natalie folded her arms across her chest and eyed him smugly. *Rat got your tongue, big pussycat?*

He dropped his hand and stood up, towering over her. He rubbed at the back of his neck. "As I was just saying, I'm...charm personified."

"Oh, without a doubt."

"I don't suppose you have any aspirin on you, do you, doll?"

Doll? "No," she lied.

"And you wouldn't give them to me if you did," Sedgewick said, almost cheerfully.

The look on her face must have said it all.

"Right." Pete cleared his throat. "Well. We seem to have gotten off on an exceptionally bad foot. Let's start over, shall we?"

Just like his head shot, Pete wore about three days' worth of growth on his somewhat haggard looking face. He also wore a rumpled black T-shirt, snug faded Levi's with frayed hems and expensive-looking but scuffed black leather shoes. He obviously hadn't yet committed to any sort of relationship with a comb.

Sedgewick was one of those guys who looked as if he should have a sign around his neck saying Born To Be Bad. He was the type cloned by Hollywood stylists, aped by adolescents and worshipped by willing women.

The headshot of Pete hadn't prepared Natalie for the force of his body or something only definable as his aura, for lack of a better word.

He was long, lean, broad in the shoulders and cocksure. He looked mysterious and tormented. And he'd been served up with a delicious amount of spice and sex appeal.

Natalie told herself she was immune to his all too familiar type. Then he smiled at her.

When Sedgewick smiled, his face transformed. She could still see the shadows under his eyes and the lines of weariness, but he lit up with mischief and humor and a shopworn faux-innocence that was hard to resist. "I can see that I had quite the wrong impression of you, Miss Moore."

She started to nod.

"You're not sweet at all."

The man certainly had nerve, didn't he?

He angled his head, perusing her. "You *are* young."

"But I'm not a thing. And despite your preconceptions, I am a professional."

"At making photographers' lives hell?"

"Your words, Sedgewick, not mine."

"Yeah." He cleared his throat and shoved his hands into his pockets. "What other words of mine did you pick up while you were eavesdropping?"

"Conversing loudly on your cell phone in a hotel lobby renders the term 'eavesdropping' moot, don't you think? It was impossible *not* to overhear you. But since you ask, I understand that you're the soul of sweetness, you specialize in "warm and fuzzy" and you're a big pussycat."

Pete had the grace to wince.

"Oh, and I understand that you're taking me to dinner one of these days. The pleasure will be all mine, I'm sure."

He laughed softly. "That's only if you'll answer to 'Miss Scarlett.'"

"I really liked Scarlett. Nobody pushed her around, and she got everything she wanted."

"Except for Rhett."

Natalie shrugged. "Well, there is that. But I hear that Rhett, or rather Clark Gable, had chronic halitosis—"

Pete choked.

"—so she was well rid of him, don't you think?"

"I think," Sedgewick said slowly, "that working with you is going to be very interesting."

She grinned triumphantly. "So this round goes to the sweet young thing?"

He nodded. "Yeah. You've definitely got me on the ropes. But watch out—I come out of the corner with a vengeance."

"I'll remember that. See you later."

"Uh—where are you going? And when do you want to start shooting this monstrosity of a hotel?"

"I'm going to explore the city. I figure we'll start shooting when you've recovered from your hangover. And I happen to think this hotel is beautiful. Those chandeliers are fabulous, aren't they?"

"Great…we're gonna get along just great," Pete muttered.

She gave him a sunny smile and sauntered off. When she reached the main doors, she stopped and squared her shoulders before turning around. "By the way, have I told you that I love your work?"

PETE SQUINTED at Natalie suspiciously when they met over breakfast the next morning. His head no longer felt as if a wrecking ball were smashing the inside of his skull. A slight improvement over yesterday.

She looked young and fresh and annoyingly optimistic about life, and as the staff brought out a platter of fruit, she exclaimed over the beauty of it. Thai chefs tended to carve fruits and vegetables into small, edible works of art, and predictably, she was charmed by this. He once had been charmed himself.

"Aren't they exquisite?" she asked Pete.

"Breathtaking."

"Isn't it a gorgeous day?"

He looked out the plate-glass window at another blue sky and high, hot sun. He tried to refrain from scowling. "It'll be sweltering out there."

She nodded enthusiastically. "Just like Atlanta in the summertime."

He didn't want to talk about Atlanta in the summertime. But he had some reparations to make from yesterday. "You grew up there?"

She nodded. "In a suburb of Atlanta called Lawrenceville. My family's still there."

"Big family?"

"Average. I have a brother and a sister. My aunt and grandmother are close by."

That sounded big to Pete.

"What about you?" she asked him.

"Just me and the old man."

Obviously curious, Natalie did him the courtesy of

not asking for details. She was indeed Southern. Because she didn't pry, Pete supplied the information she wanted.

"He and my mother were never married—they just lived together. When it came to her leaving, she knew she couldn't support me."

Natalie's mouth opened slightly, then closed. Her quick pity and conventional viewpoint amused him somewhat.

"It's really not a big deal. I hear from her every once in a while and we're all cool with it. My father lives with someone else now."

She shook her head. "How very…big city. Very New York."

He raised an eyebrow. "Funny, I hear that there are plenty of bastards down south, too."

She flushed. "I guess there are." She changed the subject. "So, is your dad a photographer, too?"

"No. He's a set designer. We lived in a loft and he tried to work from home as much as possible so he could keep an eye on me. When it wasn't possible, he stuck me in all kinds of afternoon activities. Photography classes were the ones I loved the most, and there are a lot of buildings to take pictures of in the Big Apple. That's how I chose my specialty. So how did *you* end up in New York, Natalie?"

"I wanted to work in magazines, and there aren't as many opportunities in Atlanta."

"Makes sense. What do you like about magazines?"

"Everything. The sense of a whole staff pulling together a creative visual product that will be in people's hands." She paused. "The photographs. In the case of *World Sophisticate,* the opportunity to learn about all kinds of exotic places, even though I don't have the money to go to all of them.

"I really love the photographs—and as a stylist, having a chance to influence the way they turn out. Co-ordinating a certain look. Finding just the right props and details to add life to a spread. It's a form of art, for me—same as taking the actual pictures is for you."

Pete didn't consider shopping for props art, but he didn't say it aloud. And he was curious about something. "Speaking of pictures. Why did you tell me yesterday that you loved my work? You weren't too happy with me at the time."

She blinked at him, and he became unwillingly fascinated with her hazel eyes. The left one had more flecks of green in it than the right. They were perfectly shaped, wide set, adorned by long brown lashes. One of her eyebrows was slightly higher than the left, which he liked. It added interest to her otherwise ordinary features.

He also liked the frankness in her expression, until she fidgeted under his gaze and answered his question.

"Well, it was the polite thing to say, wasn't it?"

Brutal. In spite of being Southern, she didn't pull any punches, did she? Pete palmed his breakfast roll and laughed in spite of himself. "So you don't really like the work, then." Unexpectedly, that stung.

"I didn't say that."

"Well, *I* wasn't polite in the least about you—though obviously I didn't know you were standing there. So why did you feel the need to be polite to me?"

"It's the professional thing to do." She smiled at him and calmly drank her tea.

Maddening. The girl is maddening. "Have you actually *seen* any of my photographs?"

"Yes. I bought a book of them. So you should get your fifty-cent royalty check any day now."

Pete sat back and folded his arms, eyeing her quizzically.

"Okay, if you really want to know, I do like your work. Very much."

He produced an expansive smile. *Of course she likes it. It's damned good. What's not to like?*

"Of course, it's a little dark and brooding…"

"Excuse me?"

"Occasionally bordering on melodramatic."

"Melodramatic?"

"As if you're a little cranky, and taking it out on the buildings. Giving them long, dark, gaping shadows. Shooting from odd angles so that the structures don't look as tall. That type of thing. But it's only in the photos from the past year."

Pete stared at her, speechless.

"And you should put some people in them to show scale, add a little warmth, don't you think? Of course, I don't pretend to be Robert Hughes," she said. "You know, the art critic."

"I know who friggin' Robert Hughes is," he growled.

"Oh, of course—"

"What I don't know is where you find the sheer gall to say something like that to me."

"Well, you did ask my opinion…"

"No, I don't think I did. I only asked if you'd seen any of my work."

"Oh, come on. We know what that means."

"How old are you again?"

"Twenty-four. I have a master's degree in art history from—"

"Fabulous," Pete said, standing up and tossing his napkin on his plate. He noticed that he'd made four perfect holes in the breakfast roll with his fingers, as if it were a miniature bowling ball. He would have loved to heave it at her.

Natalie stood up, too. "I didn't mean to hurt your feelings," she said.

"Don't be ridiculous, sweetheart. Do you know how many critics have reviewed my work? Hundreds." *All far more qualified than some little Southern girl fresh out of school.* "I've seen much nastier comments than yours in print for all the world to see. I couldn't care less."

"I didn't mean to be nasty. I just thought you'd appreciate an honest opinion, rather than a suck-up one."

She had a point. Pete didn't like brownnosers. But Christ! *Melodramatic?* He picked up his coffee cup and drained it, doing his best to look nonchalant. It wasn't as if her opinion mattered to anyone, least of all him.

"Let's meet in fifteen minutes to walk around the hotel and make notes on potential shots."

She nodded. "Great. By the way, I found some excellent props when I was out exploring yesterday. You'll love them."

Props. Crap to get in the way of his shoot. Fussy knick-knacks that she'd waste hours arranging. Pete scowled.

Natalie beamed at him and then tossed her own napkin onto her plate. The movement was innocuous, so why did he have the feeling that the simple square of cloth doubled as a gauntlet?

CHAPTER FOUR

NATALIE BERATED herself as she took the elevator down to meet Sedgewick. She couldn't follow a few simple rules, even ones she'd made up for herself?

Compliment his work. That had gone well, hadn't it? She smacked herself in the forehead. *Next time, keep your opinions to yourself.*

At least she was doing better on rule number two: *Do not let him get the upper hand or treat you like an idiot.* She was pleased about that. Addison would be, too.

A ding sounded in the mirrored elevator, and Natalie checked her reflection before the doors opened and she got off, walking into the lobby. Her nose was shine free and her lip gloss was intact. Not that it mattered. She didn't give a damn what Pete thought of her looks, and he'd already fixated on her crooked eyebrow at breakfast. He'd looked from one eye to the other intently, which was what had made her defensive, which was what had made her open her mouth about his work.

Sedgewick was already setting up a tripod with an expensive-looking camera on it—she had no idea what kind it was. He was also in the process of setting up lighting equipment, and had cords running everywhere.

"Pete, I thought we were going to do a walk-through first, talk about the potential of different shots?"

He nodded, then fiddled with something on the camera, muttering at it. He looked into the viewfinder. "I wanted to get some preliminaries of the lobby."

He continued to squint and adjust things: the f-stop, the backlighting, the ambient light in that corner of the room. She observed him with growing impatience. "We really should talk about this before you continue. An overall shot of the lobby will be impressive, but not necessarily welcoming without the right touches. *World Sophisticate* is a travel magazine, Pete, not an architectural or interiors magazine."

He flapped a hand at her as if she were a mosquito, and she tried to control a mounting annoyance. She waited a little longer while he puttered around, and finally stepped right into the line of his lens. "Sedgewick? Hello?"

"Please move."

"Are you listening to me?"

He flapped a hand at her again.

"Pete!"

His disheveled salt-and-pepper head popped up over the camera. "Get. Out. Of. My. Way."

She sighed in exasperation.

"Now!"

Natalie jumped at the roar and sidestepped quickly, tangling her foot in some extension cords. She lifted her foot to shake them off. Then, as if in slow motion, she felt herself lose her balance and fall backward, arms flailing. She tried to get her feet back under her, but only succeeded in yanking the cords up over her knee.

And as she fell without grace right onto her rear end, the equipment attached to the cords came with her. A lightbulb exploded on the floor next to her head, and a big silver light-umbrella tumbled on top of her. The tripod teetered, the camera on it went flying and Pete made a spectacular running dive to save it.

Unfortunately, this meant that the top of the tripod hit him square in the stomach, and he crashed down on top of her.

They lay there for a stunned moment, Pete nose to nose with her breasts and the wind knocked out of him. Natalie cautiously opened her eyes, which she'd shut to avoid the flying glass of the lightbulb.

The umbrella was crushed between their bodies. Pete coughed some air into his lungs and said, "Please, God." Then he rolled off her and gingerly lifted the camera, which rattled. The glass of the lens had broken and part of it fell out onto the floor. A stream of invective came out of Pete's mouth.

"I'm fine, thanks," said Natalie. She sat up. "And you?" She winced at his expression and hunched her shoulders. "You, um, have insurance for that stuff, right?"

His answer was another stream of invective.

She gulped. "Well, surely the magazine will replace everything that can't be fixed. I mean, we're on a job for them—"

"I *told* Addison that I didn't want one of her fluff balls here, getting under my feet!"

Nat scrambled up and glared at him. "I am *not* a fluff-ball."

"You can't even walk without destroying things."

That was it. She took a step toward him and poked him in the chest with her index finger. "You should have taped down the cords."

He stepped away from her finger but never broke eye contact with her. "You shouldn't have been anywhere near them!"

"The cords shouldn't have been set up to begin with!
You and I were supposed to meet and do a walk-
through. Discuss the shots. Even go through the props
that I spent a lot of time hunting down yesterday—and
which will set the mood for the pictures."

"You don't 'set the mood' for *my* photographs. Got
it?" He bared his teeth at her.

"It is my job as a stylist to work with you on the
mood and the details. That's why I'm here. And
they're not just your photos—they're the magazine's."

A muscle jumped in his jaw and he gritted his teeth
at that. He cast his eyes heavenward and appeared to
count to ten. Finally he spoke again. "All I wanted was
some damn preliminary—"

"When I reminded you of the walk-through you
ignored me. And when I reminded you again, you
yelled, which startled me. So I jumped backward and
tripped over your cords. You can thank yourself for this
mess, not me."

Pete sputtered at her and cradled his beloved camera
in his arms. "I can't replace this!"

She did feel bad about the camera, regardless of
whose fault the accident was. "Won't the magazine—"

"No," he said shortly. "It has sentimental value.
Han—" he stopped abruptly and shut his eyes. "Somebody gave me this."

Someone very close to him, judging by his expression. He looked...poleaxed. "Pete, look, I'm sorry." She
eyed him helplessly as hotel staff scurried around and
began to clean up the mess. Sedgewick turned away
from her and picked up the larger broken pieces of the
lens. He stared at them as if they were his heart.

Natalie swallowed. "Can I...can I pay to have the
lens replaced?"

"It's an old Bell & Howell," he said in dull tones. "And it won't be the same. There's also no way to do it out here in the field. I have to send it to someone..."

"I'll pay for it," she said again, even though she'd finished explaining how none of this was her fault. Something other than natural crankiness was causing Pete Sedgewick to behave this way. And that something caused her to feel sorry for the jerk.

Addison had asked her to cut him some slack. She'd said he'd had a hard year. What kind of hard year?

"No, Natalie. You don't have to pay to fix it." He dropped the broken lens into a nearby trash can and rubbed a hand over his face. "It was an accident."

She nodded, not knowing what else to say.

"You're not going to go pack and head for the airport, are you? Tell Addison that I eat crushed skulls for breakfast?"

"I'm not going anywhere," Natalie said. "I'm pretty grounded for a fluff ball."

A rueful expression crossed his features. "Let's take a little time to cool off, and then we'll do that walk-through, okay? I know I need to apologize to you, but I don't think I can do it right now. Can you understand that?"

Yes, in a weird way, she could. He'd obviously lost something very valuable to him. So again, she nodded. She felt tempted to apologize again herself but tamped down the urge. He did share some responsibility for the incident, and she wasn't a doormat.

Pete met her gaze and his eyes showed he was no longer angry. "Thanks," he said. His mouth twisted. "I promise to be less of an ogre when we meet again."

IN THE PRIVACY OF HIS ROOM, Pete set the injured camera down next to a framed picture of Hannah that he'd brought. He sighed.

"I used to be a nice guy, didn't I, babe? I mean, maybe a little gruff. But not the asshole I am today."

Hannah, no longer a giraffe now that he was sober, laughed at him from the picture, where she sat bare legged on a tree stump. He tried to touch her face, but in the image it was smaller than his index finger. She was shrinking, disappearing from his life.

"Hannah," he whispered. "I was grouchy today with Natalie because of that 'melodrama' comment. I yelled at her for breaking the camera lens. But..." He swallowed, and sat on the bed.

"But I think what really made me angry is that I'm attracted to her. And I feel rotten about it."

Hannah continued to laugh at him from the tree stump, her face unchanging.

"That doesn't bother you?"

A world of empathy shone from her eyes.

"Well, it bothers me."

He stared at the broken camera again. Yeah, he might be able to find another lens, but it wouldn't be the same, wouldn't be the one she'd given him for his thirty-fifth birthday, just a few short months before they'd gone to Phuket and gotten engaged.

Feeling sorry for yourself again, old man? Over two hundred thousand people lost their lives that December day. You're not the only one mourning. You're not the only one who has to pull his life together. Now get a grip.

He had to apologize to Natalie, and not just because he thought she was hot, or because of Addison. The truth was that he had enough on his plate organizing his own equipment for this job—he didn't need to be running around after props and worrying whether the fringe was straight on some scarf, or whether a dish looked appetizing enough when set against the stupid scarf, or...

Much as he hated to admit it, he needed Natalie's eye and her attention to the details.

NATALIE WAS WAITING patiently when he got back down to the lobby. "Hi," she said. "Am I talking to Ogre Pete or Pussycat Pete, now?"

That made him laugh. "Pussycat Pete."

"I have to insist on paying for the camera lens. You can replace the light-umbrella thing. Deal?"

"The light-umbrella thing?" He grinned at her. "It's just called an umbrella. And, no, you can't pay for the camera lens. But thank you. And...I'm sorry for yelling at you.

"Now, let's take a look around this place. We'll focus on the interior first, but we'll want to get a few good shots of the exterior, probably from across the Chao Phraya River."

"What about from the other side, so that the river is in the background? With one of those old restored rice barges on it?"

"That could be nice," he admitted.

"And inside, we need the lobby, a tourist being welcomed by the staff at the desk, and one of the suites."

Pete groaned. "You want those hideous chandeliers in the shot of the lobby, don't you?"

"Yes. And they're gorgeous. Why don't you like them?"

"They're showy and obnoxious. Overdone."

Natalie shrugged, her palms turned up as if to say,

What do you want me to do about it? She said, "We need some happy, smiling people in the lobby, dressed colorfully. Pillows. Drinks and hors d'oeuvres at one of the cocktail tables. Some other props…"

She stopped and looked at him. "You have something against happy, smiling people and pillows, too? Because if your lip curls any more I'll be able to tie it into a bow."

Pete put a hand up to his mouth. "Oh, come on. Lips don't really curl. That's just a figure of speech."

"Yours does. It flips up and back, and bares your left canine tooth."

He frowned at her and touched the tooth in question with the tip of his tongue.

"You sort of snarl."

"I do not. And I happen to love happy, smiling people and pillows." So saying, Pete bared his teeth to a passing female staff member. She responded with alarm, ducking her head, pulling the edges of her jacket close around her and scuttling away.

"I rest my case," Natalie said. "Remember, as Addison said, the corners of your mouth need to turn *up* when you smile."

Pete froze. "How do you know she told me that?"

Discomfort crossed Natalie's features. "I, uh—"

"Damn Addison. She had me on speaker phone, didn't she?"

"No!"

"You can't lie worth a damn." He turned away, disgusted.

"Pete, you can't say anything to her. Please! Promise me you won't say anything."

"Why should I promise that? It was an underhanded thing for her to do, and I intend to call her on it."

"She was trying to give me a taste of your personality before I met you."

Pete paused at the word *taste*. He eyed Natalie's smooth, lightly freckled skin. It looked warm, fragrant, lickable.

"She'll be so mad at me for giving her away," she said, almost pleading.

Hmm. "And I would care about that…why?"

"Pete, come on. We just cleared the air. Don't do this. We have to get through the job."

He folded his arms across his chest, leaned back on his heels and smirked at her plaintive tone. "How will you make it worth my while?"

"What?"

"Maybe you'd consider staying out of my way while I work, and not chasing me with pillows and candles and hors d'oeuvres…oh, and happy, smiling people."

She narrowed her very pretty eyes at him. "Maybe I'll tell Addison that you *do* eat skulls for breakfast and that you have all the charm of a wild boar. Do we really need to go there, Sedgewick?"

Pete shook his head mournfully, and she finally realized that he'd been kidding.

"You're no fun," he told her. "I can't even indulge in a little friendly blackmail?"

"No. Now let me do my job, okay?"

"What else did Addison do behind my back? What has she told you about me?" Pete clamped his hands in his armpits and waited for her to avoid his gaze, or outright pity him for his loss.

She did neither. "She told me nothing except that you

were a genius, a purist and could be somewhat…difficult." She thought a moment. "And to bear with you a little, because you'd had a hard year."

"That's it?"

Natalie nodded. "I swear."

"Well," Pete said, digesting this, "you're doing an admirable job of bearing with me. Thank you."

She might not be a fluff ball, but she was young enough to flush at his sardonic tone.

Quit being a bastard, Pete. Give the girl a break.

He removed his hands from their defensive position under his arms. "Let's take a look at the dining room, then, and the terrace. Then we'll need to check out a suite where you'll probably want to produce a goo-goo-eyed, kissing couple and have me take a shot of the mints on the pillows behind them."

Natalie rolled her eyes. "Do you even know *how* to be nice? Or is that kind of behavior not in your repertoire?"

Ouch. Temporarily at a loss, he went from defensive to offensive. He looked over her body, from head to toe and then back up to her breasts. Natalie's neck flushed, and pink spread across her cheeks and all the way to her ears. He liked that. "I know how to be nice," he told her softly, provocatively. "*Very* nice."

She looked daggers at him and walked away.

CHAPTER FIVE

GREAT, NATALIE THOUGHT as she flopped on her bed in the Continental Hotel. *So far I'm point-five for four as far as the list goes. I critiqued his work instead of complimenting it. I clearly lost the upper hand with him when I tripped over the power cords and broke his camera lens.*

And now I'm not at all sure that I've communicated what the magazine really wants in these pictures. The only thing I've scored at all on is forcing him to admit some of my creative ideas are good. But who knows whether he's just playing me. Will he even have film in his camera when he takes those shots?

Nat focused instead on the lovely carved ornamental screen along one wall of her room, the colorful silk draperies at the window and the framed photographs of Thai dancers in traditional costume: gorgeous brocades and elaborate gilt headdresses. They hinted at the Bangkok she wanted to see—not the modern skyscrapers and traffic of any modern metropolis, but the temples and palaces and gardens of Old City: If she and Pete could just work efficiently, she'd have a couple of days to explore before returning to New York.

It had been a long, exhausting day of aesthetic tussles, and she was both tired and wired. She was happy to have some down time that evening, but not looking forward to having dinner alone.

In spite of his words about taking her to dinner one night, Pete hadn't asked her before they quit for the day. And she certainly hadn't asked him. She wasn't even certain she wanted to spend any more time in the genius's company. He fascinated but irritated her, knocked her off balance just as she thought she'd won a round.

Just when she'd decided he was an incorrigible jerk, he said something unexpectedly kind or funny.

He's sad. Pete's mocking, sarcastic mouth contrasted oddly with something tragic in his eyes.

He's a hound. The way he'd looked her up and down a couple of times during the day had her itching to slap him first, and then…and then kiss him.

The fifth item on her list flashed neon at Natalie. *Do not under any circumstances let him know you're attracted to him.* That would be fatal for the purposes of the trip. And yet she closed her eyes, imagining for a moment what Pete's lips would feel like on hers.

The phone rang, jolting her at least a foot off the bed. Maybe it was Pete, asking her to dinner? *Oh, don't be ridiculous.* Nat got her heart rate under control and picked up the receiver. "Hello?"

"Darling Natalie," said Addison's voice, muted a little by static. "How *is* it all going?"

Natalie blinked. It was before six in the morning in Manhattan. Her boss was crazy. "Great, Addison. How early—uh, *nice* to hear from you."

"Well, I'm here at my health club for a Pilates class and then a deep-tissue massage before work."

Of course you are. Silly me. And you'll have your driver run in to Starbucks on the way to the office later, to get you a skinny half-caf white mochaccino with cinnamon on top.

"Is our Pete behaving himself?" Addison asked.

Sort of. When I'm not catching him unaware or breaking his equipment... A firm knock sounded at Nat's door before she could verbalize a reply. "Um—" She opened the door cautiously. *Speak of the devil.*

Pete stood there, freshly shaven and in a clean shirt.

"Natalie?" Addison asked sharply. "Is he giving you a hard time?"

"No, no. He's behaving himself."

Pete's eyebrows rose. *Addison?* he mouthed.

Natalie shrugged uncomfortably, heat rising in her cheeks. Pete strolled right past her, into her room, and up to the phone. Then he punched the speaker button, grinned and sat down on her bed.

Horrified, Nat gestured wildly with the hand not holding the receiver. *What the hell are you doing?*

He shrugged and raised his left eyebrow sardonically, which she interpreted as, *Turnabout is fair play.*

"I know what that means," Addison said archly. "Pete never behaves himself entirely. Which is what makes him so wildly sexy."

Oh, kill me now, Nat thought, while a highly amused Pete crossed his right ankle over his left knee and leaned back on his hands, waiting for more. Nat forced herself to look away from the sight of him on her bed.

"Don't you think?" Addison asked.

"Huhfffurmaffa," Natalie said. Or something like that.

"What was that, darling?"

Pete's grin reached to his ears now, and there was no doubt that the corners of his mouth were turning up, as per Addison's instructions.

"Er, if you say so."

"Oh, I do. And you can't be immune—no woman of my acquaintance is. The body, the eyes, that wolfish look, the rogue's unkempt hair."

Nat winced at every word, while Pete had collapsed laughing, silently. "Um, yeah. Addison, I can't really ta—"

"I remember the first time I met him, years ago. I was married then, but regardless, I just wanted to *lick* him."

Pete rolled to his side and propped himself up on one elbow, smirking like a primate let loose on a banana farm. Did the guy have no shame?

"Lick him," Natalie repeated. "I don't know, Addison. I think he'd taste bitter—like coffee grounds or cigarette butts or something."

Pete's eyes widened, then narrowed. He lifted an eyebrow, as if to say, *Moi?*

"And have you seen him lately?" Nat continued. "He's looking pretty rough…kind of *old*."

At that, he swung his legs off the bed and sat up, obviously outraged.

"Really? You're kidding. What a shame."

"Honestly," Nat continued, "I wonder if all his parts work correctly. You know what happens to these Don Juans as they age."

Pete now loomed over her, hands on his hips, foot tapping the floor. He'd shoved his tongue into his cheek, but he didn't look at all amused.

Oh, you so deserve this. Nat returned his former smirk as Addison exclaimed, *"Quel horreur!"* And then, "He does still have hair?"

"Well, yes. Though he doesn't seem to comb it, so you never know about hidden plugs—"

Both Addison and Pete gasped in tandem. Pete grabbed for the phone, apparently in a hurry to hang it up before he killed Nat with his bare hands. She hung on to it, proud of herself for not laughing out loud.

"Plugs?" Addison shrilled. "No. Absolutely not. That lovely, leonine hair!"

"I'm telling you, I have my suspicions." Nat brandished a folding metal nail file at Pete so he'd back off. "You know how men are about their hair, especially if they had a lot of it in their youth. They're vainer than women, and you have to take into account the whole Samson and Delilah complex."

Addison shuddered audibly. "If Pete does indeed have plugs, you must promise me that you'll pull them out and shave him bald while he sleeps. You have absolutely *ruined* all of my fantasies about him. Next I'll be reduced to tawdry sex toys...."

Nat's eyes widened. TMI! TMI! Too much information. She did not want to hear any more about her boss and sex toys, and she couldn't let Pete hear it, either. That crossed a line.

"Bad connection!" she sang. "Sorry, Addison, but you're breaking up and I can't hear you. I'll call you back later, okay? Bye!" She almost threw the receiver into the cradle, then wielded her nail file with menace and dodged around the bed to escape from Pete.

"Coffee grounds? Old! *Hair plugs?*" He stalked her.

"Oh, you had every last comment coming." She sidestepped him again, resisting the urge to leap across the mattress in order to get away from him.

"Maybe. But let me assure you that my parts are in fine working order, and in fact I'd be happy to give you a demo," he growled.

Sudden heat flashed through her. "That won't be necessary."

"I *guarantee* you'd enjoy it."

She did her best to look bored, then changed the subject. "How could you just invade my room and put the phone on speaker? I didn't even invite you in! And talk about eavesdropping…"

"Oh, come on. Addison deserved it, too," Pete said, running a hand through his mop of hair as if to say, *See, no plugs.* Then he amused her by checking his reflection in the room's mirror. She really had wounded his ego.

"That's not the point!" she told him. "The point is that you put *me* in a horrible position. That was despicable."

Pete thought about it. "True. But remember, I never behave myself entirely. That's what makes me so wildly sexy, right?" His teeth gleamed very white in the evening light.

Nat looked for something to throw at him, finally settling on her sandal, which he dodged.

"And women used to toss their panties at me," he said sadly, shaking his head. "Now I get an old shoe."

She threw the other one, which he dodged, too.

"Have dinner with me?" he asked, once the coast was somewhat clear.

"Are you out of your mind?!"

"I was going to take you to Spice Market."

She knew it was an expensive five-star restaurant. She'd kill to eat there. "No. Please leave."

He caught his lip between his teeth and squinted at her. "I guess that means you don't want to lick me?"

This time she threw a hiking boot.

"But…what about the *body?*" Pete gestured at

himself. "The *eyes?*" He blinked them. "That *wolfish* look of mine?" He assumed a ridiculous male model pose, one straight out of *Zoolander:* stomach sucked in, mouth a vogue O, one hand behind his head.

He looked so stupid that Natalie laughed. It started unwillingly and then took over her body. When she could speak again, she said, "You are so obnoxious."

"I know. It's one of my more irresistible qualities. So will you have dinner with me? The food is like nothing you've ever tasted before—out of this world. I promise to behave. In fact, if you'll just come with me, I promise to be utterly silent throughout the whole meal unless you speak to me first. How's that?"

She looked at him and sighed. "You don't give up, do you?"

"Nope."

"You promise not to speak?"

His lips twitched, but he nodded.

"Okay, then. But I'm only doing this because I'm hungry."

PETE STAYED TRUE to his promise. He was utterly mute while they got into a taxi, and remained that way until she reminded him that she didn't know the address of the restaurant. "Four Seasons Hotel, Ratchadamri Road," he said to the driver.

Spice Market, though it was inside a large modern building, looked like an old Thai spice shop. There were dark wood cabinets set all around the dining area, filled with old glass jars, burlap sacks and ceramic pots. Natalie couldn't help being charmed, and the aromas emanating from the kitchen had her slavering to try everything on the menu.

"This is fabulous," she said to Pete, and was rewarded with an astonishingly sweet smile.

"Permission to speak?"

She nodded.

"I'm glad you like it. I hoped you would."

They were seated at an excellent table, where they could observe everything in the room, and provided with menus by a waiter who couldn't have been more welcoming. The Thai people as a whole were friendly and warm and helpful.

Natalie stared at the menu, having no idea what to order. "Okay," she said. "Pete, you can talk. Just try to be nice, and tell me what to order since you've obviously spent time in Thailand before. Were you here for work?"

He put his napkin into his lap and examined his silverware. "The first time I came, it was for a job. The second time—for vacation."

"So have you seen Old City, then? Could you show me around if we have time?" *Wait—did I just ask that? Do I really want to spend more time in his company?*

"Yeah. I'd enjoy that. I'm actually a pretty good tour guide, when I'm allowed to speak, that is." He smiled at her, then looked at the menu.

"I'd advise ordering both bottled water, *nam kuad,* and if you're in the mood for a drink, then *bia,* or beer. The dishes here will be spicy, true to the name of the place, though you can have them toned down if you like. See, there's a chili rating. I recommend the curries or the soft-shell crab, *poo nim phad prig.*"

Nat pursed her lips. "Okay, beer it is. But I have to wonder if you're just tricking me into ordering 'poo' in a restaurant."

"Best poo you'll ever taste," he assured her.

She wrinkled her nose. "I'll start with the beer."

Over the drinks, Pete told her a little about himself at her prompting.

"I got into photography in junior high school, when my dad gave me an old Leica that had been my grand-father's. I hid behind that thing as much as possible, doing all black-and-white shots and mostly making a hash of them in the darkroom."

"You *hid* behind the camera?" Nat gave him a dubious glance.

He nodded and sipped at his beer. "Yeah. I wasn't quite as, ah, wolfish back then." His sweet smile dawned again, tinged by ruefulness. "In fact, I was skinny and awkward and had the worst haircut money could buy."

"No...you?"

"Uh-huh. But don't tell anyone. It'll ruin my reputa-tion. And you want to hear the worst of it?" He leaned forward, beckoning her closer.

Curious, she leaned forward, too.

"I was a doormat for girls."

"I don't believe you."

"God's honest truth. They wiped their feet all over me, and thought it was funny, too. But they sure loved having their pictures taken."

The revelation that Pete Sedgewick had been a geek in high school humanized him a lot. She still couldn't quite reconcile it with the Pete she saw now, though: the weather-roughened skin, the strong hands, the unapolo-getic gaze of male appreciation. She noodled over it while the waiter brought them a second round.

"So you like working for *World Sophisticate,*" he said. "Does Addison treat you right?"

"I love it. I just keep my eyes and ears open while I'm doing grunt work, and then every once in a while I get a great assignment to work with someone interesting. And, yes, Addison is very good to me."

"She's all right, Add. Underneath the layers of couture and the 'darlings.'"

"This is sooooo none of my business," Natalie said, picking up her beer and inhaling a good third of it. "But—"

"Did Addison ever lick me?" Pete's eyes danced.

"Um, I wouldn't have phrased it quite like that—"

"No. And I've never licked her, either." He paused. "Addy introduced me to my fiancée three years ago."

"You're getting married?" Nat had the sensation that a cannon had just landed in her stomach. She tried to keep the dismay off her face.

"No," Pete said quietly. "No, I'm not. That part of my life…is over." He raised his bottle quickly to his lips and then set it down again without drinking. He leaned back in his chair and finally met her eyes. But he didn't offer any more information, and she didn't feel she knew him well enough to ask.

The mystery of Pete's personality continued over dinner, which was absolutely, Nat declared after a couple more beers, the best poo she'd ever tasted.

He ordered three different Thai desserts for her to try, smiling at her and looking good enough to eat himself.

No, Natalie. You are so not going there.

They had *cha ron,* or tea and condensed milk, with the sweets, and she couldn't help wondering again what Pete's lips would feel like against hers.

"So what next?" he asked, as he paid the check.

She said nothing, and his eyes seemed to deepen.

"I could take you to a club, if you'd like. Lord Jim's, or Blue's Bar if you like an artier scene."

"We should probably get back," she said reluctantly. "We need to start early tomorrow."

He nodded philosophically and stood up, holding out his hand to her.

You could come back to my room, if you want.

No, Nat! No. Are you crazy? He's only been nice for two hours out of forty-eight.

But when she put her hand into his, and those lean, strong fingers wrapped around her own, she knew that morning wouldn't come before they shared at least one kiss.

CHAPTER SIX

PETE DIDN'T WANT the evening to end. What had started out as an attempt to avoid loneliness had turned into something remarkably like a date—complete with the desire to take Natalie to bed.

As they sat in the cab on the way back to the Continental, he was far too aware of her scent, jasmine and citrus, and wondered whether it came from her hair or her skin. He wanted to lean closer to her, bury his face in her hair or put his mouth to the nape of her neck to find out.

He admired the way her lower lip echoed the curve of her breasts in the simple dress she wore, and the dapples of light dancing from streetlamps across her small nose.

He wanted to trace the curve of her ear, right down to the soft, tender lobe pierced by a single silver earring. And these urges unnerved him, since they weren't purely sexual.

Cut it out, man. You're lonely. And no wonder—you haven't gotten laid since Christmas 2004. Now you're wanting to fondle someone who calls your work "melodramatic"?

He hung on to that insult as the cab turned corners and Natalie's body pressed against his, at one point her small warm hand even bracing against his chest.

Melodramatic. If she even had an inkling of what he'd been through, what he'd seen in the aftermath of the tsunami…entire villages destroyed, bodies floating, families racked by grief, children without parents.

If she knew what it was like to search futilely for someone you loved in the midst of chaos and catastrophe.

Pete tried to be angry, but he couldn't, because there was no explaining any of it to someone who hadn't been there. He could show her footage or photos of the devastation, but they documented none of the gaping sense of injustice, or the smells or the yawning horror that the truth held. And over it all, that goddamned sunny blue sky…he'd wanted to bomb the sun and its mockery to hell.

Pete focused on the sheen of Natalie's shoulder-length chestnut hair, trying to block it all out. No expensive blond highlights—it was just a warm, natural brown, and he wanted to lift it and let it run through his fingers.

He didn't. The taxi pulled under the portico of the hotel, and he tried to be a gentleman and not ogle Natalie's rear end as she slid off the seat and out onto the pavement. He paid the driver and then got out himself, shoving his hands into his pockets so that they couldn't touch her.

She's too young for you, and you know it. She works for Addison. She's still naive enough to believe in happy endings.

When he did date again, he'd choose someone as world-weary and jaded as himself. Someone who only employed honesty when it was useful, and kept any criticism of his work to herself.

In fact, he'd find someone who just plain didn't understand it and therefore *couldn't* critique it. She'd be unable to point out a tendency toward the morbid, the dark or the friggin' melodramatic. But she'd bake really good pies—

"Walk me to my room?" Natalie interrupted his thoughts.

He stared down at her smooth skin and intelligent hazel eyes. At that adorable—there was no other word for it—quirk of one eyebrow. He nodded. *It's not like she's asking me in for a nightcap.*

She put a self-conscious hand up to her eyebrow. "It's bizarre, I know—"

He caught her fingers and pulled her hand down. "No, it's not. It fascinates me." He traced the eyebrow gently with his other index finger.

Whoa, man. Getting into dangerous territory, now. Don't do this. Don't be such a bastard. Leave the girl alone. Pete stopped and dropped both hands. Then he kissed her on the forehead. "Come on. Let's get you to your room."

She stood completely still for half a second before nodding and turning to walk toward the elevators.

On the way up to the eleventh floor, she looked at him out of the corner of her eye while he pretended not to notice and neither of them spoke.

Ding.

"Here we are," he said in jovial tones as the doors slid open. "Now, which way?"

She pointed silently to the left and they walked together down the hall, Pete diligently inspecting anything and everything hanging on the walls. "Great mirror," he said. "And check out this weaving."

They arrived at her door, where Pete again shoved his hands into his pockets while she dug in her bag for the card key. She found it, to his relief. She turned to say good-night; he opened his mouth to repeat the words.

And then Natalie kissed him, robbing him of every good intention he'd had.

He lost himself in the warm welcome of her mouth, her sweet sexiness, the feel of her palms on either side of his jaw. Her youth and energy; the way she went after what she wanted—he drank from it. But mostly he discarded all poetic thought for a hard-on the size of North America.

Pete had been under the illusion that at the ripe old age of thirty-six, he was immune to embarrassment, but now he realized that was not true. He broke the kiss and backed away from Natalie, who raised her crooked eyebrow and stared calmly at him, amused, while he blushed like a twelve-year-old.

Pete cleared his throat. "See—my parts do still work." He looked away, embarrassed. "Sorry," he muttered. "It won't happen again."

"That," Natalie informed him, "would be a real shame. Come here, Pussycat." And she tugged him into her room.

HE WOKE UP naked at 2:27 a.m. with his arm slung over an equally naked Natalie, his fingers trailing her breast. Pete sat up and watched her breathe evenly, chestnut hair tumbled over her pillow and in a sort of rooster tail on her head.

She murmured in her sleep and rolled onto her back, looking utterly vulnerable.

What the hell have I done?

He'd taken total advantage of the girl. Or had *she* taken total advantage of him? Pete was somewhat confused. She *had* pretty much hauled him into her room by the belt buckle.

He couldn't remember the last time he'd been seduced. He always did the seducing. But little Miss Moore had pulled him inside and locked the door behind him. Then, with two flicks of her thumbs, she'd let her sundress drop to the floor so that she stood there in nothing but a tiny yellow thong.

Really, it had been a command performance. But he couldn't pretend that he hadn't enjoyed it—and very much.

Now, as he looked down at her, he felt guilty on so many levels. He'd liked it more than he should have, burying himself in her sweet, young body. Feeling her wrapped around him and begging for release.

Not once had he thought about Hannah. And that tore him up more than anything. She was fading, getting fuzzier around the edges, going out of focus. He felt disloyal in a thousand ways.

It wasn't only being with another woman, but finding her lush body more attractive than Hannah's perilously thin frame. He remembered being afraid that he'd break Hannah somehow.

Pete swung his legs over the side of Natalie's bed. He needed some air. Some time and space to think. To remember the woman with whom he'd planned to spend the rest of his life.

He'd never been under the illusion that he'd be celibate forever. But he hadn't planned on jumping into bed with someone this soon, either.

It's been over a year. Don't beat yourself up.

Pete moved silently around the room in the dark, picking up and putting on his clothes. Natalie didn't stir again, not even as he quietly opened the door and slipped out.

It was 7:19 A.M. when he heard the soft knocking and let Natalie in. She deserved an explanation for why he'd disappeared in the middle of the night.

"I'm sorry," he said immediately. "I didn't mean to sneak out. I just had to get some air."

Her eyes were cool and her hair was wet, though she was fully dressed in a cream tank top and khaki pants. They were sensible clothes, not wild, monkey-sex clothes. The soft, romantic girl of the night before had vanished.

"I woke up around four," she said, "and you were gone." She elevated her chin and her nostrils flared slightly. She looked him square in the eye. "I figured you'd pulled the typical bang-and-run maneuver."

Whew. She'd cast aside her Southern courtesy for sure. He gritted his teeth. "I did not 'bang' you, Natalie. Last night was incredible. It just…knocked me off-kilter a little."

Her eyes had been casually taking in the elements of his room, which was a lot like hers. But now they widened, then narrowed at a spot behind him. "Who is that?" she asked.

The photograph of Hannah stood on his nightstand, along with a roll of film and some crushed crackers in cellophane.

"My fiancée."

Natalie's breathing quickened and goose bumps bloomed on her bare arms. She said slowly, "I thought you said that part of your life was over."

"It is."

Her silence swept into the room like high tide and swirled around his ankles while he tried to think of something to say. He couldn't.

She swallowed. "Then why would you travel to a foreign country with her picture?"

Because I couldn't come here without it.

Her voice rose. "And then sleep with *me?*"

He sighed.

Her hands now shaking, she asked, "Did you dump her and now you regret it?"

Pete shook his head.

"Did she dump you? What is going on here?"

He detected tremors behind her words, and a pulse beat irregularly in her throat. "Whatever it is, you leaving in the middle of the night without waking me— it made me feel cheap!"

"Natalie, listen to me—"

"Were you thinking about her the whole time you were with me?"

"No. That's part of the problem."

"What? Are you some kind of sick—"

"She's *dead*, Natalie. She's dead. Okay?"

He dropped his words into the room like a grenade.

She covered her mouth with her left hand, hazel eyes reflecting shock, and then remorse and last, the most unwelcome emotion: pity.

He looked away, unable to stand it. There was nothing you could do with pity. What a useless, humiliating bitch of a feeling. You couldn't share it. You couldn't give it back. You just had to endure it.

"Pete, I'm so sorry. I can't—oh, God. I'm sorry."

"It's okay. It's been a year."

She walked over and put her arms around him. "I'm sure it's not okay, and I shouldn't have been nasty on top of it all."

"You didn't know." Pete stepped out of her arms and

went to sit on the bed, while she stood rooted, obviously not knowing what to do.

Finally he said, "Come 'ere."

She did, sitting next to him on the mattress, but not touching him. He waited for her to ask what had happened to Hannah, but she didn't, again respecting his privacy.

And so he told her anyway: about the monster wave itself, the horrific aftermath, the agonizing days and weeks after it, wretchedly hoping and praying for some word that Hannah was alive. Then the months he'd spent waiting for proof that she was dead. And the months after that, battling a vast desert of nothing after he returned home.

Night fell every evening; the goddamned sun rose every day. Commuters streamed to and from their jobs, the mail got delivered, his landlord still wanted the rent.

Everything was so sickeningly normal. Pete had wanted to scream from the roof of his building. *Just stop! Just fucking freeze! Can we have five minutes of silence, of acknowledgment, of respect?*

But the city and the world went on. And so, eventually, did he.

CHAPTER SEVEN

NATALIE AND PETE WORKED side by side for the rest of the day. She threw herself into the job, providing interesting props and bringing in enough happy, smiling people to make Addison happy but Pete not too crazy.

They didn't speak of the night before or of their morning conversation, working around the clock with only brief breaks for food.

Nat wanted to touch him, smooth the dark circles out from under his eyes, massage the tension from his shoulders, ease his memories a little. But she could see clearly that he didn't want her pity and couldn't accept her comfort—he felt guilty enough about sleeping with her. It was an impossible situation.

Finally, Pete decided that they should call it a day since the light was fading. He began packing up his equipment. Then, to her surprise, he said casually, "So, would you like to have dinner with me again?"

She hesitated. Things hadn't been too awkward throughout the day, because they'd both been studiously professional. But should they take it into the evening again? What was she saying yes to if she did say yes?

Then again, an evening alone in her room sounded dismal, if less challenging. "Okay," she told him. "Where do you want to go?"

"I'll take you to Old City, if you'd like. The way to do it is really to take a dinner cruise on one of those old rice barges, but it would be impossible to get a reservation right now. So we'll go to Sorn Daeng, near the Democracy Monument. It's not as fancy, but still good. And maybe the concierge can get us tickets for the Bangkok Playhouse or the Patravadi Theatre."

His voice was flat, carefully neutral, without inflection or excitement. He sounded like a tour guide, not a man she'd made love with the night before. Something twisted in her gut at his emotional disengagement, even though she understood it intellectually.

"I'm really tired. Let's just do dinner," Natalie said.

If anything, he looked relieved, and that hurt worse than the bland tone. She certainly didn't want to force herself on the man.

She excused herself to go and get ready, on the verge of backing out altogether. But she had to eat, she wanted to see more of the city and she was stuck with Sedgewick for another couple of days anyway. There was no hiding from this one-night stand, as she had from the only other one in her past.

In her room, she thought again about the photograph she'd seen on his nightstand. Hannah. He hadn't said all that much about her, but there was no escaping the fact that she'd been drop-dead gorgeous—model material. In fact, she probably *had* been a model. Addison knew plenty of them from the New York fashion shows.

Nat avoided the mirror—she really didn't want to compare her looks with Hannah's, for God's sake. That was one competition she was going to lose before it started.

Even without seeing her reflection, though, she ran her hands over the excess flesh of her upper arms. She sucked in her stomach, all too conscious of the small tire encircling her waist and the couple of inches of padding on her hips.

Her legs were fine, but they weren't nearly as long as Hannah's. She didn't have thick honey-blond hair or wide-set eyes under perfectly symmetrical, groomed eyebrows. Or that lush, plump lower lip.

About the only thing she had on Hannah was a cup size, but with it a couple of inches of back fat. Ugh.

Nat closed her eyes and Addison's words, spoken before the trip, came back to her.

Cut him some slack. He's had a tough year. What an understatement! She could cheerfully kill her boss right now, for not filling her in…before she went and slept with the guy.

Had Addison sent her here on purpose, figuring this might happen between them? Had she bundled off Nat to Thailand as some kind of sick *therapy package* for Pete Sedgewick? It was all too possible.

Natalie's fingers itched to call "Addy," as Pete referred to her. But what was the likelihood that she'd get a straight answer out of her? And who wanted to confess to her boss that she'd gotten naked with the photographer on a job?

She'd have to return Addison's call at some point, but first, she needed to get her head straight.

She put on a soft blue cotton tank dress and the sandals she'd thrown at Pete, grimacing at them. She pulled her hair back in a clip and grabbed her straw bag. She took a deep breath. The three of them would have a great time tonight—she, Pete and the ghost of his fiancée.

HE SURPRISED HER by reaching for her hand across the table. "Natalie, I didn't mean to hurt you." The shadows under his eyes had deepened, and for once no trace of mockery marred his lean face.

She looked down at their hands, hers lying under his much larger, strong fingers. The heat and the frisson of electricity were hard to resist. "I realize that, Pete. And I'm a big girl, anyway. Don't worry about it."

"Look, I want you to know that you're the first woman I've even wanted to be with since Hannah. The only one who's gotten under my thick skin."

"Well, that's a compliment," she said, keeping her voice light. She pulled her hand out from under his, picked up her menu and tried to decipher anything at all on it, but the words blurred.

He sat silent for a moment, then pulled her menu down gently to get her attention. "I don't want last night to go down as a one-night stand."

She elevated her chin. "What are you saying, then, Pete? That you want to sleep with me again tonight?"

He exhaled audibly. "If that's what feels natural."

"Feels natural," she repeated. "Well, it feels natural to me to have sympathy for you—what you've been through is horrific. But—"

"You think I want you in my bed for the sake of *sympathy?*" he asked, his voice tight.

"What else do you want to call it? Loneliness? Comfort? Do you want a *three-night* stand? We go our separate ways again once we get off the plane at La-Guardia?"

"Natalie, you're reducing this to something simplistic and pathetic, and that's not what it is!"

She took a deep breath, trying to inhale serenity and patience to replace her despicable jealousy over a dead woman. "Then what is it, Pete? Tell me. Because despite what it may have looked like to you, I don't pull men into my room casually."

"You think I don't know that? Look, Nat, I can't define what this is between us. But I know that it's worth pursuing. I've never been the wham-bam-thank-you-ma'am type. I've never treated women as if they were disposable."

She took a sip of the *bia* they'd ordered again, and ordered herself to calm down.

"I'm sorry this isn't easy," Pete said.

"Is it because you feel guilty?"

He nodded.

"But why the guilt? You said it yourself—that it's been over a year. You're not betraying her."

"I know. I know that it doesn't make sense on the surface of things. I can't explain it. But it's hard to reconcile my feelings for you…"

So he had feelings for her? She tried not to let the little flicker of euphoria get out of control. "Pete." She set down her beer bottle. "Why me?"

"What do you mean, why you?"

She shrugged. "I'm ordinary, not model material. You've only known me two and a half days. I piss you off. I get in your way."

He grabbed her hand again. "You're by no means ordinary. You're beautiful. Yes, you piss me off and get in my way. But I love that you won't back down. I love that you're still fascinated by the world and not horrified by it. I love the fact that you're not afraid to criticize the great Pete Sedgewick's work—"

"God, I'm sorry about the 'melodramatic' comment. I had no idea…."

"No apologies," he said seriously. "Did it annoy me?

Hell, yes. Do I agree with the assessment? I'm not sure I'm ready to admit that. And every viewer of art brings his or her own context to meet it. Your context doesn't include catastrophe."

"Yeah, but—"

"I *really* love," he said, "the way you kiss."

She tightened her fingers around the beer bottle. "You do?"

He smiled and nodded. "And the fact that you look like you just stepped out of an Ann Taylor catalogue, but you're all Victoria's Secret or Frederick's of Hollywood in bed."

That little flicker of euphoria burst into flame. Nat blushed.

"The topper, though, is how you turned the tables on me when I put Addison on speaker phone in your room." He grinned at her, and she found herself reluctantly grinning back.

They finished the meal in harmony, and held hands all the way back to the hotel.

"Want to walk me to my room this time?" he asked.

Natalie nodded, and they rode the elevator to his floor. Pete fished for his room key, and this time *he* tugged *her* inside, where they wrapped the exotic Thai atmosphere and the darkness around them and made love all night long.

Natalie completely forgot about Hannah's picture on the nightstand.

THE MORNING LIGHT revealed his fiancée's smile to Pete, as she sat casually on her stump with her knees drawn up to her chin. She seemed to approve of his activities, and that kicked him right in the stomach.

Natalie still slept beside him, tangled in the sheets.

Pete sat up, lifted Hannah's photograph and out of habit, traced her face with his index finger. He whispered, "I'm so sorry, baby. So sorry…"

Behind him he heard the breath catch in Nat's throat and turned as she sat up and vaulted off the bed, beginning a wild search for her clothes. He dropped the picture, ignoring the soft thump it made as it hit the thick rug next to the bed. "Hey," he said. "Where are you going? I wasn't—you don't understand."

She swiped her forearm across her eyes and kept getting dressed. "Don't."

"Natalie—"

"Don't say anything." Her voice was thick. "Because I'll *never* understand, will I, Pete? I can't possibly imagine what you've gone through. The pain you've endured. The love you've lost. I can only feel what *I* feel inside, deal with my own pain." She pulled her dress over her head and shoved her feet into her sandals. She dashed a hand under her eyes again and tried to smooth her rumpled hair.

"Please understand. I'm not trying to be bitchy. I'm not unfeeling. I can't blame you. But…" She stared at him helplessly, regret in her eyes, along with tears.

"But I cannot compete with a dead woman whom you still love."

She picked up her straw tote from where she'd dropped it the night before, while he leaned his hands on his knees, not knowing what to say. What could he say? How could he make this right and still be true to himself and to Hannah?

"We'll have to work together today," Natalie continued. "There's no getting around it. But—no hard feelings—make your own dinner plans, okay?"

He tried to move toward her, but she held up a hand. "See you around nine." And she was gone.

PETE STARED at the closed door for what seemed like hours. It began to take on an odd symbolism, that door. It had a handle and hinges and a latch.

If he could find the key to his feelings, maybe he could get a handle on *them* and find…closure. Shut the door on the whole awful ordeal.

That was it: he'd had no closure of any sort regarding Hannah's death. Her parents had decided not to hold a funeral or go to Thailand for any kind of ceremony. They'd held their own memorial service in their small Nebraska town, and he hadn't gone, feeling responsible for her death. He'd convinced her to go to Phuket, after all. He'd purchased the plane tickets and made all the arrangements. And he was the one who'd left her alone on the morning of December 26.

"It's not your fault, son," her father had said woodenly on the telephone. Her mother said nothing, but Pete had heard her breathing on the line. He'd ended the call with the strong impression that they did indeed think their daughter's death was his fault. And he couldn't entirely blame them.

Pete's way of dealing with it all had been to either ignore the yawning emptiness or get drunk, and neither of those choices worked.

He needed the closure of a ceremony—he really did. But what kind? A traditional service wouldn't fit the circumstances for him. And he didn't want to grab some unknown priest or pastor or Thai monk and explain the situation to him.

He dropped his head into his hands and saw

Hannah's picture lying where it had fallen on the rug.
He picked it up and stared again into her smiling face,
tried to brush away the strand of blond hair that had
fallen into her pale blue eyes as he'd taken the photo.
As usual, it didn't work.

He set her down on the nightstand again and rubbed
at his eyes.

"It's not your fault, darling," Addison had said over
and over. *"What could you have done if you'd been
there? Taken her in your arms and leaped over the tall
wave in a single bound?"*

"You're grappling with survivor's guilt," said another
friend of his, one he played hoops with every other
weekend. Pete had blocked his pass and told him in a
friendly way to blow his pop psychology out his ass.

Maybe if he'd been a woman, he thought gloomily,
he'd have sat around eating an entire pan of brownies with
a group of girlfriends and cried it all out of his system.

Too bad he wasn't a woman.

Pete went back to the concept of survivor's guilt and
smacked it around like a handball. It wasn't tough to understand: he felt bad that he was alive and Hannah was dead.
He would have given up his life for hers. But God hadn't
given him that choice. So where did that leave him?

CHAPTER EIGHT

BEFORE MEETING Pete to wrap up the job, Natalie steeled herself to return Addison's call. She'd been very abrupt when she'd hung up the other day. Fresh out of the shower, she sat on the bed. She picked up the phone and dialed the number, which she knew by heart.

"Hi, Addison, it's Natalie."

"Darling! How are you?"

"Fine, thanks. Sorry about the other morning—the connection went bad."

"No worries. I don't think we were discussing anything of more importance than Pete's pecs. How are they, by the way?"

Chewy. "Um…"

"I simply don't believe he's looking old. Is he being decent to you?"

"Oh. Yes. Yes, he is. No problems at all."

"Are you getting some fabulous shots of the Continental? Warm, personal, engaging shots?"

"I think so. Of course, I'm not the one behind the camera, but I've provided plenty of props and we've been working with the staff and some cooperative tourists. I didn't have to hire anyone—I've just tipped well and bought people drinks."

"Excellent. Now, have you had any chances to do a

little sightseeing? Bangkok is truly marvelous! I remember going to the Grand Palace and the National Museum, The Temple of Dawn and Jim Thompson's house…oh, and I *adored* the flower market."

"We've been really busy," said Natalie. "Though I did see the Grand Palace the first day I was here."

"Getting busy, did you say?"

"No! No, no. We've *been* busy," Nat corrected.

"Has Pete said anything about Hannah?"

"Yes. Addison, I wish you'd told me. I would have tolerated a lot more from him if I'd known—"

"He's experienced too much toleration from too many people at this point," Addison said in acerbic tones. "It's time for our sweet Pete to move on. So tell me, does he still make all the right moves?"

"Excuse me?"

"Oh, don't be coy, Natalie, dear. I know Sedgewick, remember? He'd never have said a word to you about Hannah unless you'd been in his bed. Hair plugs, my foot. I should have known when the lady did protest too much."

Natalie held the phone away from her ear and stared at it. She took a deep breath and said, "I don't know what you're talking about. I'm a professional."

"You *charged* him? Darling! I didn't think you had it in you." Addison chuckled.

"What? No, I didn't charge him! I didn't mean professional in that sense, and you know it."

"You're ever so much fun to tease, Natalie. Anyway, I'm glad to hear that you and Pete are getting along so well."

Nat sputtered. "Addison, did you—" But she couldn't

ask the question without revealing that she had indeed been in Pete's bed.

"Did I make it possible for two like-minded souls to meet? Well, I think that's obvious, darling. Have you fallen in love with him, then? It would be easy to do, if you can get past the desire to murder him."

Natalie had to laugh, even though her boss had torn through the envelope—forget pushing it—of what was appropriate between employer and employee. "No, Addison, I'm not in love with Sedgewick." But her words lacked conviction. She had to bolster them somehow. "And even if I were in love with him, it wouldn't do any good, since he's still attached at the hip to a gorgeous ghost."

"Hmm. I wouldn't be so sure about that. They didn't have enough in common. But you…"

Natalie was only human. Part of her was elated at the words. But this was Addison talking, and Addison tended to change facts and figures for her convenience.

Her boss said, "It's really an awful shame that you haven't had time to see the important sights. What's the point of going to Bangkok if you can't experience it? I'll just have Debbie change your tickets to…let's see, we'll add on two extra days, all right?"

Not all right! "No, really, it's very kind of you, Addison, but I couldn't possibly—"

"That's perfect, since I'm in meetings and then tied up with the board on Friday. So you'll even have the weekend to recover from your jet lag."

Forty-eight more hours of Pete, plus another twenty-four on the plane? No way. "I can't stay extra days. I *can't.*"

"Why not?"

"Because…because…I have a…family reunion," Nat said lamely.

"On a Wednesday? Come on, you'll have to do better than that. Oh, look! I'm on the British Airways Web site and they have two seats available for Friday, right next to each other. Isn't that just brilliant?"

Natalie tried again. "I think I'm getting a kidney stone. I should have immediate medical attention."

"Lots of cranberry juice and water," her boss said briskly. "Do they have cranberry juice in Thailand? I can't remember. You'll be fine, darling. We'll see you here at the office on Monday. Bye, now!"

And Addison disconnected.

Nat glared at the phone and then stabbed herself repeatedly in the forehead with its short, stubby antenna. Her boss was unbelievable!

She checked to see if there were strings attached to her arms and legs, because she'd never felt more like Addison's little puppet.

AFTER SEVERAL STRAINED hours of work with Natalie, Pete could barely stand the distance between them. And something in his gut told him that it was wrong to throw away the connection they had. Something, perhaps even Hannah herself, told him that he had to let go. He had to let the past slip away and address the present and the future.

He racked his brains to think of a suitable ceremony for saying goodbye to Hannah. Stymied, he left the hotel and wandered aimlessly, eventually finding himself on New Road, or Charoen Krung, the first paved highway in all of Thailand. He stopped at the brown stone General Post Office, fascinated as always by the *garudas* carved in relief on the facade of the building. A *garuda* was a mythical beast, half bird and half human. It made him think of Hannah's spirit, flying off to roost somewhere in another sky.

He photographed the statue of King Chulalongkorn, as well, and then continued on to the Bangrak market. It was there, among the stalls of fruit and clothing and various other things, that he found what he was unconsciously looking for.

One vendor displayed small wooden replicas of public buildings, houses and different boats to be seen on the Chao Phraya river. He even had models of *tuk-tuks* and *samlors,* the three-wheeled conveyances that were more visually appealing than safe for tourists.

Pete stopped, greeted the man in his pidgin Thai, and picked up one of the larger boats, a varnished teak model of one of the royal barges. "How much?" he asked.

The man named a sum triple the boat's value. Pete shook his head with a smile. "How much?" he asked again.

Giving him a toothy grin, the guy came down about twenty percent.

Pete offered him roughly seventy percent of what he wanted to pay, and got laughed at. He shrugged and set the model down on its shelf again, preparing to walk away.

The man eyed him shrewdly and after a little more haggling, they came to an agreement. Pete paid in baht, the Thai currency, and left with the little barge under his arm.

He made his way back to the river and took a short ferry-boat ride back to the Continental Hotel, trying to enjoy the bustle around him on the busy river. But he kept seeing Natalie's face, struggling with a hurt she felt guilty about even feeling.

He stroked the edge of the lacquered little barge on his lap and thought about guilt. It could be a useful emotion for reforming the immoral, but in his case and in Natalie's, guilt was simply destructive.

When he got to the hotel, he went to his room and gathered together what he needed for later that night, putting everything into a small canvas duffel. An odd assortment of objects, the collection meant nothing to anybody but him.

Then he went down to Natalie's room and knocked.

"Who is it?" she called from the other side.

"Just a garden-variety idiot."

A few moments passed; then she opened the door. "I thought you were a misunderstood genius." She stood there barefoot in a long T-shirt with no makeup on, and she didn't move out of the way so he could go in.

Pete shrugged. "Same difference, in my case."

She gave him a weak, obligatory smile. "Is there something you need from me?"

"I was hoping I could talk you into meeting me later by the river."

"I don't think that's a good idea."

"I promise you, it's a great idea."

"Pete, I'm not sleeping with you again, because this is an impossible situation. You're still in love with Hannah, and I can't tolerate being her stand-in for you. I just can't."

"You're in no way a stand-in for her, Natalie."

"Come on, Pete. You talk to her picture first thing in the morning. I might as well have been a blow-up doll."

"That is not true! But let's say for an instant that it was. Why would you be upset?"

She aimed a blistering stare at him. "Why? You really are an idiot, Sedgewick!"

"Probably. But what I'm asking is whether it's your ego or your feelings that would cause you to object?"

"I fail to see the point of this discussion," Natalie said, trying to close the door.

He stuck his foot in it. Literally, because he already had done it figuratively many times over.

"Move your foot."

"Tell me whether it's ego or emotion."

"Ego!" Her tone expressed exasperation.

"Ouch. But are you sure? What I'm trying to ask, here, is whether you have feelings for me. Because I do have some for you."

"Pete, surely you don't expect me to believe that you're in love with me after what happened this morning!"

"Maybe *love* is too strong a word right now. But, yes, that's what I'm trying to tell you."

She stared at him. "I don't buy it. We've known each other three days, now. Even if you didn't have more baggage than Paris Hilton, you can't feel anything for me after only seventy-two hours."

Pete stood his ground. "I can and I do."

"Does this have something to do with us being stuck here for two extra days? You want to make sure you don't sleep alone?"

That made him angry. "Would you get a clue? We are in Bangkok. I could hire fourteen willing young girls— or boys, if I were bent that way—to pleasure parts of me I didn't even know I had. While I could kiss Addison for her amazing ballsiness at extending the trip, I'd rather kiss you."

"Well, you can't." She tried to close the door again. "Move out of the way!"

"Not until you tell me the truth. Was it just sex for

you? A cheap thrill to screw a big-name photographer?" He searched her face, tried to get behind those hazel eyes and the stubborn expression on her face.

Finally, she dropped her gaze. "No. It wasn't just sex for me. I thought you knew that."

He exhaled a bit shakily. "I'm an idiot, remember? It's all part of the Pete Sedgewick charm." He removed his foot from the doorway. "Okay. I have a few things to do. But I'm asking you to give me the benefit of your doubts—all of them—and meet me down by the river on the hotel grounds in a couple of hours. Around nine o'clock."

She looked miserable and confused. "I'm not promising anything, Pete."

He nodded. "I understand. Just think about it."

She shut the door firmly, leaving him with the impression that she didn't want to think about it at all.

CHAPTER NINE

DAMN THE MAN. Her plan had been to pull the covers up over her head and enjoy a world-class pity-party, even without a tub of ice cream to gorge herself on. But now Pete had her restless and curious and *yearning,* for God's sake.

He had her hoping that maybe things could actually work between them, that he could miraculously remove a memory chip from his thick head and forget all about the past and his gorgeous swizzle stick of a fiancée.

Then she felt horrible for thinking about Hannah negatively—the poor woman had drowned in a natural disaster, after all, and had done nothing wrong. She didn't deserve jealousy or snarkiness from anyone, especially not postmortem.

Nice. You're a real sweetheart, aren't you, Natalie? Full of compassion and goodness.

In an attempt to distract herself, she stared into the mirror and began to fixate on her crooked eyebrow, a habit she'd indulged in much more often at the age of thirteen. She remembered the time that she'd plucked it entirely and then redrawn it with an eye-pencil.

Her sister Nancy had shrieked with laughter, and her mother made Nat go to school anyway, even though she cried and begged to stay home until the eyebrow grew back.

She touched the offending feature now. Pete had said he loved her eyebrows.

Yeah, but Pete doesn't know what—or who—he loves. One minute he's in love with a dead model, and the next he says he has feelings for me. And after seventy-two hours! Ridiculous.

But why was it so unbelievable when she herself had fallen for *him?*

Natalie looked at her watch. She had enough time to make herself presentable and go meet Pete, see what he was up to, and whether or not he'd just gone nuts, been struck with malaria by some giant Thai mosquito. See if he'd changed his mind again in the past couple of hours. See if he'd repeat what her ears hadn't believed. *Pete and Repeat were walking along a bridge...*

HE SAT on a teak bench, in his typical faded jeans and black T-shirt. His hair had gone a little frizzy in the heat and humidity and curled, damp, against the back of his neck. He leaned forward, hands loosely clasped between his knees, staring across the water.

"Hi," Natalie said.

He turned and wrapped her in a smile so sweet that she struggled to reconcile it with the grumpy, sarcastic, mocking man she'd met in the hotel's lobby three days ago. The shadows under his eyes had lightened; the grooves bracketing his mouth had eased. He got up and held out his hand to her. "Thank you for coming."

A toy boat and a blue canvas duffel rested on the bench where he'd been waiting, and she eyed them, curious. He followed her gaze with his own. "It was the only boat big enough, and with the right configuration."

"For what?"

"You'll see. I wanted you to join me tonight for a ceremony. It means a lot to me that you did. I know it's not easy for you."

A ceremony? With a toy boat? What was in the duffel? Frogs? Little plastic sailors? She couldn't begin to guess.

"I want to talk to you about Hannah," he said.

She dropped his hand and backed up. "No." How could he? After he'd said he cared for *her*, Nat?

"I want to tell you about our relationship—"

She whirled and began to climb the slope that led back up to the hotel.

"—and answer any questions you may have about her."

Natalie told herself she was too mature to stick her fingers in her ears and chant, "Lalalalalalala! I can't hear you!" But the temptation was strong. She kept walking.

"And then I'm going to say goodbye to Hannah for good. I want you to help me do that. Please."

Nat stopped.

"I want to say goodbye to that time in my life, get some closure so that I can move on. And I'd like to move on with you."

A faint breeze blew the hair around her neck; she could almost imagine that it was Pete's breath, soft and warm and gentle. He stopped speaking and she heard the zipper of the canvas bag. She turned to see what he was doing and her heart tumbled forward, stopping at the base of her throat.

Pete had set Hannah's framed photograph in one end of the boat. A closed minicabin of sorts took up the center of the little royal barge. And in the other end, he set a candle with some fresh blossoms. He glanced up at her and kept talking.

"In seventy-two hours, you've turned my attitude around, Natalie. I had to get drunk to even come to Thailand, did you know that? I had no desire to move on. I festered with anger and grief and resentment and self-pity. Everyone I know has been walking on egg-shells around me for the past twelve months. Putting up with me, pitying me, indulging me. And then you walked up to me in that lobby and got in my face, made me see you as a woman instead of an annoyance."

He put, of all things, a bottle of Dr. Pepper behind Hannah's photograph. Then, leaving the laden model boat balanced on the bench, he rounded it and took her hands, tugging her back down the riverbank.

She didn't resist.

"Do you know how long it's been since anyone got in my face?" Pete asked.

She shook her head.

He sat down again next to the little barge and pulled Nat onto his lap. He put his arms around her and inhaled the scent of her hair. "You get well-known, and you develop a certain mystique. It's all bullshit, of course, but people defer to you and look at you wide-eyed, trying to figure out how the hell you got on top. They want to know the secret handshake, and they'll do any amount of sucking up to learn it from you, the wizard." He snorted. "They don't want to hear that it's just hard work."

"I've had my fill of deferential, Nat. I needed you to take me down a peg. I'd have laughed and ap-plauded if you'd done it to anyone else. But I do have a bit of an ego—"

She put her finger under his chin and met his eyes in mock surprise. "No, *you?*"

"Yeah. I know it's hard to believe. Anyway, because of my little ego problem, your words didn't go down like a spoonful of sugar. But you did jolt me out of my blues and make me sit up and pay attention."

She ran her fingers through his hair, tangling them in the curls at the nape of his neck. "I had no idea my words had such power."

He nodded. Then he said judiciously, "Well, it was also your breasts."

She smacked him and he laughed. Nat slid off his lap and put her hands on her hips. "But why me, Pete? Why not some flight attendant, or darkroom staffer or girl on the street?"

"I don't know why," he said. "But I'm trying to explain it to you. Why you? Because you won't take any crap from me. Because you've got those great eyebrows. Because you don't believe me when I say that it only took three days for me to fall for you...."

"When was it?" she asked.

He looked at her. "Oh, I was three-quarters of the way there after day one. But the capper was this morning, when you tried so hard not to resent Hannah. When it was clear that you felt guilty for wishing she'd never existed. It told me a lot about what a good person you are."

She stared at him. "How do you know I felt guilty?"

"It was written all over your face. You never said a bad word against her, but you kept looking at her photo as if you wanted to throw it out the window."

Natalie averted her eyes and rubbed at her arms.

"Let me tell you something. There are times that I

wish she'd never existed, either. My life would have been a lot easier, you know?"

That shocked Nat.

"Look, my point is that you shouldn't feel guilty for resenting her. And I shouldn't feel guilty for being alive when she's not. It's time to move on. Time to put our guilt on that little boat with her and let it sail away with the current."

"Are you sure?"

He nodded. "I'm sick of being drunk and morose. I'm sick of being an asshole. It's time I stopped depressing my friends. It's time," he said, "for me to love someone else."

Natalie absorbed this. It was one thing for Addison to say those words. It was quite another for Pete to admit them. She reached up and kissed him on the cheek, a little tentatively. Then she pulled away and looked at the little barge again. "What's the Dr. Pepper for?"

"Her favorite drink. She'd starve herself for half the day to justify the calories of one."

"She was a model, wasn't she?"

He nodded. "Hard to feed. Starving all the time so she could get and keep jobs. But she loved food. God, I remember her deliberately eating one of those fried insects you can get here, just to make herself sick. So she wouldn't want to eat dinner."

Natalie shivered, remembering the vendors she'd passed in the taxi on her first day in Bangkok. While she loved the exotic culture as a whole, there were certain "delicacies" that she'd never, ever try.

Pete dropped a ticket stub, single key and a champagne cork into the little boat. "My first date with Hannah was a Mets game. The key was mine to her apartment. The champagne cork—it's from when we got engaged. The day before the tsunami."

Nat couldn't help her curiosity. "Did you get down on one knee, do the whole Mr. Romance thing?"

He shook his head. "No. She proposed to me."

She couldn't help but be happy about that. "She did?"

"Yeah. It was a pretty spontaneous thing."

She'd imagined the opposite, an elaborate courtship of roses and diamonds.

"Do you have any more questions?" Pete searched her face. "You can ask me anything."

Anything? Did she want to know Hannah's darkest fears and secrets? Did she want to know about their sex life? Did she want to know if they'd planned to have children?

Yes…but no. Hannah had already shadowed the beginning of Nat's relationship with Pete. Did she want her to disturb it further? Did she really want to know her intimately and therefore think about her for longer?

"Really," Pete prompted. "Bring on the questions."

Slowly, Nat shook her head.

"You sure?"

Surprisingly, she was.

Pete brushed her cheek gently with the backs of his knuckles, then he dug into a pocket of his jeans for a lighter. He flicked it on and touched the flame to the wick of the candle in the little boat.

Supporting it in his right hand, he took Natalie's with his left and they walked to the edge of the water. Pete bent down.

He stared for a moment at the picture of Hannah's beautiful face under the halo of golden hair. Natalie tried to mentally put her jealousy and insecurities on the little boat with the photo, where they belonged. It was time for them to depart, too.

Pete set the craft into the swift-running current. "Goodbye, Hannah," he whispered. And then he released it. The barge bobbed and rocked in the rough water, looking frail and insignificant.

Nat thought it might overturn and sink right then and there. The candle flickered wildly and a couple of the blossoms went overboard; the cork rolled and the key slid. But the little boat persevered, hurtling its odd cargo downstream.

They watched it slip away, the varnished red paint glowing in the candlelight. Within moments, it became a tiny red dot in the distance, and then disappeared.

Hand in hand, Pete and Natalie walked up the slope to the hotel together, no further words necessary.

Frame by frame, they'd start a new life together.

EPILOGUE

Six Months Later

ADDISON FRY PUSHED her sapphire-blue glasses up to the bridge of her nose and looked severely at Pete. "This is how you reward my kindness? By poaching my brilliant stylist?"

Natalie covered her mouth and coughed to hide her laughter. Addison's eyes sparkled with annoyance, as did the half-carat diamonds embedded in the upper outside corners of her spectacles.

Did her jeweler design her eyewear to coordinate with her accessories? Because today the blue frames were the exact color of the large sapphires—also punctuated with diamonds—that encircled her right wrist.

Even more peculiar, the thick, nasty *green* liquid that her boss used to drink had now become a thin *blue* liquid roughly the color of Windex. Was she trying to sparkle on the inside, too?

"I don't mean to poach Natalie," Pete said. "But we work so well together. She's the only person who'll put up with me, and the only stylist I can tolerate. Besides, she always finds the right props."

Nat couldn't resist. "And happy, smiling people. Your favorite."

"Riiiight." Pete aimed a long-suffering look in her direction. Then he turned back to Addison.

"Look at it this way," he said in his best snake-oil salesman's voice. "Every time you hire me for *World Sophisticate*'s architectural shots, you'll be getting a two-for-one deal." He flashed a big, cheesy white grin at her.

Addison snorted.

"Besides, you've been paying her a wage below the poverty line anyway—in another few months you'd have to give her a decent raise. I'm saving you money."

"Saving me money...?"

"Yes. Because you can bring in fresh meat again at the bare minimum."

"Well, goodness, Pete, I just can't thank you enough." Addison's sarcasm was so thick that Nat could have accessorized it while Pete photographed it.

"I knew you'd come around to my way of thinking. Now, we have a pitch for you. We think you should send us both back to Thailand in six months, for a working honeymoon."

"Oh, you do, do you?" Daggers shot through the blue eyeglass frames. "Well, congratulations. Now, let me tell you what *I* think. Since I set you two up, *I* think that you should pay me a big fat fee, just like an Internet dating service."

"Why?" Pete volleyed back. "So you can buy more strange art?" He gestured around the office.

This time Natalie laughed out loud—she couldn't help it. "Sorry, Addison. Really. We are so grateful to you for making it possible for us to meet. Thank you."

Her boss unbent a little. Then she turned back to Pete. "My art is not strange, you philistine. It is *conceptual*."

Pete eyed the green brick in the Lucite box with faux

reverence. "And what a concept it is," he declared. "Complex. Mysterious. Rectangular. Green."

"Natalie, where is his leash? At least *you* respect my taste. I see you analyzing these pieces every time you come into my office."

"Um. Yes."

"Enlighten him."

Nat opened and then closed her mouth. "Well," she said carefully. "The steel bucket and the brick in particular are very…cogent…and, and…pragmatic in terms of their visual communication."

Pete squinted at her. "Say *what?*"

Her lips twitched. "What you see is what you get. There's nothing deep or *melodramatic* about them."

This time it was Addison who laughed. "Oh, touché, darling Natalie."

Pete shot out of his chair and loomed over Nat's. "My work is *not* melodramatic. And you told Addy about that? We've got to be going now, so I can throttle you in the elevator."

"So soon? I wanted to tell Addison all about our wedding plans."

"And I want my matchmaking fee. You owe me, Sedgewick, especially now that you're poaching her."

"Will you waive that if we give you twenty percent off the next gig?"

Addison drummed polished nails on her desk and frowned at him. "Oh, I suppose. But you can also find me a new stylist. Your track record regarding them is abominable, so you can bloody well stay away from the next one."

Pete shoved his tongue into his cheek and assumed a soulful expression. "Well, okay. But if she sees me, I can't be held responsible for what might happen. Because I have it on very good authority that no woman is immune to my charms. It's something to do with my sexy, *wolfish* look and my, ah, rogue's unkempt hair."

Natalie cringed as the eyes behind her boss's blue glasses narrowed. Skewered by Addison's gaze, she yelped, "Speaker phone! And he's the one who switched it on, not me, I swear."

Her boss looked for something to throw at him, while Pete tugged Natalie to her feet and out the door. He blew Addison a kiss. "Payback is a bitch, ain't it?"

While Addison called him something colorful and unprofessional, he gathered Natalie into his arms and put his lips on hers. "I may be a low-down, dirty poacher but I sure do love you, Nat."

She smiled up at him. "I love you, too. Even though you never behave yourself and probably never will."

THREE WISHES

Colleen Collins

Thanksgiving
Present Day

TRAVELING BACK toward Bangkok on Thailand's peaceful Chao Phraya River, the cruise ship *Manohra Song* rocked gently in the slipstream from a passing ferryboat. The three couples lounged on the deck, sipping their chilled fruit drinks and tea as they watched the last day of their three-day cruise turn to dusk. From a nearby stilted village, hanging temple bells chimed as they caught on breezes. Scents of fried fish and curry wafted from a floating house moored on the shore.

The couples had been chatting comfortably about their tour that day of the colorful Bang Pa-In Summer Palace and its ornamented tile floors, massive ebony furniture and impressive acquisitions of gold, silver and porcelain. These being their remaining few hours together, a sentimentality had descended over them as they quietly reminisced about the trip's highlights as well as some of the personal stories they'd shared.

Dot and Henry had told more stories of their Peace Corps work, past travels in Thailand and the language. *"Mai pen rai,"* Dot had explained, "is a Thai expression that characterizes their general focus of life. And that is, life is to enjoy."

Pete Sedgewick chimed in about an upcoming project he knew he'd enjoy—a black-and-white architectural shoot in Los Angeles.

"Black and white is perfect for you," teased Natalie, as she tousled his shock of salt-and-pepper hair.

Dot turned to Christie Griffin and her husband, Mac, who were leaning against the teak railing.

"I've heard about your journalism work, Christie, and your distinguished career in the military, Mac—"

"My hat's off to you and those daily push-ups," said Henry, raising his glass of juice in a toast.

Mac grinned. On the first day of the trip, Henry had caught Mac doing his early-morning one hundred push-ups on the deck. Later at breakfast, Mac had explained to the couples that "the morning one hundred" was a habit indoctrinated after his years in the air force.

"But you never told us what exactly brought you two to Thailand this Thanksgiving," finished Dot.

Christie turned, a breeze blowing wisps of her shoulder-length hair into her eyes. The setting sun caught hints of silver in the dark brown strands, which she brushed back as she smiled, looking younger than her fifty-six years.

"I suppose the simplest answer is destiny. Because Thanksgiving, and this part of the world, are what brought us together." She looked up at her husband, a teasing glint in her sable eyes. "Should I tell them how we met?"

Mac wrapped an arm around her and feigned a weighty sigh. "Has my saying no ever stopped you?"

Tonight he wore a pair of khakis and a beige polo shirt that emphasized his trim, athletic build. He looked conservative next to the green silk sarong Christie wore, a dress she'd purchased that day at a bustling outdoor market.

"Blame it on the journalist in me," Christie said with a laugh. "I never take no for an answer." She nestled closer to her husband. "Our story isn't quite as dramatic as a bucket of water being tossed—" she looked at Pete and Natalie "—or a shoe for that matter, but it comes close. A few hours after Mac met me, he had me jailed."

Dot gave a startled gasp. "I call that every bit as dramatic, if not more so!"

"You had your wife *jailed?*" asked Pete. "In what states is that legal?"

Natalie, her straight chestnut hair pulled back with a stylish barrette that complemented her chic outfit, playfully punched his arm.

The couples laughed, then waited for Christie and Mac to continue.

"In my defense," said Mac, "I posted her bail a few hours later. It was, after all, the night before Thanksgiving and I knew she had a bus to catch."

"Unfortunately, I was sprung too late and missed it," added Christie. "So Captain Mac, as I sometimes called him back then, offered me a ride partway home." She held Mac's gaze for a long moment. "I suppose that journey is responsible for where we are today, although we didn't see each other for an entire year after that night."

On the far side of the boat, the large, dark shadow of one of the *Manohra Song*'s poorer cousins passed, a barge emptied of its cargo after a day of trading. A steward appeared on the *Manohra*'s deck, announcing they'd be docking in Bangkok in an hour.

After he exited, Natalie said, "I know what I want

before this cruise ends—I want to know why Mac had you jailed!"

Christie set down her drink. "Let's see…it all started one fine, foggy day in San Francisco as I was gathering material for an article, one I hoped would get me promoted from writing obits and fluff pieces to real stories…."

CHAPTER ONE

San Francisco
Day Before Thanksgiving, 1971

IT WASN'T THAT the cold encroaching fog bothered twenty-one-year-old Christie Doyle. After all, she was wearing her favorite thermal tie-dyed shirt plus a pair of woolen bell-bottom pants, topped with her blue peacoat to ward off the November San Francisco chill. And it didn't bother her—well, not too much—that the dank weather was coaxing unmanageable curls in her long, preferably straight hair. Or that she'd run out of her Market Street apartment this morning without eating breakfast, unless one counted the forgotten half of an Abba-Zaba candy bar she'd found tucked in the pocket of her coat.

No, what bothered her were those heavy footsteps announcing yet another arrival of Mac Griffin, air force captain and government-bureaucracy pundit and warlord.

She blinked into the thickening gray fog. Didn't he have better things to do than spy on her from within the inner sanctum of his Air Force recruiting office? With the increasing fog, she'd thought he'd have lost sight of her by now. But he hadn't, which meant he'd not only seen her asking passersby to sign her antiwar petition, he'd also seen twenty of them sign it.

She smiled to herself. Twenty. *Probably freaks the hell out of him.*

The swirling gray parted as a shadow materialized into a tall, dark, all-business guy in blue air force slacks and long-sleeved shirt.

"You're still here," he said.

"Nice to see you, too."

He looked around, as though it were possible to see anything other than fog and more fog. "Weather report says rain." He looked back at her. "Thought you'd have given up by now."

"Me?" She scoffed, fighting the urge to shiver. The cold was seeping right through her coat, all the way down to her bones. "Never."

"Don't you have enough material for your story?"

When she'd arrived three hours ago, at eleven this morning, he'd come outside and interrogated her on her activity. She'd thought by confessing she was a junior reporter at *The Chronicle,* doing firsthand research on what it was like to be an antiwar protester—an article she'd explained could open the door to her getting a promotion at the paper—he'd realize she wasn't a real threat. Just a writer gathering background material.

So much for assumptions.

Three hours ago, he hadn't told her she *couldn't* stay, just to wrap up her business quickly. She'd pondered that comment after he'd left and had decided "quickly" was a relative term.

"No," she answered to his question, "I don't have enough material for my story yet." *Although twenty people signed my petition!* She bit back a smile.

He ignored her comment as he glanced at the clipboard and flower she held. Their eyes met again—his steely, no-nonsense blue, hers brown and steady. The man must be freezing wearing no jacket or coat. She had to hand it to him, he was tough.

Which made her all the more determined to show him she could be tough, too. After all, this was 1971, and women were fighting for equality.

"Time to give it up, don't you think?" he asked.

"A little fog never stopped me before."

"I imagine much doesn't," he muttered, cocking an eyebrow.

When he did that eyebrow thing, without shifting his steely gaze even one iota, he looked a bit like Sean Connery as James Bond in the recent movie *Casino Royale*. Sexy, deliciously sardonic, disgustingly in control. She hated herself for the small hot thrill that zig-zagged through her. She was a liberated woman, not some bygone-era stereotype who went weak-kneed over some tall, dark, and handsome guy.

He must have sensed his edge because he took a step closer. A citrusy aftershave teased her senses.

"You're interfering with my business," he murmured in a low, rumbling voice.

Damn her quickening heartbeat. "How can I interfere with your business when you haven't had any?"

Sassy. Mac liked that in a woman. Liked her fresh looks, too, which were a study of her life. A face clean and pink, without pretense. Big brown eyes that sparkled with intelligence and will. A spray of freckles across her nose that evoked the girl. The full, plump lips of the woman who'd tasted passion.

He took in a lungful of cold, bracing air to steady himself. He had to keep his head on straight with this fireball. He had four more hours to go before he could close up the office and head home for Thanksgiving, and the last thing he needed was trouble. Not just the trouble Christie was bound and determined to give him, but the kind of trouble that made his blood run hot and his head lose all sense. Such entanglements only complicated life, and he needed to keep things simple.

Simple meant no more bull. Time to nail this problem and get back to work.

"I'm expecting a busload of recruits, so it's time to pack up your gear and leave."

She didn't budge.

"You have fifteen minutes."

Those brown eyes widened in disbelief. "This sidewalk is public property."

"Which means people are free to walk on it, not park on it."

She huffed a breath that escaped in a plume of white. "I'd hardly call my standing here *parking.*"

"No, to be more exact, it's positioning yourself so that you are impeding business at a government facility, in this case a United States Air Force Recruiting Office."

"Impeding?"

"Stopping recruits by asking them to sign a petition against the Vietnam War."

She looked around. "What recruits?"

"The ones arriving this afternoon."

Her eyes searched his, and he swore he could see the wheels turning. "Look, I won't talk to the recruits," she finally said. "Deal?"

"I don't make deals."

She shuffled a foot, exposing hand-painted clogs that were bright yellow and orange, and had pink flowers with purple peace symbols. Why someone would make their shoes look like a Grateful Dead concert was beyond him.

"What if I put away the clipboard and petition when the recruits arrive?" she asked. "Then they won't have a clue why I'm here. Is that copacetic?"

"No, it's not fine," he said. "You've got fifteen minutes."

"You don't waver once you've made up your mind, do you?"

"No."

She blinked. "Never?"

"Once I've made up my mind, not much gets past the decision."

"I imagine much doesn't."

He cracked a half smile. "Touché."

Jumping on the moment of goodwill, she smiled. "But this might. You seem to forget I'm exercising my First Amendment rights."

"Spoken like a true journalist." After she'd first shown up, dressed in more colors than a rainbow, she'd explained her goal of nabbing a more senior position at the paper. She was fervent, articulate and obviously new at demonstrating.

He'd suggested she join one of the antiwar rallies across the way in the Civic Center Plaza—those seemed to happen at least once a month these days—but no, she'd insisted she needed to do her research now or she'd lose this career opportunity. Seemed some senior reporter was leaving *The Chronicle,* and all the young cubs were vying for the open slot. She had to be here. Today.

All Mac had wanted to do was fill in for his buddy Jim, the real recruiter, for one day so Jim could have extra time with his wife and kids over Thanksgiving. Just his luck to get straddled with a wet-behind-the-ears, starry-eyed first-time activist.

"There's a difference between First Amendment rights and breaking the law," Mac said calmly.

"There's a law about impeding the government?"

"Impeding government business, yes. In fact, it's a federal offense."

He looked into those soulful brown eyes, so full of zeal and idealism. He recognized that look, had seen it a hundred, a thousand times in young men eager to serve their country. There was a time when he had blindly bought into that same premise, even been willing to give his life for the cause. After a tour in Vietnam, though, his idealism had been tarnished, although he still supported his government. He couldn't *not*. To do so denigrated the memory of friends lost, buddies left behind. Ultimately, he'd learned that the men were family. And you never let down your family.

But rather than going into all that, he'd keep it simple. "You have fifteen minutes." He turned and started walking away.

"Or you'll what?"

Sassy and obstinate. He pivoted to confront her, stared at the blur of color topped with that sweet face.

"Or I call the police."

As he walked back to the office, he heard her call out behind him. "They'll have to catch me in the act of impeding business, which I won't be doing."

What a handful. "They'll arrest you for trespassing," he yelled over his shoulder. "Add the evidence of your petition, and they'll tack on impeding government business."

She snorted self-righteously.

"Fifteen minutes," he said, before closing the office door behind him.

CAPTAIN MAC GRIFFIN, twenty-six, sat down in the swivel chair behind the massive wooden desk that dominated the recruiting office and glared out the front window at the long-haired, bell-bottomed free spirit whose true goal, it appeared, was to be more than a senior reporter.

She was also damn determined to be a pain in the butt.

"Never knew a flower child had thorns," he muttered under his breath as he picked up his book. He glanced at the page he'd been reading, but all he could see in his mind's eye was Christie, who looked similar to the actress Susan Saint James who played a housewife-investigator in that new TV show *McMillan and Wife*. She and Christie both had big brown eyes, long dark hair and more energy and spunk than a roomful of cadets.

He thought back to her clog shoes and wondered if she'd painted on those neon-bright flowers and peace symbols herself. Surely she hadn't bought them looking like that. He'd also caught the edge of a tie-dyed shirt peeking over the collar of her coat. Not that he was against hippies or their peace-and-love philosophy—the world certainly could use more peace and love—but Ms. Free Spirit was marching all over *his* day of peace.

He figured she'd have given up by now, especially as dark clouds were rolling in, ready to fulfill the weatherman's prediction of rain. Winds gusted, fog swirling in their wake. The birds outside were a frenetic wind ensemble as they announced the incoming storm. He imagined Christie tightening the belt of her coat and standing stiffly in the wind, braving the elements to get a few more precious signatures. Determined, brave, goal oriented. The type of recruit the Air Force loved to sign up.

He took a last swig of black coffee, then set down the mug. It was cold out there. Soon she'd be drenched. He imagined one of her photographer pals at the paper dropping by and snapping a picture of her soaked to the bone, straining to keep her balance against the roaring winds and lashing rains, her arms outstretched with the clipboard for just one more signature. He could see the caption now—Young Woman Battles Pneumonia After Gathering Twenty-One Signatures Against the War.

Just what he needed.

He sighed heavily, got up from his seat. She'd burned up five of her fifteen minutes. He'd burn up the next ten.

He reached the door and opened it. "Christie," he yelled to the outdoors, "it's getting worse out there. Want to come inside?"

He had to force the door to stay open as a blast of air passed.

"I have hot coffee and sweets," he yelled.

On Market Street, a car honked. Tires squealed.

"Heat is cranked up, room is toasty."

"Do I resume my fifteen minutes when I go back outside?"

He knew he'd flush her out, one way or another. She was, after all, a woman who appreciated the basics— food, heat, drink. He smiled. He, who never made deals, prepared to make one.

"Yes, you resume your fifteen. Now, get your behind in here before you get soaked."

Christie scurried through the fog toward him, her

head bent, clutching the clipboard to her chest. An oversize tapestry bag, almost as big as she was, hung from a strap over her shoulder, bouncing against her body as she ran.

Minutes later, she sat near the desk on one of the folding metal chairs, wearing her peacoat with the flower—missing half its petals—sticking out of one of its buttonholes. She'd set the clipboard on the edge of the desk. The bright, floral-design tapestry bag had been dropped in a pile on the floor.

Across the room, Mac poured steaming coffee into a mug. "Sugar? Milk?"

"Both, please. Lots of each." When he gave her a look, she shrugged. "Sweet tooth."

"You don't look like you have a sweet tooth."

"If I had the money, I'd be rolling in chocolate."

Like he needed that image. "Go ahead and help yourself to those candies, then." Jim, notorious for his own sweet tooth, had left a bowl of assorted candy bars on the desk.

"Thanks." She pawed through the bowl. "Groovy. Mallo Cups. I love these."

As she chewed, she emitted a low moan that made it next to impossible for him to turn off the spigot on the twenty-cup coffee urn.

As Mac watched her nibble and devour the rest of the candy bar, he fought a sudden craving for sugar. "Take another if you want," he said. She immediately dove back into the bowl. "When did you last eat?"

"Bit-O-Honey!" she exclaimed, extracting a red-wrapped bar. "Last night. Two cans of chicken noodle soup."

He waited to hear what else, but she was busy eating again. This time, she carefully unwrapped the candy and rather than toss the paper, folded it into a neat rectangle that she slipped into her pocket. When she caught his look, she explained, "Good to hold gum."

He nodded, a little embarrassed he'd been caught staring, but couldn't stop doing more of it as he watched her pink tongue lap lovingly at the candy before she slid the piece whole into her mouth, making him think how her lips were expert at getting what they wanted.

He was still waiting to hear what else she'd had for dinner when he'd realized she'd finished telling him. Two cans of soup, period. From the threadbare edges of her coat collar, and the fact she was famished, he concluded her junior reporter salary was barely above a pittance. The newspaper probably knew they could pay little better than dirt to those eager for an entry-level reporter position. People who were willing to pay their dues and starve until they got a coveted promotion.

He'd never struggled like that. Not that he didn't live on next to nothing in college, but his mom's care packages, full of baked goods, had made him the envy of his pals.

Thinking of his family made him anxious to wrap up the day, get on the road. Tomorrow was going to be a feast, one he wouldn't see again for another year.

"Having Thanksgiving with your family tomorrow?" he asked, setting her steaming mug in front of her.

She wrapped her hands around it and smiled beatifically. "Warm. My fingers were *freezing* out there. Yes, I'll be with my family." A look crossed her face. "I missed last year," she continued, a slight hitch to her voice, "so this year is all the more important. I'm catching a bus later tonight."

He wondered what had happened last year but didn't

want to pry. "Have some coffee," he said gently. "It'll warm you up."

She nodded, took a sip. Swallowing, she closed her eyes, a look of immense pleasure crossing her face. "Outa-sight coffee," she murmured appreciatively. "Takes the chill right out of me."

And in that moment, he realized how much he liked pleasing her. Liked taking care of her. Which surprised him. Not that it was unusual for him to feel or be that way with a woman, but it surprised him he'd open that door with a women's libber. Those types never wanted men to do *anything* for them.

"Where's your family?" he asked.

"Flagstaff, Arizona. You?"

"Visalia." When she looked confused, he explained, "About two hundred and twenty-five miles southeast from here, in central California. Right at the base of the Sierra Nevadas."

"Must be pretty."

"Miles of rich basin under a California sun. Yeah, it's pretty. My parents moved there a few years ago, after my dad retired."

She took another sip. Her low, guttural sound of pleasure made him think it best if he sat down quickly.

"Unbelievable!" She nodded at the book he'd been reading, lying facedown on the desk. "I thought your reading tastes would be, well, uptight."

"You think *The Godfather* is a loose story?"

She gave a small laugh that momentarily made the room even brighter.

"Or are you pigeonholing me because of my uniform?" As if he had room to talk. It'd been easy enough for him to judge her based on the flash of tie-dye, psychedelic clogs and those dangling moon-and-star earrings.

"Not loose, per se, but I was surprised you'd be reading such a dramatic, hedonistic thriller. I mean, you—" she gestured to his uniform as though her point was obvious "—come across as so...stern."

"Stern?"

She shrugged. "Inflexible, then." The way she nibbled on another piece of honeyed taffy, he had the sudden wish to be reincarnated as a Bit-O-Honey.

"Keep sweet-talking me," he teased, "and I'll make it twenty minutes."

"Sweet-talking?" Pink crept up her neck. "Thought you never wavered."

"Yeah, I thought so, too," he said, watching the flush fill her cheeks.

Their gazes held for a long moment, broken by a crack of thunder that startled them both.

Christie glanced at the window and the fat drops of rain splattering against it. "Looks like the storm's here." She gave a small shiver. "My coat is damp from being in the fog for hours. Mind if I take it off, let it dry some?"

"Sure," he mumbled, realizing she hadn't asked his permission as much as let him know her intention. Kind of like what had happened when she arrived this morning.

She removed her coat with great care, laying it across the back of a chair with the sleeves hanging so they didn't touch the rest of the coat, which efficiently exposed all the coat's surfaces to the air. How pragmatic. He wondered what other practical streaks lay underneath that free-spirited exterior.

When she stretched and yawned, he had an ample view of her purple-yellow-and-red tie-dyed shirt.

And the fact she wasn't wearing a bra.

He tried not to stare, again, but only a man with Jell-O for blood wouldn't have been drawn to the round, pert shape of her breasts.

He cared about many of the issues of women's rights. Absolutely agreed a woman should be treated fairly and believed both sexes should be paid equitably for the same work. But he'd never understood why women's libbers were so hell-bent to burn their bras.

Although, at the moment, he'd fight to the death for them to have that right.

She glanced up at the wall clock. "You said my time in here doesn't count, right? I still get the rest of my fifteen minutes when I go back outside?"

It took him a moment to remember whatever they'd agreed to. "Correct."

"I'm down to ten minutes? Nine?"

"You make it sound so—"

"Stern? Uptight?"

"Look, Christie, I'm not a bad guy."

"No, just a military one wanting me to leave so I don't interfere with business. Is that what you call the Vietnam War? *Business?*"

It wasn't just the cynicism of her remark that rankled him. It reminded him of all the idealistic know-it-alls who'd never witnessed war firsthand yet felt uniquely entitled to pass judgment.

"Business," he repeated, the word tasting bitter. Agitated, he stood, not wanting to say something he'd regret. Instead, he picked up his almost empty cup and walked across the room to the counter and its small sink. "I never called it that," he mumbled.

She followed. "Then, what do you call it? A just cause?"

"Christie, let's not do this."

"Do you ever think about how many young men have lost their lives over there?" she asked, her voice tight, high. "Over forty thousand."

He turned and looked into those brown, sparkling eyes fervent with a cause. His head hung momentarily, then he looked back up.

"Three times that many disabled," he said evenly, keeping his emotion in check. "You're not even counting the POWs and the MIAs. I think about them every day. Every night."

Startled, she paused. "How can your conscience allow you to do this job?" She glanced up at a poster of several air force cadets working on the engine of a plane. "How can you encourage men to go?" She looked back at Mac. "Are you blind to what's really going on?"

He swiveled, set his cup down on the counter, then turned back to her. They were less than a foot apart. "Blind? To what? The world? The war?"

They were close, so close he could smell her patchouli perfume, see the dewy sheen on her face from the fog, sense her need, which was as strong as his own.

"To us?" he asked huskily.

The rain suddenly fell in a dull roar. Beyond the window, there was a wild riot of thrashing tree limbs. A pop of lightning momentarily froze the outside world in a purple incandescent glow, followed by a crash of thunder.

He looked down at her, acutely aware of how her shirt fell just below her collarbone, the spot where her pulse wildly throbbed. A hot ache ripped through him. Incisive, deep, as though his chest had been hacked open with a machete and everything he'd been fighting not to feel came rushing in to fill the wound.

And when he gathered her in his arms, and felt her body press willingly against his, he was lost...lost in the softness of her lips, the taste of coffee and sugar, her muffled moan of pleasure. And when she finally pulled back, her eyes glazed over, those plump lips wet, he realized he was far from lost. For the first time in weeks, months, years, he felt found.

"I...should...go," she whispered.

"Like hell." He bent for another kiss.

CHAPTER TWO

CHRISTIE PULLED BACK, her eyes closed. She didn't know at what point the kiss ended, just that the sensations continued after their lips no longer touched—the exquisite pressure of his mouth on hers, how he tasted of coffee and heat and sin, the way he moaned deep in his throat. She wanted more.

She raised up on her toes and tipped her head, inviting him to kiss her again. When he didn't, she blinked open her eyes in time to see him cup her head with his hands—his big and warm and incredibly gentle hands—and tilt her head oh so slowly. She willingly dropped back her head and closed her eyes as she waited for the kiss.

But this time his mouth barely brushed hers, the contact like a passing wave of heat. Then she felt his lips press against her neck and trail a slow, sizzling path down the middle of her throat. When he nuzzled the pulsing hollow at the base of her neck, she released a long, shuddering moan that carried his name.

And then the phone rang.

With a small gasp, she rocked back onto her feet and met his eyes. His hands still cushioned her head, and she marveled how his touch was both protective and sensuous all at once. How their kiss this moment felt so right. She had the crazy thought that she never wanted to leave this room. Or him.

Brring. Brring.

Mac stared at her, unable to move, to think, to speak. If he wasn't still standing, he'd swear he'd just been sucker punched. The way she looked at him, those brown eyes soft with invitation, those sweet lips trembling, it was all he could do not to sweep clear the desk and ease her back down and...

"I think you should get it," she whispered.

"Get what?"

"The phone. It keeps ringing."

With a soft curse, he glanced at it. She was right— the damn thing was ringing again. With Herculean effort, he released his hold on her, amazed how his entire body ached from the sheer act of holding back. Hell, *he* was trembling. He clenched and unclenched his fingers as he took several deep, deliberate breaths.

Brring. Brring.

"Don't move," he whispered huskily.

Christie murmured agreement as he eased away from her and crossed to the far side of the desk. He caught the phone mid-ring.

"Recruiting."

She'd promised she wouldn't move. As though she remembered how. She'd never been kissed like that before. *Never.* Either she'd been dating the wrong guys or Captain Mac had signed a pact with the devil to learn the secret of being the best kisser on the planet.

She managed to float back to her chair and sit, where it took all her concentration and then some to focus on a poster on the far wall—an air force jet soaring over a bank of bright, swelling clouds. The photographer had made the distant sun a pulsing red, the clouds so white one's eyes hurt looking at them, the sky a fathomless blue. Red, white and blue. Air Force. Career military. She was at the opposite end of the spectrum with her tie-dyed, liberal ways, her determination to carve her own career.

I've kissed the enemy. Worse, I liked it. A lot.

She toyed with a pen holder positioned on the edge of the desk, the words "One Over All" burned in black letters into the wood. Those words, which had to be the air force motto, were elsewhere in this office. She looked up at Mac, who winked at her as he continued talking on the phone to someone named Jim.

Funny how not so many minutes ago she'd sworn his eyes were the frostiest blue she'd ever seen. Cool, guarded, territorial. Now they'd melted to a warm azure. Like the balmy, vibrant waters she'd once swum in off the Gulf of Mexico. For a man who'd initially come across as cold, he'd sure turned hot. Like fire and ice. Which, come to think of it, summed up Mac perfectly. All that heat and need wrapped tightly in ironed creases and rules and duty. Unleashed, he'd be a power to be reckoned with.

"Enjoy your Thanksgiving," Mac said into the receiver. "Hey, no sweat, I'm happy to have filled in. Think of it as an early Christmas present—I helped you have an extra day with the wife and kids." Listening, he suddenly looked serious. "I'll be safe, buddy," he said quietly. "Not to worry."

I'll be safe? How dangerous was it to run a recruiting office?

She glanced around the room. The dull white walls were plastered with plaques, photos of President Nixon and other air force officers, and enough posters to wallpaper a smaller room. Posters of men training dogs, fixing engines, sitting in cockpits. Career-training promised to the recruits, no doubt. Looking at these photos, one would think the Air Force only accepted men, although she knew differently. Although the Air Force Academy, built in the mid-fifties, *still* hadn't opened its doors to women. Another good-ol'-boys club.

Christie's focus dropped to the desk, its gunmetal surface covered with stacks of forms, a cup filled with pens, a compartmentalized tray filled with paper clips, rubber bands, tacks. The only thing out of place was the paperback, *The Godfather,* a wrapped stick of gum doubling as a bookmark. A few months back, she'd spent a weekend devouring that story cover to cover, caught up in its world of Mafia blood ties, gangland killings and steamy sex.

The Mac she was getting to know seemed as out of place here as that book. But as soon as she had that thought, she backtracked. Of course he belonged here. He was a man who placed service to his country above himself, which was what she fundamentally railed against, the notion of it being noble to subjugate oneself to another being or entity.

The rain suddenly ceased, as though someone had turned off a faucet. Sounds that had been drowned by the deluge, sharpened, seemed almost too loud. A popular song, Marvin Gaye's "What's Going On?", blasted from a passing car radio outside. In the corner, the coffeepot sputtered. Across the desk, Mac's voice dropped as he talked in earnest about something with Jim.

It wasn't that she took Mac's private conversation personally; it's that it symbolized how much of an outsider she really was to his life. She didn't belong here. Perhaps just as he'd never belong in her world, either.

It was time to go.

She stood and started putting on her coat.

Mac made a "hold on" gesture to Christie. "Jim, gotta go, buddy. Have a great holiday." He hung up the receiver. "Why are you leaving?"

"It's...stopped raining."

He glanced through the window. "So it has. Fog's lifting, too." He looked back at her. "And what does that have to do with...?"

She reached for her clipboard. "I need to go."

He looked almost pained. "Stay."

"Can't."

"Why?"

"Priorities." She pretended to busy herself with the last buttons on her coat, though she never bothered with those last few anyway.

"What priorities?"

"Work."

"You mean, your story?"

She nodded as she vainly attempted to stick the broken flower back into her coat lapel.

"If you want to know about antiwar activists, I can provide plenty of details. I've witnessed demonstrations firsthand. And although many might find this view debatable, I believe it takes the same set of skills to organize a successful antiwar demonstration as it does to organize a successful military campaign."

She jerked up her head. "That's ridiculous."

He shrugged. "It's true."

"The same skills for war as for peace?"

"Not everything's as black-and-white as you want

to make it, Christie. We're more complex creatures than that."

The words stung. She didn't like the feeling *he* was lecturing *her.* She scanned the room and its Air Force he-man posters, the ponderous American eagle paperweight on the bookshelf, the "One Over All" motto plastered everywhere. She bit back the impulse to ask what was so complex about creating men to be killing machines.

He obviously picked up her vibe, because he suddenly looked contrite.

"Come on, Christie, I wasn't—" A chugging sound from outside snagged his attention. He craned his neck to look out the window. "Damn. They're early."

She turned and looked. Outside, a dark blue van with United States Air Force in gold letters on its side pulled up. It had to be the recruits. The reporter in her came to the forefront. Now *this* would make a compelling piece in her story. A great opportunity for interviews. Extremely copacetic.

"Gotta go," she said, heading toward the door.

"Christie!"

She stopped, her heart racing. "I can't."

"Can't what?"

"I have a job to do."

"That's not what you can't do."

She felt a sharp little jab in her ego, and was glad her back was to him so he wouldn't see that on her face. Or see that what had happened between them made her feel more than a little crazy, and a lot confused. What had happened back there, she wasn't ready for. Because she knew, despite their similarities and differences, what they'd shared was more than just a kiss. It was something that could sidetrack her, disrupt her life.

Make her something she didn't want to be.

Make her feel things she wasn't ready for.

"Gotta go," she mumbled.

A moment later she breathed in the brisk air, welcoming the rush of cold against her still-overheated skin. The fog had thinned to wisps of gray floating in the air. She watched the van come to a stop, the side door open. Young men began getting out, bags in hand.

She positioned herself near the recruiting office front door and waited. The first young man, a boy really, approached. He walked as though overly determined to meet his fate head-on. Didn't these men-children know what lay ahead?

"Hi," she said, stepping closer. "May I talk to you for a moment?"

He halted, looked surprised. "Yes, ma'am."

She wished she'd thought this through better. It was one thing to ask passersby to sign her petition, another to ask a military recruit.

"Why are you going in there?" She'd read the best way to get people to talk was to ask open-ended questions, although the words leaving her mouth sounded lame. She was pondering what to ask next when he spoke up.

"To serve my country," he said proudly, standing straighter.

She could run with that. "But your country is misleading you…."

He let her talk maybe two or three more seconds before he mumbled some kind of apology and stepped around her to enter the recruiting office. Undeterred, she stopped another recruit, who seemed more interested in flirting than hearing what she had to say, so she moved on to the next one. Third time was, as they said, the charm, because the guy actually set down his duffel bag and talked with her for a few minutes.

She'd pulled her steno notebook out of her tapestry bag, was taking some notes, when the young man—who'd introduced himself as Jerry McCormick from Walnut Creek, California—suddenly halted.

He nodded to the side. "Police."

She looked over. Sure enough, a black-and-white unit had pulled up to the curb, its cherry-red light swirling and flashing. The driver's door opened and an officer stepped out. Static spurts from a police radio crackled, abruptly cut off when the door shut again.

"This is the woman," said a familiar voice behind her.

She turned, spied Mac approaching the officer while gesturing toward her. He'd called the cops? Sure, he'd threatened to, but she didn't think he'd actually do it. After kissing her, no less!

The officer looked her over. Probably decided anyone dressed in a shabby peacoat with flower-painted clogs couldn't be that much of a threat, because he lumbered over as though this were more a waste of time than a true civic duty.

"You'll have to leave the premises, miss," he said.

Miss. She hated that. "I have a right to be here."

"You're trespassing."

"This sidewalk is public property."

"Not when you're interfering with business."

Here we go again. "I'm hardly interfering—"

"Make it easy on yourself and don't argue with the officer," interjected Mac, suddenly at her side.

She narrowed a look at him meant to convey every mean thought she could muster and then some.

"This is about business, Christie."

She recalled asking if that's what he called the war—business. His response had surprised her, because he'd actually seemed to care about what was happening to the men sent to the slaughter.

He didn't seem to care what was happening to her, though.

"You could have waited," she accused. "You didn't have to be so impatient."

"Impatient?"

"That's right. Impatient and inflexible. Uptight. This only would have taken me a few more minutes."

Crossing her arms under her chest, she returned her attention to the officer, who leveled a look at Christie maybe meant to be no-nonsense, but all she saw was how tired he was. Probably this incident was his last call in a long day before a holiday weekend, and he'd really like to make this short and sweet and get home to his family. Unfortunately, she wasn't in the mood to cave in and be a good girl.

In a weary voice, the cop said, "Move along, miss."

"No."

"Christie," Mac said under his breath, "don't make this a bigger issue than it is."

"I'm a peaceful protester."

He sputtered something that sounded suspiciously like *peaceful his ass.* "You don't need to go *this* far for a story."

"I'm not doing this for a *story.* I'm doing it for *them.*" She looked toward the window, through which was seen a handful of recruits, all of them staring back at the unfolding drama.

"Them?" Mac rolled his eyes. "You don't even know what I'm going to say to them when…" He stopped himself and sucked in a breath. "Look, I have to get back inside, talk to these guys. It's not too late to end this three-ring circus. Don't you have a bus to catch?"

"I didn't start this three-ring circus. And my bus doesn't leave for a few hours."

"Just enough time for you to go home and get packed."

"I'm ready to go." She glanced down at her bulging tapestry bag, the edge of a paisley-printed blouse sticking out where the zipper didn't quite close. When she looked up, Mac was frowning at the remnant of clothing. She could just imagine how he packed—everything folded neatly, everything in its place.

Although he sure didn't kiss like that.

"Do you want to press charges?" the officer asked Mac.

He cocked his eyebrow at her, and she steeled herself for the verdict. Welcomed it, in fact. This was truly how it felt to be an activist, to be strong and ready to face the consequences for your conscience.

"No," said Mac.

What? Christie frowned at him. "Why not? I'm trespassing, interfering with government business." She looked at the officer. "That's a federal offense, you know."

"Christie," Mac warned between tight lips.

"Go ahead," she urged the officer. "Arrest me."

"You got that right."

The officer clamped a firm hand around her arm above the elbow. She flashed her best peaceful smile as he began reading her Miranda rights.

A FEW MINUTES LATER, five to be exact, Mac stood in front of the men gathered in the recruiting office. All were sitting on the folding chairs as he'd requested, none of them talking although he'd invited them to relax and take it easy. They hadn't helped themselves to the coffee or the bowl of candy, either, despite his making the offer several times. They all sat looking up at him, their eyes wide with the zeal and idealism he'd seen at least a hundred, a thousand times.

He wished to God he'd never see that look again.

Over the recruits' heads, through the plate-glass window, he saw the officer handcuffing Christie before leading her away. If only she'd listened to Mac. No, he took that back. She'd listened all right; it was just that Christie marched to her own beat. And in a few minutes, she'd be marching straight into a jail cell. *I shouldn't have made that call.* But she'd pushed him, flagrantly interfered with the recruits' right of entry. He'd had no choice.

Maybe he was more black-and-white than he liked to admit.

As regrets churned within him, he talked to the boys. Asked their names, where they were from—all the while watching the police unit drive away and disappear into the distant fog.

Everything in his life was doing that. Disappearing to some far point he couldn't see and might never see again. Viewed that way, life became stripped of weight. Few things mattered. It seemed every day he was trying to decide what those few things were. Family, certainly. Friends. Not an unimpressive list, but it still seemed short. Or maybe the lack was within himself.

He couldn't see the unit anymore.

Christie was gone.

Outside, the haze of business lights that lined Market Street seemed to waver, and he had to take a moment to get his bearings.

Mac drew himself up as he faced his small audience. Nice group of kids, waiting for him to take the lead.

He leaned against the desk, crossed his arms. "What I'm about to say will surprise some of you, maybe upset others, but you'll remember me for the rest of your lives because I'm going to talk to you straight and not sell you a line of bull. Listen up, and listen well, because my words will decide your future."

"CHRISTIE DOYLE?" barked the police sergeant, peering through the jail bars.

"Here!" she croaked, rising from the stone bench she'd been sharing for the past few hour with several prostitutes and one woman who reeked of whiskey.

"Your bail's been posted," he said, opening the creaking door. "You're free to go."

"Told ya," said one of the prostitutes, a scrawny woman named Velvet whose black-lined eyes overwhelmed her gaunt face. She'd divulged her entire life story to Christie, who'd wondered if Velvet rarely got to talk, or rarely had anyone who took the time to listen.

"I can contact your family," offered Christie, although she already knew the answer. Velvet had made it clear her family had no interest in her.

"Been here before, sweetie, no big deal." Velvet touched her chipped, red-tipped fingers on Christie's hand. "My old man always gets me out. He'll be here soon."

As Christie followed the officer down the cement hallway, she wondered why Velvet had never given a name, just kept referring to some guy as her "old man." Maybe she meant her pimp? Sad to think the one person Velvet could turn to for help was a man who used her.

As Christie and the sergeant turned down another hallway, she asked who'd posted her bail. He didn't know. She'd used her one call to leave a message with the paper's editorial secretary. Even though it was the night before a holiday, and most people had left the office for the next few days, a newspaper always had a skeleton crew holding down the fort. Christie figured Danny in production had come through. Or tough-talking, chain-smoking Gail who never left the crime desk.

But as Christie and the sergeant stepped into the processing area, she nearly stumbled to a stop when she saw who stood there.

Captain Mac. Damn, he looked good. Even if his brows were pressed together, giving her a cautionary take-it-easy look as though she didn't have a right to be thoroughly pissed off after what he'd put her through.

And then he smiled, those blue eyes so warm and caring that something unfurled in her heart.

The sergeant was spouting instructions, pointing to where she'd pick up her bag and sign release forms. She barely nodded, a mix of emotions coursing through her as she stared down Mac. She was tired and out of sorts, pleased he was helping her out of this mess, and trying her best to hold on to her justified anger because he was the one who had put her here in the first place.

He crossed to her, a sheepish look on his face. One corner of his mouth lifted in a teasingly contrite smile. "I'm sorry."

She rolled back her shoulders, a feat in itself, as she felt sore all over after sitting for hours on cold, cramped benches. Her nostrils still smelled the stench of unwashed bodies, booze and a hint of disinfectant. She'd love to give Mac a piece of her mind, but she was too tired to argue. Too tired and too hungry. God, what she'd give for a hot bath, a big glass of red wine and James Taylor crooning softly on her eight-track.

Mac took a step closer. "I didn't want you to miss Thanksgiving with your family."

She glanced at the clock on the wall. Seven-twenty. "My bus left over an hour ago."

He paused, looking surprised and sad. "I'll buy you another ticket, then."

"It was the last bus to Flagstaff."

"You sure?"

"That's what they told me when I made my reservations." She shrugged and headed toward the desk where she was supposed to sign forms. "Look, I've had over five hours to think this through, and getting me to Flagstaff in time for Thanksgiving is not going to happen unless I hijack a bus. I'll use the next few days to write this story, so all's not lost."

"What will you do for Thanksgiving dinner?"

If she told him it'd be a feast of potato chips, canned soup and leftover wine, he'd probably get all guilty and apologetic and she really wasn't in the mood to comfort him when *she* was the one who needed some solace.

"I, uh, have friends I can join for dinner," she lied.

He frowned, then suddenly smiled. "I have an idea. Let me give you a ride home."

"All the way to *Arizona?*"

"Well, almost. I have an appointment in Las Vegas day after tomorrow. I can drive you that far. I have a good buddy in Vegas who'd be happy to take you the rest of the way to Flagstaff."

She snorted. "Oh, I'm sure he'd be *real* happy stuck driving a total stranger over a hundred miles."

"I've helped him out of some jams. He'll be glad to return the favor." He gave her an odd look. "If it's your safety you're worried about, I can vouch he's a stand-up guy. You'll miss the turkey dinner with your family, but at least you'll have the rest of your vacation with them."

She had a twinge, thinking of who in the family wouldn't be there. Her beloved grandmother passed away six months ago after a bout with cancer. This Thanksgiving was a time when their family needed to be together, and her mother had made it crystal clear that she wanted all four of her children home for the holiday. Especially Christie.

She hadn't gone home last year. Because she had an important deadline at the paper, she'd missed the last Thanksgiving when the family was all together. If she didn't make it this year, her mother would pour on the guilt, as usual. Nothing Christie accomplished pleased her mother. She was the black-sheep child, the trouble-maker who always questioned authority and wouldn't settle down to a normal life of being married and having children. She refused to compromise her ideals or her career goals. In that way, she and Grammy Louise had been very much alike. Her grandmother had traveled the world as a nurse in World War I, and when she was widowed, she kept her career. Christie wanted to go home to honor her memory. And she wanted to be with her family.

While she was stuck in the jail cell with Velvet, she had been counting the minutes until she knew the last bus was gone. Frustrated, she'd finally resigned herself to the guilt and regret of missing the holiday with her loved ones.

But Mac had given her another chance.

He was her opportunity to go. Really, her only op-portunity. A cross-country ride with the man who'd put her into jail, but he'd also posted her bail, so everything was on the up-and-up, right?

Sure, this could work.

She sucked in a shaky breath.

This could be one big, hairy disaster.

Considering the emotional wringer she and Mac had already put each other through, could they survive a road trip? What would they talk about for hours? God help the man if he brought up the war or women's rights. Or what if he hogged the radio and she was forced to listen to marching-band music hour after hour. Or what if he tailgated or didn't make pit stops when she wanted or what if he…

Kissed her again.

She licked her lips, remembering how delicious it'd been to kiss him.

"I'll be stopping along the way to eat Thanksgiving with my family," continued Mac. "We always have room for guests, and you'd be very welcome. My mom cooks a great spread—big fat turkey, homemade pecan stuffing, the whole deal." He dipped his head and flashed her a smile he'd probably used to break many hearts. "You'll love her. She's the heart and soul of the family."

Regret reared its head again. It was more than wanting to be with her family, she *needed* to be with them. Grammy would have wanted her to reconcile the past, make her peace.

She began fussing with her tapestry bag, not wanting Mac to read the emotions on her face.

"Let's go," she said quietly.

CHAPTER THREE

CHRISTIE WOKE with a lurch as Mac's Jeep turned a sharp corner. Gravel crunched under wheels.

"Good morning, sleepyhead."

"Morning *already?*"

"Technically. It's almost O one hundred hours."

She frowned at the string of numbers and words. "It's what?"

"Almost one in the morning."

She yawned, wrapped her arms around herself. "Much better when you speak English." She peered out the passenger window at the black sky littered with stars. "Morning?" she muttered. "It's the dead of night and somebody turned off the lights."

She looked over at Mac, the outline of his silhouette etched with faint blue light from the dashboard. She knew his smile before she saw it—the full lips pulling back in a half grin, the slight movement of the eyes as he gave her an amused look.

"What?" she asked.

"Somebody turned off the lights?"

She glanced outside into the desolate countryside. "Like it's not dark?"

"It is, city girl."

"City—?" She feigned a dramatic gasp. "What, you think I never leave the streets of San Francisco?"

"No." But his smile didn't waver. "It's just...you sometimes come across as naive."

He parked on a paved driveway outside a two-story wood-frame house that looked like a piece of old-fashioned Americana. Mac had told her that his father was retired from the military—no big surprise there—but seeing this picturesque home in the middle of nowhere she thought they might do a bit of farming. Though only a few lights were lit, he tapped gently on the horn. "Folks said they'd be waiting up."

He cut the engine and quiet surrounded them. She heard distant howling and shuddered.

"Coyotes," he said.

"Please tell me they're in another county."

"They're all over these hills, but you hear them more than see them."

Mac suddenly sat very still as he stared into the dark. She followed his line of vision, but saw nothing except for the clumps of trees visible in the moonlight.

"What are you looking at?" she whispered.

For a moment, she wondered if he'd heard her question. The seat creaked as he shifted his weight. "The shadows."

She waited to hear more. Nothing.

"That's a little pessimistic," she murmured. "Where there are shadows, there has to be light."

He looked at her as if she had said something profound.

"Mac, my boy!"

The front door of the home was open, golden light spilling around the form of a man. His white hair didn't match his ramrod-straight carriage, as though age dusted but didn't bow him. The man grabbed hold of something and pushed it in front of him. The porch light caught on the silver rails of a walker.

"My dad," said Mac, lightly thumping the horn again. The older man paused, looked at the Jeep and smiled broadly.

A woman followed, her hands fluttering around her short, curly blond hair. She wore a pair of slacks and a white blouse, and a pair of glasses dangled on a chain around her neck. She waved at the Jeep and nearly skipped toward them.

"I'll get your door," Mac said, opening his.

"That's okay, I can get it—"

But he was already bounding around the front of the Jeep. She watched him, thinking how he moved with a grace most men didn't have. And how happy he looked. For all their differences, they both felt the ties to home.

Opening her door, Mac extended his hand to help her down.

"That's all right," she said, gathering her bag, "I can get down by myself."

"I'd like to help you."

"I'm not helpless."

"I didn't say you were—" He stopped himself, gave his head a shake. "I forgot. You're a women's libber."

"City girl. Women's libber." She purposefully took his hand and stepped down. "Maybe you're judging me too harshly."

They stood for a moment in the dark, coyotes howling in the distance. The quarter moon, curved and yellow like the last remnant of the Cheshire Cat, hung in the northern sky. Scents of fireplace smoke traced the cool night air.

But the greatest sensation was the heat of Mac's hand holding hers. She looked up into his eyes. They no longer were blue but a dark indigo, as though they'd absorbed the night itself. And that's when she felt his sadness.

"Mac, what is it?"

He shifted closer, his hand squeezing hers. "Christie," he whispered, "there's something I need to tell you—"

"MacArthur!"

They turned their heads just as his mother approached, her arms open wide. Christie released Mac's hand. She stepped back to make room, catching the whiff of White Shoulders perfume as his mother grazed past her to hug her son. She threw her arms around him and he lifted her, making her laugh.

"Mom, you haven't gained a pound in years."

"Yes I have, now put me down."

His mother patted her hair as they separated, shaking her head as though taken aback, although her smile said enthusiastic greetings were the family norm.

She looked at Christie expectantly.

"Mom," Mac said, turning more serious, "I'd like you to meet Christie...." He squeezed shut his eyes, reopened them. "Sorry," he muttered under his breath. "I had this same problem earlier when I went to post your..."

His mother raised an eyebrow, waiting.

Of course. She'd never told him her last name. He must have had quite a time trying to post her bail without knowing it. She wondered if his parents sensed some of the missing words in Mac's stilted introduction and what might they be thinking. Had her son brought home a felon for Thanksgiving?

Christie reached forward and shook his mother's hand. "Doyle," she said. "Christie Doyle."

If his mother caught anything, she didn't let on. Shaking Christie's hand, she welcomed her warmly.

"Nancy Griffin, but please call me Nan. And this—" she stepped back to make room for her husband as he approached "—is my husband, Paul."

The soft thump of the rubber-tipped legs of the walker announced his father's arrival. When one of the legs hit something on the ground, the older man teetered for a moment.

Nan reached out and helped her husband steady the walker.

The man grumbled something under his breath about doing it on his own before nodding a greeting to Christie. "Any friend of Mac's is a friend of ours. Welcome."

Mac leaned over the walker and gave his father a hug. Christie marveled at how the walker seemed to melt away, as though it wasn't a barrier at all.

As the two men walked ever so slowly back to the house, she sensed the deep bond between father and son. Mac paused to look into the miles of desolate darkness and comment on how good it was to be back home, subtly giving his father a chance to catch his breath. He was kind without being condescending.

She could hardly believe this was the same man who had been so impatient with her when he called the police. She'd accused him of being stern and upright.

Maybe she'd been too quick to judge.

THE NEXT MORNING, Mac sat at the kitchen table chopping walnuts as his mother checked the cooking turkey.

"She's a dear," she said, opening the oven door. Scents of turkey and pecan stuffing filled the air, making Mac's mouth water. Containers of prepped foods— chopped apples, peeled yams—dotted the table and countertops. Next to a silver set for milk and sugar sat the ever-present pot of coffee, its dark-roasted scent mingling with turkey and yeast bread.

He sometimes thought he liked this part of the holiday the best. Sitting at the kitchen table, chopping this or that to help his mother in the preparation for Thanksgiving dinner. Occasionally, his kid sister Stephanie walked in, singing some tune about "gypsies, tramps and thieves," checking if it was time to set the table yet. Outside in the driveway his brother Grant, home from college, dropped hoops with a buddy. Sometimes his dad wandered into the kitchen, helping himself to a taste of something and to plank a kiss on his wife's cheek. The walker wasn't part of Mac's holiday memories, but an acceptable addition because it symbolized his father's recovery from a stroke. It had only been a few months and his dad swore he'd be completely recovered in time for spring, but he complained loudly about his loss of independence and called the walker an "abominable curse."

Nevertheless, he'd caught the small ways his father allowed his wife to help. It made Mac feel better about leaving, knowing his dad, Mr. Independence himself, was strong enough to accept assistance. No, not just feel better. Mac needed to know his family would be all right in his absence.

"I'd say a penny for your thoughts, but I already know what you're thinking," Nan said. She didn't look up as she siphoned the juices from the pan with the baster and squirted them over the turkey. That had always been his mom's style—biding her time, waiting for the response she already knew the answer to.

Of course, it had always been his style to pretend she didn't know. They'd been playing this push-and-pull game as long as he could remember, and would probably do it for the rest of their days.

The last thought filled him with a cold foreboding that was tangible, as though he'd swallowed a tray of ice cubes. No. He'd promised himself his thoughts wouldn't go there, and they wouldn't. He wanted this Thanksgiving to be easygoing, nothing out of the norm, so its memories would comfort him for the many difficult days to come.

"Awfully sure of yourself, aren't you?" he teased before taking another sip of his coffee.

"I'm your mother, it's my job." She closed the oven door and straightened, brushing a curl off her forehead. "We'll be all right, son."

He nodded. "Good to know."

She tossed the pot holder onto the countertop. "She doesn't know, does she?"

He paused. "No, she doesn't."

"Why not?"

"I barely know her, Ma."

She flashed him a knowing look. "Sell that baloney somewhere else."

He guffawed a laugh that was more embarrassment than mirth. He looked up at the kitchen clock, shaped like a teapot with spoons for hands. "It's eleven o'clock. I've known her exactly twenty-four hours."

"Some people you know in a minute. Others you know for a lifetime but you never really know them." She lifted a glass bowl from a cabinet. "She likes you, you know."

He thought about that kiss. If he thought of that alone, he'd swear Christie was head over heels in love with him. Heated, off-kilter moments could be deliciously deceiving, although he couldn't remember when he'd ever experienced one that knocked the air out of him and damn near brought him to his knees.

Although, it was a waste to reflect on a single event. In the bigger picture, he and Christie were as different as night and day.

"We have…different views."

"So? If your father and I agreed on everything, we'd have left each other years ago. Boredom is death, you know. A good marriage is a mix of interesting personalities."

He shot her a look. "How'd we get on the topic of marriage?"

She handed the bowl to Mac. "Pour the chopped apples and celery in here and stir. I'll get the raisins." She headed to the pantry. "I simply made a reference to your father's and my marriage. You're the one who seems interested in the general topic of matrimony."

"No, I'm not."

She retrieved a small box and returned to the table. "You're stirring too hard."

He paused and looked at her. "You know how I feel about getting involved with anyone. Especially right now."

"Your sister says I put too many raisins in my Waldorf salads," she said, shaking some from the box. "What do you think?"

He watched the raisins fall into the bowl. "I think you know exactly what you're doing."

"And you're exactly right. I put enough raisins in, not too many." Carrying the box back to the pantry, she said over her shoulder, "Love is never planned, my darling son, it just happens."

He knew this conversation wasn't about raisins. "It's not happening to me. Not now."

"That sounds suspiciously like a plan."

"And a good one, too."

"What plan?" someone asked.

Mac looked up and his breath caught. Christie had stumbled into the kitchen, her face soft and sleepy, her long hair tousled and a little curly in spots thanks to yesterday's bouts of fog and rain. She probably ironed her hair straight as many young women did, but he liked Christie's hair natural. A little unconventional, just like her.

She wore the pink chenille robe his kid sister had loaned her. It had always looked good on Stephanie, but never as good as it looked now on Christie.

She inhaled deeply, her eyes closed, and emitted a hungry moan that made him shift in his seat. "What plan?" she repeated, blinking open her eyes.

Their color reminded him of all the good things of the season—rich pecan pie, the heat from a roaring fire, leaves turning a golden brown. Good things that return and repeat, year after year, affirming the best life had to offer.

And for a crazy moment, he wondered if it was true.

Could love just happen?

His mother crossed his line of vision, flashing him another look, one that said she'd read his mind again.

"THAT'S SO GROOVY you live in San Francisco," said Stephanie, Mac's baby sister—fifteen wishing she were twenty—as she waggled her blue metallic nails at a ceramic bowl filled with her mother's homemade cranberry sauce. "I'm moving there this summer, after I turn sixteen."

"Over my cold, dead body," barked Mac's father from his seat at the head of the table. "You're graduating from high school before you move anywhere, and as we've discussed, that anywhere will be college."

Christie stuffed half a buttered roll in her mouth as she witnessed what obviously was an ongoing debate. It reminded her of butting heads with her mother, old fights that still stung. It seemed like only yesterday she'd been a rebellious sixteen, informing her mother what time she'd be home after a date, how she planned to study writing *not* accounting in college, and that her miniskirts were not too short.

Besides the choice of college majors, the rest seemed so silly now. All those confrontations were simply an excuse to declare her autonomy, which she did often and loudly. Too often and too loudly, which only exacerbated the fights between her and her mother.

It had been different with Grammy Louise. The older woman had a way of listening to Christie that calmed her down, made her feel valued.

Christie glanced at Stephanie with her thickly madeup eyes and pale lips. She seemed to be going for the look Cher made popular on the new TV series *The Sonny and Cher Show.* Grammy Louise would have gotten a kick out of Stephanie, known how to talk with her, even provide a dash of wisdom to the young girl's conflicts.

"That anywhere will be wherever I want," Stephanie muttered under her breath, still miffed with her father's edict.

The table was so quiet Christie was certain everyone had heard the sullen retort, but surprisingly, no one said anything. She met Nan's gaze and the two women exchanged a small smile. Small, but it said a lot.

After tossing back her long, straight hair, Stephanie

asked loudly to no one in particular, "What does college have to do with my being a singer?"

Christie cringed a little inside. *She sure doesn't know when to let sleeping dogs lie.*

Mac handed his baby sister the cranberry sauce. "I thought you wanted to be a writer."

She took the bowl and spooned some of the rich red mixture onto a corner of her plate. "I want to be a singer who writes her own songs. Like Joni Mitchell or Carole King. And I don't need no diploma to do that."

"*A,*" said her father. "I don't need *a* diploma. Which just goes to show you do need one."

From the radio playing the background, Sinatra crooned "All the Way." The family ate in silence for several long moments, Paul Griffin glaring at his obstinate daughter, Nan watching Paul, Grant oblivious to the drama as he drowned half his plate in gravy, Mac giving Christie an "every family has its moments" look.

"I'm thinking of hitchhiking around Europe this summer," Grant suddenly said. "Anybody want more?" He held up the gravy bowl.

"Is there any left?" joked Mac.

Grant tipped the bowl, looked inside. "There's enough."

"Europe?" asked his dad. "What's wrong with vacationing in the United States? How come everybody wants to leave and go overseas? Isn't it bad enough we're sending—" He paused, a pained look on his face.

"Give me that gravy bowl and let me see just how much is left," said Mac, taking it from his brother. "Should've named him Gravy instead of Grant," he said in a stage whisper to his mother.

Nan smiled and patted her younger son's hand. "Which country do you want to visit?"

Grant shrugged. "I was thinking of getting a Eurail pass and just traveling spontaneously in a region. Maybe Scandinavia. Or the Mediterranean. Youth airfares to Europe are solidly cheap. With a backpack and a tent, I could do the whole trip for several hundred dollars."

"You'd sleep *outdoors?*" asked Stephanie, a look of horror on her face.

Grant stabbed turkey and stuffing onto his fork, which he swirled in a pool of gravy. "Sure. There's lots of campgrounds and youth hostels. It'd be way decent." He shoved the forkful of food into his mouth.

"Can you go with a friend?" asked Paul. "Hate to think of your being alone, so far from home."

Christie noticed the older man's hands were trembling slightly, and she wondered if it was distressing him that his children were growing up and leaving the nest. Must be difficult to finally retire and settle down, then watch your family go their separate ways.

She'd never thought about it before, but her mother probably felt that way, too. Especially after losing her own mother, the house must feel especially empty. Christie made a mental note to herself to be home for the holidays from here on out. And to not argue with her mom. Not much, anyway.

"I'll go alone, Dad," Grant answered his father. "No big deal. Lots of kids are doing it. Plus, it'd be great for my major."

"What does biology have to do with hitchhiking through Europe?" asked Mac.

Grant loaded another mound of food onto his fork. "Biology sounds different over there, dude."

There was laughter around the table. Even Paul chortled, his light blue eyes sparkling.

Now that the mood around the table was lighter, Christie decided to broach a topic she'd been thinking about. She set down her glass of water and asked Stephanie nonchalantly. "What kind of songs do you write?"

"Sad ones," teased Grant.

Stephanie rolled her eyes at him before looking back at Christie. "Some are sad, some are happy. I write what I feel." She plucked an olive off her plate. "Mac says you're a writer."

Christie nodded. "Newspaper. I'm starting out, so they have me writing fluff and obits—meaning I'm a junior on the staff—but I'm working toward being accepted as a serious journalist. It takes time to pay your dues."

"What kind of stories do you want to write?"

"Political issues. Social commentaries. Some sad, some happy," Christie added with a smile.

Stephanie blinked, unsure if that was a joke. "When I move to the city, maybe you can introduce me to some people in the music business."

Christie thought about the staff writer at the paper who handled all the concert reviews. He'd know all kinds of people in the local music business. "Love to. Be sure to send me your résumé." Christie busied herself buttering another roll.

"Résumé?"

"You know, a list of songs you've sold, places where you've performed, stuff like that. Business people— even in the music business—like to know your background before meeting you."

Stephanie looked taken aback. "Well, I don't have that kind of experience yet."

Christie nodded. "True for most people starting out, which is why you also list your education on a résumé. If music producers see you studied music, they'll take you more seriously. As far as writing songs or poetry, you'd better have a college degree. And even with that, you're still competing with a ton of other college graduates."

Stephanie snorted. "Here we go again. Everybody thinks I need a diploma."

"When you're breaking in," Christie continued calmly, "it's critical. Talent is raw, like a lump of clay that needs to be formed. Whatever one can do to shape themselves, show they know their craft, puts them ahead of the game."

"Really?"

"Big cities are full of talented unknowns who earn their livings waiting on tables."

"That's heavy." Stephanie grew quiet as she intently ate her cranberry sauce, but Christie knew she'd made an impression on the girl.

When she looked up, she saw Mac's father, Paul, staring at her with steady blue eyes. She saw Mac in the older man. No secret where he'd gotten his staunch character.

"Miss Doyle," said Paul, breaking the silence, "I hope you visit us again."

She smiled. For the first time since she didn't know when, she didn't mind being called Miss.

THE THANKSGIVING FEAST ended in a rush when Christie and Mac returned to his Jeep in the driveway. As she climbed into the passenger seat, allowing Mac to hold the door for her, Christie felt she was waddling, stuffed with good food and good feelings. She wouldn't have minded spending more time with the Griffin family, but Mac insisted they hit the road. He was supposed to report for duty by nine o'clock tomorrow morning at Nellis Air Force Base outside Las Vegas.

Watching through the windshield, Christie sensed a tension in the family goodbyes to Mac. His mother wrapped her arms around her tall, broad-shouldered son and held on tightly. He lifted her as he'd done before, making the same comment how she hadn't gained a pound in years, but this time she didn't laugh.

Instead, after he lowered her to the ground, she stepped back and wiped away a tear. Mac's brother and sister also gave him prolonged hugs. Then Mac turned toward his father, who stood at attention behind his silver walker.

Paul cleared his throat, but there was still a note of huskiness. "Make me proud, son."

"I will, sir."

"Take care of yourself."

Paul raised his hand to his forehead in a salute, which Mac returned. Though Mac was dressed in worn Levi's and a blue oxford cloth shirt with the sleeves rolled up, he looked as if he could have been in uniform.

As Nan handed over a picnic basket packed with sandwiches, Stephanie scampered to the passenger side of the Jeep and leaned in. Her long straight hair hung around her cheeks like dog ears. "I'm glad I met you, Christie."

"Same here."

"What you said about college kind of…" She frowned, searching for the right words. "I guess I really do need a résumé. Your advice was…"

"Copacetic?" Christie suggested.

Stephanie beamed. "Right on. It was copacetic."

Mac opened his door and stashed the picnic basket in the rear. Without saying a word, he started the engine and backed down the driveway onto a two-lane road.

His jaw was set in a firm, stubborn line as he stared straight ahead and drove in silence. His strong hands gripped the steering wheel too tightly. Tension radiated from him in waves. In the brief time she'd known him, Christie was surprised by how well she could read his mood.

"Something wrong?" she asked.

"I hate goodbyes."

There was something more that he wasn't sharing with her, and she was curious to find out what it was. Her reporter's instinct kicked in. "Is there something about this particular goodbye?"

He shrugged. Purposely changing the subject, he asked, "Did you get hold of your family?"

She exhaled a regretful sigh. "My mother isn't too happy with me for missing the big dinner. But she's never been too thrilled with my behavior."

"Not copacetic?"

"Not a bit." She appreciated his use of her word. "This is a rough time for my family. My grandmother died six months ago. That's why it's so important for me to make it home for the holiday."

"Sorry for your loss," he said. "Tell me about your grandmother."

"Grammy Louise." When she said the name aloud, happy memories flooded back to her. Although she and her mom had a knack for crossing wires, it hadn't been that way between Christie and her grandmother. "Everybody in the family says I look just like Grammy when she was young. She was a nurse and supported the family for years after she was widowed."

"A career woman. Like you."

"For her era, she was a free spirit. Independent. She always did things her own way, not caring about what anybody else thought."

"Uncompromising," he said. "Like you."

"And you," she shot back. "You had me arrested rather than admit you were wrong."

"Technically, I didn't press charges. You were the one who dared the officer to arrest you. And, for the record, I wasn't in the wrong."

Though she could have argued her point, she let it go. Her real purpose in this conversation was to uncover Mac's big, hairy secret. The reason for his tension. She knew it was somehow connected with saying good-bye to his family.

"Compromise," she said, "is an interesting word. Your mother and I had a little chat about compromise."

"Did you now?"

"She was telling me what it was like to be a military wife."

"You were talking about marriage." Mentally, he cringed. Mac wasn't sure he wanted to hear what his mother had said to Christie. Mom already had them married off, living in a house with a white picket fence and having babies. Dreading the answer, he asked, "What did Mom say?"

"To tell you the truth, Nan shot my stereotype all to hell. I thought being a military wife meant constantly moving and being subservient to your husband's career at the cost of your own dreams."

That opinion didn't surprise him. Mac figured that introducing Christie to his family was a guaranteed clash. Like Woodstock meets West Point.

She continued, "And Nan agreed. The moving around was difficult and she didn't have much time to develop her own talents. But she said there were compensations. An opportunity to see the world. Plus, your father's career gave them financial stability. She knew his time in the service wouldn't last forever, and she'd have plenty of time to pursue her own dreams."

That sounded like his mother. "She's always encouraged us to think big. And to dream."

"Here's what she told me. 'Wisdom isn't always about what's right or wrong. Sometimes, it's in the act of compromise.'"

"There's that word again."

He looked through the windshield at the hazy skies over the distant Sierra Nevadas, wanting to imprint the memory of this wide-open countryside in his mind. Tomorrow he'd be shipping out for Vietnam, and he didn't know when he'd see this land again. He'd miss home. "Do you mind if I roll down a window?"

"Why?"

"The smells." He wanted to remember the dry wind and the scent of sagebrush.

"Oh, sure. There's nothing like the bitchin' stench of diesel fuel in the afternoon." She reached into the back and pulled out her pea jacket. "Go ahead."

Though he hated to see her cover up the gauzy little peasant blouse that she wore over a brown turtleneck, he needed to breathe the fresh air. Through the open window, a cool breeze washed over him.

When Christie reached over and touched his arm, he glanced toward her. With a shock, he realized that he would miss her, too. He had no right to feel this way. They hardly knew each other. Yet, she intrigued him. He was fascinated by the serious expression in her dark amber eyes, the way she licked her lips and tilted her head when she was about to ask a question.

And despite his concerns about how she'd interact with his family beforehand, the actual visit had gone well. In fact, he'd say she damn near won over everyone. He'd never had a first-time meeting between his parents and a girlfriend go that well.

Of course, Christie wasn't a girlfriend.

Although he seemed to be the only one holding on to that theory. Within his family, anyway.

"Is there something you want to tell me, Mac?"

More than telling, there was something he wanted to show her. Another kiss. A long, deep kiss and a sweet embrace.

"Nothing in particular." He lied.

"Your mother wiped away a tear when she said goodbye to you. Why?"

"She wasn't crying," he said. "That's not our family tradition. Even when feelings run deep, we keep things simple."

"Why were feelings running deep?"

Tearing his eyes away from her, he looked back at the road. "The real question here is why are you so persistent?"

"I wouldn't be much of a reporter if I didn't make an effort to dig for the truth." She tugged on his sleeve. "Tell me, Mac. You've been tense ever since you said goodbye to your family."

"Have I?"

"It's kind of freaking me out," she said. "What's going on?"

He was usually good at keeping his emotions hidden. Never had he been one to wear his heart on his sleeve, but she brought out a different side to him. She made him want to open up.

"The truth," she demanded.

"Tomorrow. At nine o'clock in the morning. I report for duty at Nellis Air Force Base."

"I knew that."

"From there, I ship out for another tour in Vietnam."

CHAPTER FOUR

STUNNED, Christie slammed backward in the passenger seat. Of all the secrets he could have told her, this was the least expected. He was going to war. Tomorrow.

A chill went through her, and she pulled her wool jacket more tightly around her. All that wonderful Thanksgiving food turned to a rock in her belly.

She'd known guys who had been drafted, others who had spent time in Vietnam. Someone who graduated two years ahead of her in high school had been killed over there. But she wasn't close to those other men, hadn't spent time with their families. Though she read all the articles and knew the body-count statistics, the war hadn't seemed personal until this moment.

She should have guessed before he told her. There had been that phone call at the recruiting office when he promised his buddy that he'd keep safe. Plus there was the very obvious fact that Mac was a captain in the United States Air Force. And when they left, his father told him to take care of himself—ah, now she understood why the older man grew sad during Thanksgiving dinner when Grant talked about traveling to Europe. It was too similar to Mac going overseas.

All the signs had been there, but that didn't mean she wanted to believe them.

It took her a moment to find her voice. "I thought you already did a tour in Vietnam."

"And they're sending me back."

"But they can't. It's not fair. I mean—"

He interrupted her protestations with a chuckle. "It's almost worth another tour of duty to see the look on your face right now. If your eyes get any wider, they're going to pop out of your head."

How could he laugh at a time like this? How could his family send him off without dissolving into hysterics? This stoicism must be the way they coped. It had to be a military thing. But it wasn't her thing. She fought an urge to throw herself into his arms and beg him to go AWOL.

Mac reached over and turned on the radio. After flipping through several stations, he settled on a pop station that was playing a Beatles tune from a few years back.

"I always liked this," Mac said, singing softly along with the refrain.

She shook her head. "And that's that?"

He stopped, looked at her. "What?"

"We listen to a song as though you didn't just drop a bomb?" She winced, hating her slip. Bomb. War. Vietnam. Sometimes she could put her foot into it. "Sorry, I didn't mean to say that particular word, but you know what I mean."

"Sure. I know."

Here he was comforting her, and *he* was the one going halfway around the world, willing to give his life for his country. Their country. Suddenly she felt selfish and little and sad. Very, very sad.

"I feel like crying."

He touched her arm lightly. "Please don't. I want this time before I go to be...normal."

She barked a laugh. *"Normal?"*

He shrugged. "Best word I can come up with. Let's put it this way. Today will have to last me for a long time, so I want it to be good. I want to look back and remember laughter and the smells in my mom's kitchen and the way Stephanie tossed back her hair like Cher."

"Don't forget the blue nail polish," she said, her voice breaking.

"Blue." He shook his head in disbelief, his mouth crooked in a half grin. "And I want to remember you. Your laughter, your cockeyed optimism—"

"Cockeyed?" She turned her head so he wouldn't see her swipe at the corner of her eye. "I beg your pardon."

He chuckled under his breath. "And the way you looked when you stumbled into the kitchen all sleepy eyed, and how you charmed the hell out of my family, and…"

A drawn-out moment of silence fell between them as the Beatles kept singing.

She knew what he'd left unsaid. *And how it was when we kissed.*

She glanced over at him as his head bobbed in time to the beat. His attitude couldn't have been more cool, and she wanted to match him. She nodded along with the tune, struggling to maintain her own cool, listening to the music and not knowing what to say. Talking to the new recruits on the sidewalk in San Francisco seemed so long ago. She realized how glib she'd been, how it was easy to talk about the war when it was faraway.

A sign on the highway said Bakersfield was forty-two miles away. They were making good time.

The next song on the radio was "Me and Bobby

McGee" by Janis Joplin. Much to her surprise, Mac turned up the volume and sang along. He'd kept his voice low during the Beatles tune, but this time he opened up and sang, his smooth, rich baritone harmonizing with Janis Joplin's raw emotion.

At the chorus, he turned to her. "Don't you know the words?"

"You bet I do."

She joined in. She rolled down her own window and belted the lyrics into the wind. At the *la-di-dah-dah-dah* part, she threw back her head and wailed.

Mac did the same, letting off steam. At the end of the song, he turned down the radio. "Now this is officially a road trip."

She agreed. Nothing like riding across the highway, belting out a song, living for the moment. "I loved Janis Joplin."

"Me, too. I was really broken up when she died."

"You? Liked Janis Joplin? The quintessential wild woman. The hippie chick?"

"First time I heard her was over the radio in Saigon."

Another stereotype shattered. "That's hard to believe."

"Just because I wear a uniform doesn't mean I like marching bands. Or Mitch Miller. Those tunes are fine for my parents, but when it comes to taste in music I've got a lot more in common with my sister."

"And it's Stephanie's dream to be a singer and songwriter."

"By the way," he said, as he reached over and took her hand, "I really appreciate what you told her about going to college and getting a degree."

He raised her hand to his lips and brushed a thank-you kiss across her knuckles. The unexpected tenderness of his gesture sent a shiver along her arm.

"Cold?" he asked, releasing her hand.

Her tremble had nothing to do with the temperature. If anything, she felt warmer than usual. Any physical contact with Mac had that effect on her. Still, she said, "Maybe we should roll up the windows."

He was quick to comply. "Is there anything else I can do to make you comfortable?"

Maybe stop looking at me with those intoxicating blue eyes. "I'm fine," she said. "I wasn't just shooting off my mouth when I told Stephanie that college was important. If she hopes to fulfill her ambitions, she needs to prepare."

"Like you. Paying your dues as a reporter."

"That's my dream." They had come full circle, back to their dreams again. "What's yours?"

"Given my current situation, I'm taking things day by day, not thinking too much about the future."

Starting tomorrow when he shipped out for Vietnam, she imagined his dream would be simply to survive. A difficult thought, and she didn't want to dwell on it. "Then let's take today." All she had with him was one day. Not even twenty-four hours. "What's your dream for today?"

He gave her one of those sensual, raised-eyebrow looks that clearly indicated he was thinking about sex. "My dream for the day?"

"Not every dream has to be on a grand scale. Think of it as a wish. More than one wish." Her words tumbled out as she got excited about this plan. "Pretend that you found a magic lamp, like Aladdin, and you have three wishes."

He looked at her for a long moment, reminding her

of every time they touched. The heat of his kiss. A low growl rumbled in his throat.

"What?" she asked.

"I was thinking of you dressed up in an *I Dream of Jeannie* outfit."

Harem pants and a bare midriff? "I really hope that's not one of your wishes."

"Yeah, I knew it would never work. If you were Jeannie, you'd have to call me 'Master,' and I don't see that happening."

"Not in this lifetime."

They exchanged a smile that said for all their differences, they accepted each other. Maybe didn't quite accept each other's viewpoint all the time, but accepted the person behind it.

However, she wasn't sure how he was accepting her plan. Suddenly she was more determined than ever to see it through. He wanted this day to be memorable because it was normal, but she wanted to make it better than that. She wanted to make it fun, exciting, adventurous…something he'd want to remember over and over.

"Try again." When he shot her a questioning look, she reminded him, "Your three wishes."

"Oh, right." He mulled it over. "I always wanted to fly. Not in an airplane, because I do that all the time. But to fly like Superman. To be suspended up in the air."

He was making this really hard. "How about something a little more down-to-earth?"

He pointed to a roadside billboard advertising Cora's Diner and their famous hot, buttered corn on the cob. "That's it," he said. "I wish my mom had served corn on the cob with dinner. That's one of my favorite foods."

"Then you shall have it," she proclaimed.

"It wasn't that long ago that we ate. We really shouldn't stop for—"

"We're going to Cora's Diner," she said. "And you will have corn because that's your wish. And you deserve it."

"And if I don't stop?"

She brought her fists up even with her ears and flexed her biceps. "I'll go ape on you."

"That certainly is a terrifying vision," he said drily. "You as a primate. I guess I'd better set a course for Cora's."

THE INTERIOR of Cora's roadside diner wasn't much to look at, so Mac took his order of corn to a picnic table outside. Though Christie insisted she was still full of turkey, he got another order for her.

He sat on top of the table with his square-toed boots on the bench. The arid foothills leading to the Sierra Nevadas spanned the horizon. With the late-afternoon sun warming his back, he stretched and yawned.

Christie nudged his arm. "Go on, eat the corn."

"I like to go real slow and savor every bite. You're always in a hurry, city girl."

She rolled her eyes. "I can go slow."

"Bet you can't." He remembered how she'd scarfed down the Mallo Cup and Bit-O-Honey in the recruiting office. All that gooey sweetness devoured in the blink of an eye. At his parents' house, she'd cleaned her plate right down to the shine. "You're a speed eater."

"Oh, yeah?" She tossed her head defiantly. "Well, watch this."

She lifted the corn by both ends and looked directly into his face. A mischievous light glimmered in her eyes as she looked across the yellow corn glistening with fresh butter. Her tongue darted out for a taste, then she licked her lips. "Mmm."

Did she have any idea how sexy she was? Her lips puckered into a tight bow as she pressed them against the corn with another long, low moan. When she bit into the corn, he felt the snap of her teeth all the way down to his toes.

She chewed slowly, and he was mesmerized by watching her, imagining those lips tasting him. Better yet, he'd like to dip her in butter from head to toe and lick it all off. Slowly.

Beaming a smile, she said, "Now it's your turn to savor."

Forget the corn. His mind was stuck on the image of her delectable body and warm butter. Still, he managed to pick up the corn by the ends. When he took a bite, he thought of nibbling on her earlobe, tugging at the fullness of her lips with his teeth. The rich, buttery flavor melted in his mouth. He echoed her low moan. "Mmm."

"I can tell you like it. There's butter all over your chin."

Using a paper napkin, she dabbed around his mouth. Her casual gesture surprised him. Though he hadn't purposely avoided touching her, he had been keeping her at a distance. The intensity of their first kiss had been a warning. This was a woman who could drive him wild, get under his skin. He didn't want that kind of involvement. Not now.

With an effort, he looked away from her. His tone was abrupt when he said, "Eat your own corn, city girl."

"Don't call me that."

Distance. He needed to put miles between them.

"Maybe I should call you Lois Lane or Brenda Starr because you're a girl reporter."

Her mouth pulled into a scowl that was supposed to be intimidating, but he thought the curve of her mouth was adorable.

"Never call me 'girl,'" she snapped. "I'm a woman."

"Oh, I'm aware of that." Too damn aware. He'd have to be six feet under not to notice how womanly she was, especially since she'd shed the wool jacket. Her brown turtleneck fit like a second skin, and the gauzy peasant blouse added an enticing layer of softness that made him want to slide his hands over her slim torso then up to her...

"That's a song you should keep in mind," she said huffily. "Because 'I'm a Woman. *W. O. M. A. N.*' And I'll say it again."

"What do you want me to call you?"

"Christie." She leaned toward him and bared her white teeth in a sharp grin. "I'm unique. There's nobody else quite like me."

He could say that again. She was special.

When he took another slow bite of the corn, the butter oozed across his lips.

Slick.

Warm.

Delicious.

There was only one way this could taste better.

For all his preconceived decisions, he was still at heart a man desiring a woman. A very special woman. Add the warmth of the sun, the succulent food and the tantalizing Christie, he'd have to be made of stone to not want more. Sure, he might be making a huge mistake, but at the moment he was willing to take the risk.

He placed his corn back in the paper container and watched as Christie took another bite. Predictably, the butter dripped down her chin.

Mac quickly took advantage. Napkin in hand, he reached toward her. "Let me clean up that drip."

She lifted her chin. At the last moment, he substituted his lips for the napkin. His mouth slid across hers. The taste of corn, butter and *W. O. M. A. N.* was indescribably sweet. Better than he imagined. Though he wanted to go on kissing her for hours, he lingered for only a second, then pulled away.

Inches apart, he looked into her soft mocha eyes and saw a reflection of his own desire. Fading sunlight flickered across her face. This was a moment he would never forget. Sitting in the sun outside a diner, eating buttered corn with a sassy, beautiful woman who had given him three wishes.

He wanted this moment to last a long time. A lifetime.

BACK ON THE ROAD, the radio played a sound track for their travel across California. The day faded into a brilliant golden sunset and night descended as they came to the edge of the Mojave Desert. The time passed too quickly for Mac. He was a man who liked to savor the good times, and this was one of the best.

Christie kept him on his toes with her clever wit and verbal jabs. Never boring. His mom had been right about her. They were different enough to keep things interesting.

They'd gotten into a huge debate about the lyrics for "Riders on the Storm" by the Doors. Her jaw dropped when he told her that Jim Morrison, who had died earlier this year, was one of his favorites.

"Jim Morrison, the Lizard King," she said. "I can't think of anybody who is more opposite of you."

"How about John Lennon?"

"The former Beatle who did an antiwar sleep-in with Yoko Ono?"

"The famous bed-in protest." When he remembered the newspaper photographs of John and Yoko in bed, surrounded with reporters, he couldn't help laughing. "I always thought staying in bed for ten days with your wife was a fine way to protest anything."

"Didn't it tick you off?"

"I'm not crazy about his politics, but he's got a right to act like a jerk if he wants to." Personal rights and freedoms were why Mac was ready to fight for his country. "And I like John Lennon's music. Have you heard that new song of his? 'Imagine.' It's all about dreamers."

"Stop!" She put her hands over her ears. "My head is going to explode. I can't take all the contradictions."

"Compromises," he calmly corrected. "I can hate the poet, and, at the same time, love his poetry."

"Heavy," she said. "Maybe you should become a poet."

"Yeah, right. I could grow my hair long and trade in my combat boots for sandals."

Instead of laughing, she seemed to take his comment seriously. "Is that your long-term dream?"

While he was in the Air Force, he tried not to think long-term, but it seemed important for her to know more about him. They had so little time together. "I want to go back to school. Law school."

In the glow from the dashboard, he could see only the outline of her features, but he recognized the curious tone in her voice when she asked, "Prosecution or defense?"

"Defense." Though Vietnam had made him cynical

and world-weary, he still had enough idealism to believe that he could help people who had been trampled by circumstances and hard luck.

"You'll make a really great attorney. I'd like to see that happen for you."

"Not likely. After tonight, we'll probably never see each other again."

That realization cast a shadow darker than the night on the Mojave. To never see Christie again? To never hear her laughter and the way her words jumbled together when she got excited?

To never kiss her again?

A pang of regret tightened in his gut. He hadn't expected to become so attached to her. His vow to keep his distance was fading fast.

"We'll stay in touch," she said.

"Sure."

People always promised to keep in contact with each other, but it seldom happened. He knew better than to believe she'd remember him while he was gone for a year in Vietnam. Last tour, he'd seen what had happened to some guys. No expectations were better than a Dear John letter.

The lights of Barstow lightened the sky ahead of them. This was the last town of any size before they hit Interstate Highway 15. From here, it was only about a hundred and fifty miles to Las Vegas.

"Almost eleven o'clock," she said. "Are you tired?"

"I should be, but I'm not."

"Want me to drive?" she asked.

"Hell, no."

Approaching Barstow, she sat up straight and pointed through the windshield. "Look at that. A carnival."

Strings of lights danced around several tents. Neon scrawls outlined several rides on the ground, and the pink-and-green lighted Ferris wheel loomed over it all.

"It's magical," she whispered.

He had to agree. The appearance of this frenetic, brilliantly lit oasis in the midst of the sparse, arid Mojave seemed strange and extraordinary. Like his chances of finding a woman like Christie when the landscape of his future held little more than strife and loneliness. "Doesn't even look real."

"We have to stop."

"Not a chance. We're only three hours out of Vegas."

"Don't you get it?" Her voice rose excitedly. "A Ferris wheel. This is the answer to your second wish. You wanted to fly, to be above the land but not in an airplane."

Her logic was really stretching the envelope. He wanted to soar like Superman. Not ride a Ferris wheel. "It's just a carnival."

"The last one you'll see for a long time. Come on, Mac. Let's make this a night to remember."

That hit hard. Where he was going, there wouldn't be Ferris wheels or carnivals or a woman like her with bright eyes and petal-soft lips. This was turning into a day of goodbyes. Might as well say one more. He turned onto the exit leading to the carnival. "This is the last time we stop before Vegas."

"Yes, sir." She snapped off a smart-aleck salute. "Do you always have to be the boss?"

"How do you think I got to be a captain?" He was only half joking. "I'm good at what I do, and people tend to pick the best man for the job."

"Or the best woman."

He parked in the dirt lot outside the carnival grounds

and turned toward her. The pinkish glow from a kid-size carousel shone on her upturned face. Enough light for him to see her smiling happily at the Ferris wheel. She was obviously pleased that she had found a way for him to fly without an airplane.

He cracked open his car door. "Let's do it."

Christie sat quietly and watched as he circled the hood of the Jeep. After two days with Mac, she'd learned to accept this particular compromise: She would wait for him to come around to her side of the car and open the door. Not because she needed to be helped from the car but because it gave him pleasure to treat her like a lady. And she liked pleasing him. Quite possibly she liked the feeling too much.

This road trip had turned into one of the best times she'd ever had. He made her laugh and sing. He made her mad, too. But even when they argued, it was fun because she caught hints of sensitivity—an attribute Mac would never admit to having. And when he kissed her…it felt like everything she'd ever wanted in life. The way she was drawn to him went deeper than friendship. Soul deep.

Strolling onto the carnival midway, she blinked at the lights. Though they were mostly bare bulbs dangling from wires, she saw fireflies and magic lanterns. In any other context, the reporter in her would have noticed the grime and the tawdriness of the carnival booths, but tonight she saw it through rose-colored glasses. In this enchanted mood, she found the popcorn aroma to be as exotic as a fine perfume. The spun pink cotton candy seemed a gourmet delight.

Then she linked her hand with his. His fingers tightened in a gentle squeeze. Walking side by side, the top of her head barely came up to his chin, but she thought they fit together very well.

Few other people were here tonight. Eleven o'clock on Thanksgiving was a time when most families would be home in bed, digesting their turkey dinners. But the carnival folk were out in full force, working their booths, waving and shouting above the tinny music that played over a loudspeaker system.

A skinny guy with a huge mustache approached Mac. "Hey there, buddy. Step this way. Knock down the bottles and win a teddy bear for the little lady."

Raising an eyebrow, Mac asked her, "Are you too offended for me to play?"

She frowned.

"He called you a lady. Want me to correct him, say it's 'woman' not 'lady'?"

"No," she said quickly, feeling rather silly to be having this whispered conversation within earshot of the carny. "He doesn't mean anything derogatory by it."

"So, a person's intention is what matters?"

She gave him a small, self-deprecating smile. "I get your point, Captain Mac. Not that I'm changing my ways entirely, but I get your point."

"I always liked a woman who's willing to compromise," he said, squeezing her hand. "Now, let's go get one of those stuffed animals."

"You're pretty cocky. Are you sure you can win?"

"Damn straight."

He pulled her over to the red-and-white striped booth where three stands of plastic bottles were stacked in pyramids.

The carny informed him. "Three balls for a buck. Seven for two bucks."

"I won't need more than three," Mac said.

"Suit yourself," the carny said with a sly twitch of his mustache. "You've got to knock down all three stands to win the big prize."

"No problem."

Mac unzipped his brown bomber jacket and picked up one of the baseballs. He gave her a confident wink, drew back his arm and fired a direct hit. The center stand of bottles fell.

Christie gave a victory whoop and applauded.

"Lucky throw," the carny said. "But you've got a good eye. Two more and you win the prize."

Though this was only a game—probably a crooked game—she saw Mac's competitiveness come to the fore. It was obvious that he didn't like to lose. His second shot knocked down the second stand of bottles.

"Holy cow," the carny said. "You are one lucky fella."

"Got to be lucky at something," Mac said, "because I'm shipping out for Vietnam tomorrow."

"Army?"

"Air force."

"Is that so?" The carny stepped in front of the remaining bottles. "Hold on there, flyboy. Let me make sure these bottles are balanced just right."

From her vantage point, Christie saw him make an adjustment at the back of the pyramid. Cheating? She was about to complain when Mac threw the ball and the bottles fell. He was a winner.

She selected a two-foot-tall garish red teddy bear with a huge yellow bow around his neck. As they were walking away from the booth, she said under her breath, "I thought that guy was going to cheat."

"Most of these games are fixed. There's a brace that keeps the bottles from falling."

"Then how did you—"

"He let me win," he said with a grin. "I saw the navy tattoo on the back of his hand and mentioned Vietnam. I figured the carny might be sympathetic to another uniform."

"He shouldn't be allowed to gyp somebody else." Her sense of fair play came to the fore. "He's a con man and ought to be exposed."

"Yeah, right," he said drily. "You should organize a protest. Maybe get some people to sign a petition."

"I just might do that."

"It's a carnival. Different rules apply."

She knew he was right. But whenever she faced injustice, it sparked a stubborn flame. "What if he cons an innocent kid out of his last nickel?"

"Then the kid learned an important lesson. Life isn't always fair."

A hard lesson. "The world would be a better place if nobody lied or cheated. If people took care of each other instead of going to war."

"You can't change the world, Christie."

He was right. She couldn't stop bad things from happening, couldn't keep Mac from following orders and reporting for duty tomorrow. The only thing she could control was tonight. And she meant to make it special...for Mac's sake.

"I'll let it slide." She hugged the teddy bear closer. "If I protested, I'd have to give up my prize."

In the nearly deserted midway, there were only two other couples riding on the Ferris wheel. Mac pulled out his wallet and gave the operator a ten-dollar bill. "I want to stop at the top so I can take a good long look around."

"You got it, buddy."

When the ride stopped, the carny escorted them up a ramp to the gondola seat and fastened the safety bar across their laps. She placed the teddy bear on the seat beside her and snuggled close to Mac, pleased when he placed his arm around her shoulders. Though this was only a carnival ride, excitement bubbled inside her. She felt that something wonderful was about to happen.

They swooped backward and circled a quarter of the way up before the operator stopped the ride to let another couple disembark. Creaking, their gondola car swung back and forth. The sensation of being suspended in air delighted her. "I haven't done this in a really long time."

"Me, neither."

"It's chilly out here."

"I'll keep you warm." His arm tightened protectively around her, and she found a cozy niche in the crook of his neck. Her cheek rubbed against his cotton shirt, and she inhaled his masculine scent.

With a whoosh, they ascended a hundred feet in the air, then plunged downward so suddenly that it took her breath away.

She heard a delighted scream from the other couple as they rose again to the pinnacle. "We're going fast."

"The carny who's running this ride must figure that we're all adults. He's giving us a treat."

Around and around they flew at an exhilarating pace until—at the highest point—they stopped, rocking gently in the wind. To their left were the lights of Barstow. In every other direction, the rugged desert landscape stretched for miles. The moonlight cast pale swaths against the deep blue shadows of the arid hillsides. Overhead was a canopy of stars and a sliver of moon.

She looked up into Mac's ruggedly handsome face. The faint lines at the outer corner of his warm blue eyes deepened as his mouth curved in the sexiest smile she'd ever seen. "Happy?"

"Very."

"Does this feel like flying?" she asked.

"When I'm with you, my feet never touch the ground."

When he reached up and stroked a wisp of hair off her forehead, his slight movement caused the seat to rock with a loud creaking noise. He pulled her closer, and the seat emitted a huge squawk.

She had the feeling all the carnival folk on the ground must be staring up at them. "Do you think anybody can see us up here?"

"I don't care."

He cupped her face in his warm, big hands and kissed her.

Not in the tender way he'd held her face in the recruiting station. Not like his teasing kiss when they'd stopped for corn. This was real passion.

Strong.

Demanding.

Challenging.

At the top of the Ferris wheel, she was flying.

CHAPTER FIVE

MAC COULDN'T CONTROL his desire for her. Not for one more second. Her lips burned against his. Molten lava spilled through his veins, setting fire to any hope for restraint. He wanted this woman. Struggling with the safety bar, he tried to pull her closer.

The gondola seat swung wildly as she threw her long legs across his lap and pressed against him. The squeaks and squawks of the Ferris wheel played counterpoint to her low, sensual moans.

She deepened the kiss, plunging her tongue into his mouth. Nothing slow and savoring about their kiss. They devoured each other, satisfying a desperate appetite.

With a hard jerk, the Ferris wheel started up again. Gasping, they plummeted toward earth. He held her on his lap. His hands inside her pea jacket pulled her close. Her firm breasts were crushed against his chest.

They swept upward again at a dizzying speed that made it impossible to separate the sensation of the Ferris wheel's motion from the racing of his own heart. Dipping her head, she nipped at his earlobe. Sensation pounded through him.

She threw back her head, laughing—her cheeks, rosy; her eyes shiny like dark amber. She was the picture of joy unfettered.

When the ride stopped, he threw off the safety bar and lifted her in his arms. She clung to him, her arms wrapped around his neck.

The carny who had been operating the Ferris wheel gave Mac a thumbs-up sign, and he was glad that Christie didn't see the gesture. The last thing he needed right now was a lecture on women's lib.

She shifted her weight. Breathlessly, she said, "You should probably put me down."

Ignoring her, he strode along the midway, carrying her and the big red teddy bear. He couldn't handle the thought of separating from her. After a full day of keeping his distance, he needed this closeness. If he couldn't smell the clean, floral scent of her shampoo, he didn't want to breathe at all.

"Mac?" She tossed her head and her soft, dark curls brushed against his cheek. "Put me down."

Gently, he lowered her feet to the ground, and she rewarded him with another kiss. Her slender body wriggled in his grasp, setting off a burst of fireworks inside his chest. The blood rushed to his groin.

Although he wanted to lower her to the ground and take her right here, that wasn't possible. He needed a plan.

Somehow they made it to the Jeep. He sat behind the steering wheel. Overwhelmed by desire, his brain was numb.

"We need to find a place." She leaned across the seat. Her delicate hand quested across his chest. "A place where we can be alone."

"Motel?"

Her hand dipped lower. She cupped his hard erection. "Someplace closer. I can't wait one more minute."

He drove erratically into the night, taking the first

turnoff he saw. Then another. Mac was usually good at planning and strategy. He'd told Christie that it took the same skills to plan a war and an antiwar protest. And making love? That required planning, too. Damn it, he wasn't even sure he had a condom with him. "I'm not prepared."

"I didn't expect this, either." She had unbuttoned his shirt. Her fingers traced swirls on his bare chest.

"What I mean to say is…I don't have protection."

"I'm on the pill."

"Thank God you're a liberated woman."

His headlights cut through the desert. It was a damn good thing that he was driving a Jeep, because this dirt road wasn't on any Rand McNally map. At the edge of a wide ravine, he parked beside a Joshua tree.

A flash of sanity momentarily froze him. Making love to her was a mistake. They had no possible future together. He was shipping out tomorrow. "Christie, do you—"

"Yes." She threw herself into his arms. "I want you. Now."

She had never felt this way before. Though she was a card-carrying member of the free-love generation, she had never given herself so completely to her desires. This was pure, unadulterated lust.

When Mac swung open his car door, she couldn't sit—quiet and ladylike—waiting for him to open her door. She stepped out onto the sandy earth and dashed around the Jeep.

He'd found a couple of army green sleeping bags in the rear and held them up. One in each hand. "Ta-da."

"And you said you weren't prepared."

He tossed one to her. "Unzip it."

She followed him to a waist-high rock formation of

red sandstone and watched as he spread out the sleeping bag. "This is our bed." He rested his hand on the rocks. "This is our headboard."

She tossed her own sleeping bag onto the other one. "And this is our night."

"We own the stars."

"And the moon."

He tore off his jacket and his already unbuttoned shirt. Moonlight shone on the broad outline of his shoulders and his lean, muscular torso. He carried himself with masculine confidence as he came toward her. His arm snugged tight around her waist. With his other hand, he caressed her hair and shoulders. His laser-blue gaze compelled her attention, and she gave a little whimper.

He slipped the peacoat off her shoulders. Though she knew the night was cold, she burned. In sure, swift moves, he tugged the peasant blouse over her head. Her turtleneck followed. Naked from the waist up, she faced him.

"Beautiful," he murmured.

He lavished kisses on her cheeks, her forehead, her nose, her eyelashes. His mouth descended along her throat, tracing his way down to her breasts. When he took her nipple in his mouth and suckled, an electric thrill fizzed along her nerve endings. She was gasping, writhing against him.

He stood and tilted her head up toward him. His lips took hers again with another fierce, demanding kiss.

His passion overwhelmed her. Tremors tightened her muscles. An earthquake of sensation rumbled through her legs. Her knees went weak, but he held her even more tightly as he lifted her off the ground and fitted her against his erection. His hardness between her thighs set fire to her passion. She had to have him.

Wrapping her legs around his thighs she rubbed against him. Oh, God, she wanted him, ached for him.

They collapsed onto the sleeping bag. Frantically, they tore at the zipper and yanked off the restraint of clothing. Their naked bodies met. Flesh against flesh. Their bodies like liquid heat.

Her hand grasped the length of his erection. He was long, thick and hard. When she stroked, he exhaled a gasp that became a growl of pure desire. His fingers stroked the juncture of her thighs, and she knew she was wet, ready for him.

She saw his heat, his need. And something more. She saw a future for them. They were meant to be together. They would make love like this a thousand times and then even more. She saw her destiny.

He rolled her onto her back and rose above her. With one hard, exquisite thrust he penetrated her, and she screamed his name. Again and again.

He moved inside her, and she tightened around him. Her muscles fluttered as he pulled back and thrust again. His motion stimulated her beyond all reckoning. He rocked against her with a hard rhythm, pushing her to the edge. In perfect accord, they climaxed. The delicious trembles were almost more than she could stand as she sank into a world of pure sensation as the warm Santa Ana winds swirled magically around them.

They lay side by side on the sleeping bag, and he pulled the second bag over them as a blanket. Her utterly contented gaze rested fondly upon his face.

When he stroked her cheek, she playfully nipped at his finger.

"She bites," he said.

"She does a lot more than that."

"And very well, too." His hand slipped down her throat to cup her breast.

"What are you doing?" she asked.

"Remember how I told you that I like to go slow and savor every moment?"

She nodded.

He flicked his thumb against her taut nipple. "That's how I want to make love this time. Real slow."

"We're going to do this again?"

"Oh, yeah."

Though she couldn't imagine any experience that would surpass the intensity of their first time, she was willing to try. Snuggling against him, she asked, "Where have you been all my life?"

A GUST OF WIND blew against his shoulder, and Mac wakened, shivering in the darkness. Christie was in his arms, wrapped snugly in both sleeping bags while his backside was exposed to the elements. It figured that she'd be a blanket hog. When she saw something she wanted, she grabbed and held on stubbornly.

He liked that about her. Leaning down, he kissed her forehead. What a long, strange journey this had been. When he first saw her pacing on the sidewalk in San Francisco, carrying an antiwar petition and a wilted flower, he never thought they'd end up here. Making love in the Mojave Desert.

And now he had to say goodbye.

Ever since he'd committed to another tour in Vietnam, he'd told himself a serious romantic commitment was out of the question. Despite what he'd experienced with her, had even entertained in his thoughts about a possible future with her in a few over-the-moon moments, it just wasn't possible. He didn't want to go overseas with complex ties back home. It wasn't fair to her. Or to him.

He looked at his wristwatch. Almost 0400. Four in the morning. He was due at Nellis Air Force Base at nine, and they were still a long way from Vegas. They needed to get back on the road.

When he glanced back at Christie, her eyes were open. Dreamy brown eyes and a gentle smile. She rose up on one elbow and kissed him.

Her lips were soft and warm, reminding him of their slow, savory lovemaking. The best ever. The mere thought aroused him again. He wanted more of her. But it wasn't right. He had to change gears and start thinking like an Air Force captain. With a major exertion of willpower he scooted away from her. The time had come to disengage.

She frowned. "What?"

"We need to get going."

Though she grumbled, she didn't give voice to her complaints. As he got dressed, he watched her every movement. Her arms arched gracefully as she slipped into her turtleneck. She was even sexy when she was putting her clothes back on. How the hell could he say goodbye to this incredible woman?

Pulling on her socks, she sat in the middle of the sleeping bag. A soft, sexy purr escaped her lips. "Last night," she said. "It was…"

"Copacetic?"

She laughed. "Mucho copacetic. And it wasn't just the sex. Although that was pretty amazing. When we were making love…" Her hands fluttered as if trying to grab the right description. "I never felt that way before."

Though he didn't want to hurt her, he had to push

her away. It was the best thing for both of them. His lips pressed together. There were no words for what he had to say.

Her alto voice whispered softly, "Do you believe in soul mates?"

A dangerous question. One he couldn't answer honestly because he wanted to say yes. He wanted to tell her that she was the only woman for him, the woman he wanted to spend the rest of his life with. Maybe after he came back from Vietnam he could say that. But not now. The timing was wrong.

"Soul mates? No, I don't believe in that stuff."

Clearly taken aback, she sat up straighter. "Then we're...what?"

"Friends." The word tasted bitter in his mouth. "We're friends."

She bounced to her feet and glared daggers through the moonlight. For a minute, he thought she was going to punch him. Instead, she jammed her feet into her shoes and stormed toward the Jeep.

Gritting her teeth, Christie stifled the urge to scream. Or throw something. Or dissolve into tears. Friends? He thought they were just friends? Last night, she'd experienced what love was really about. She knew what she had felt in her heart and soul—they were meant to be together.

He knew it, too. Why was he denying the most wonderful gift in the world? How could he calmly tell her that they were nothing more than friends?

She watched as he stashed the sleeping bags in the rear of the Jeep and fired up the engine. The headlights illuminated the rugged desert landscape and the twisted branches of a Joshua tree. Against all odds, this tree grew in the desert. She needed to be like the Joshua, finding a way for these feelings she had for Mac to take root and flourish, even though it seemed impossible. If she lost him, she'd regret it the rest of her life.

Stoically, he stared through the windshield, back-tracking across the wild route they'd driven last night when they were both crazy with passion. Then they were back on the highway, on their way to Vegas.

She had to say something. Remembering her inter-viewing skills, she decided it was best to ease him into conversation gently. "You know, Mac. You never actually made your third wish."

"I didn't?"

"No, you got the corn and the Ferris wheel flight, but you still have wish number three."

He shrugged. His jaw was granite.

"Come on," she cajoled. "You still have dreams, don't you? There must be something you want."

"I'd rather not talk."

"Not at all?"

"That's correct."

A tense silence fell over them. Not even the radio provided relief. They were out of range for any of the popular stations.

Not knowing what else to say, she counted the miles and read the road signs. One hundred and thirty miles to Las Vegas. Ninety-eight. Seventy-two. Her anxiety rose to an unbearable level. She didn't want their time together to end like this, but she didn't want to argue with him.

Nearing Vegas, billboards advertised the buffets at various casinos and announced the dates of Elvis's next appearance at the MGM Grand.

Unable to hold back any longer, she blurted, "You

know we're more than friends. We have a connection. Something deep and precious. I know you felt it."

"Leave it alone."

"Or else what? You'll have me arrested again? Good luck finding a police officer out here." She was on a roll. The words she'd been repressing came out in a rush. "Don't do this, Mac. Don't turn back into an unfeeling, tight-ass military guy."

"That's who I am."

"No." He was sensitive and funny and sexy as hell. "You know you're supposed to be with me. Last night you felt it. I know you did. Please, Mac, don't leave me like this."

"It's not my choice." His words were clipped. Terse. "I have my orders."

"You can get around those orders. You've already done one tour of duty and you have seniority, I'm sure there's some way you can arrange to—"

"Maybe I don't want to."

"What?" She was honestly shocked. "Are you telling me that you want to go back to Vietnam?" Disbelieving, she shook her head. "I know you're not one hundred percent behind the war. Why are you saying this?"

"It's not about war. It's about the Air Force, honoring my commitment, supporting the other guys who are involved."

"That's very noble, but what about you? Your dreams? Your hopes for the future?"

The desperation in her voice touched him. Mac knew he was doing the right thing by ending this, but he was torn up inside. When he turned to her, he was hurt by the pain he saw in her eyes. "You want me to admit there's something special between us?"

"Yes, I do."

"Granted," he said. "You touch my heart. You turn me on. You make me want to fly. I want to carry you away to a distant star where we can make love all day and night."

"I feel it, too."

They were entering Vegas, driving into the rising sun. Their night together was over. "Now we have to forget about it. Be realistic. Nothing between us would work out long-term."

"It would."

"You like to talk about dreams. Well, what about your goals? You have a career to conquer, and I'm not a part of that."

"You could be."

"Somehow I don't see you as a military wife."

"Wife?"

Her voice was high and surprised. Apparently, she hadn't been thinking about marriage. "Some kind of hippie free-love relationship would never work for me," he said.

"Because you need commitment."

"Damn right."

"What about compromise?" she asked. "If there's one thing I've learned being with you, it's the wisdom of compromising."

Her simple words punched a hole in his logic. Realization dawned with the sun. Why hadn't he seen this before? They could follow their own paths and stay true to themselves with compromise.

Somehow, he had to make things right with Christie. And he had less than an hour to do it.

Spotting a telephone booth, he pulled over. "I need to call my buddy. The guy who's going to take you the rest of the way to Flagstaff. I need to make sure he's awake."

She caught hold of his arm, and he turned. Her eyes were soulful. Her lips trembled. "I love you, Mac."

He left the Jeep and went to the phone booth. Across the street, he saw a little white chapel, one of dozens in Vegas. The sign over the door read, "Open Twenty-Four Hours A Day."

He flashed on his parents' marriage, the sacredness of belonging to something bigger than himself.

In the Jeep with the motor still running, Christie watched him walk away. It couldn't end like this. It just couldn't. She turned on the radio, adjusted the dial. The song—the last music of their road trip—was John Lennon singing "Imagine." A song about dreamers. She was not the only one. Mac had dreams, too. Together, they could make something wonderful.

A tear slipped down her cheek.

She looked across the street to the chapel. How many couples had passed through those doors? Hundreds, maybe thousands. And when they married, their dreams didn't end. They got bigger.

Mac opened her car door and leaned inside. His lips pressed gently against hers. "I love you, Christie."

Her heart soared. "That was all I needed to hear."

"There's more." He dropped to one knee. "I want you to marry me. That's my third wish. So you have to do it."

She tumbled out of the Jeep and into his waiting arms. "Or else, what?"

Current Day on the Manohra Song

CHRISTIE LEANED her elbows on the railing of the cruise ship *Manohra Song* and looked lovingly at her husband of thirty-five years, observing how the deck lights were reflected in the blue of his eyes. Mac was still as sexy as the first day they met. Marrying him at that chapel in Las Vegas was the best decision she'd ever made.

"It hasn't always been easy. But never boring." She turned toward the other couples and admitted, "We've learned a lot about compromise."

"Amen to that," echoed Dot and Henry.

"What happened next?" asked Natalie, her enthusiasm for the story unabated. "Did Mac stay in the military?"

"Not for long," he answered. "After my last tour of duty in Vietnam, I didn't re-up. You see, I had this dream to be a defense attorney, and this woman who kept pushing me toward it."

"And you?" Natalie turned to Christie. "What happened to your article about antiwar protests?"

"Funny thing about that. That article put me on the path to promotion, but it wasn't about protest. I wrote about compromise. Seeing both sides of the war and still staying true to yourself."

Mac draped his arm around her shoulders. "I can't say I've always been happy about some of the dangerous trouble spots my wife has gone as a journalist, but I try to be supportive."

"You are." She reached up and touched his cheek. "When I'm with you, everything is…copacetic."

The steward announced they would be disembarking in a few minutes. In the distance sparkled the lights of Bangkok, its skyscrapers like dark monoliths against the dusky sky. The buzz of distant city traffic mingled with the sounds of barking dogs and laughter from the boats crowding the shore.

The couples said their final goodbyes to each other with promises of staying in touch. Phone numbers and e-mail addresses had already been exchanged. As Natalie and Pete, first down the gangplank, headed to shore, Natalie waved at Dot, Henry, Mac and Christie over her shoulder.

"Don't forget to check out our shoot in *World Sophisticate Travel and Lifestyle!*"

The two couples promised they would as they waved goodbye.

Christie and Mac exited next. Hand in hand, they were walking down the plank to shore when Christie felt a soft tap on her shoulder. She paused and looked back.

Dot, arm in arm with Henry, smiled. *"Mai pen rai,"* she whispered. "Don't forget, life is to enjoy."

"Mai pen rai," Christie repeated under her breath. She squeezed Mac's hand as they continued walking. *Mai pen rai.* Three words. Like three little wishes.

nocturne™

HER BLOOD WAS POISON TO HIM...

MICHELE HAUF

FROM THE DARK

Michael is a man with a secret. He's a vampire
struggling to fight the darkness of his nature.
It looks like a losing battle—until he meets
Jane, the only woman who can understand his
conflicted nature. And the only woman who can
destroy him—through love.

On sale November 2006.

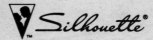

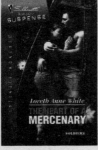

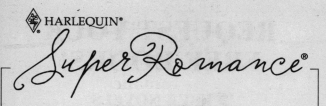

Join acclaimed author

Tara Taylor Quinn

for another exciting book
this holiday season!

MERRY CHRISTMAS, BABIES

by Tara Taylor Quinn

#1381

Elise Richardson hears her biological clock ticking loudly and, with no husband on the horizon, she's decided to have a baby on her own. But she begins to depend more and more on her business partner, Joe Bennet, who's also her best friend—especially when she finds out she isn't having one baby this Christmas, but four!

On sale November 2006 from Harlequin Superromance!

Available wherever books are sold including most bookstores, supermarkets, discount stores and drugstores.

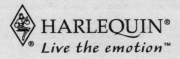

HARLEQUIN®
Live the emotion™

REQUEST YOUR FREE BOOKS!

2 FREE NOVELS
FROM THE ROMANCE/SUSPENSE
COLLECTION PLUS 2 FREE GIFTS!

YES! Please send me 2 FREE novels from the Romance/Suspense Collection and my 2 FREE gifts. After receiving them, if I don't wish to receive any more books, I can return the shipping statement marked "cancel." If I don't cancel, I will receiv...

U.S.,...

appli...

unde...

to bu...

neve...

mine...

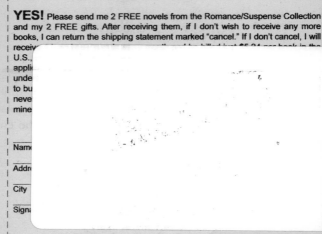

Name

Addr

City

Sign

IN U.S.A.	IN CANADA
P.O. Box 1867	P.O. Box 609
Buffalo, NY	Fort Erie, Ontario
14240-1867	L2A 5X3

Not valid to current subscribers to the Romance Collection,
the Suspense Collection or the Romance/Suspense Collection.

Want to try two free books from another line?
Call 1-800-873-8635 or visit www.morefreebooks.com.